PRAISE F[illegible]KLEY

'Adam Rackley is one of the very few who has both the literary skill and the sensory intelligence to make the rest of us understand exactly what is out there, and why.'

Peter Nichols, author of
A Voyage for Madmen

'American Psycho *has a British cousin.* White Collar *shines the torch of satire on the City's toxic, hyper-competitive nihilism.'*

Simon Evan-Cook, Citywire
columnist and fund manager

Also by Adam Rackley

Salt, Sweat, Tears

WHITE COLLAR

Adam Rackley

The Book Guild

First published in Great Britain in 2026 by
The Book Guild Ltd
Unit E2 Airfield Business Park,
Harrison Road, Market Harborough,
Leicestershire. LE16 7UL
Tel: 0116 2792299
www.bookguild.co.uk
Email: info@bookguild.co.uk

The manufacturer's authorised representative in the EU
for product safety is Authorised Rep Compliance Ltd,
71 Lower Baggot Street, Dublin D02 P593 Ireland (www.arccompliance.com)

Typeset in 11pt Minion Pro

Printed and bound in Great Britain by CMP UK

ISBN 978 1835743 942

British Library Cataloguing in Publication Data.
A catalogue record for this book is available from the British Library.

Find what you love,
Love what you do,
And to yourself
Be true.

Nosce te ipsum.

CAST

Andrew Waite
analyst at Green Knight Asset Management

Aurelius Blois
billionaire, hedge fund manager and founder of Livermore Capital

Dan Trench
finance lecturer with an appetite for violence

Francis Portnoy
pugnacious founder of Green Knight Asset Management

Gareth Eary
salesman with a secret at Gresham Street Capital

Hugh Holmes
straight-talking accountant, CFO of Albourne PLC

'Jabba' (Nigel Oakheart)
trader at Gresham Street Capital

John Gruff
deal junkie, CEO of Albourne PLC

Jude Delaney-Hall
writer working undercover

Marianne Bleekman
graduate investment banker at Gessner Bank

Martin Fowey
graduate salesman at Gresham Street Capital

Paul Todd
investment banker, Marianne's boss and John Gruff's confidante

Richard Newbury
octogenarian fund manager at Green Knight Asset Management

Sarah
Dan Trench's former fiancée and climbing partner

Patrick
Jude's publishing agent and family friend

CHAPTER ONE

Thursday the 22nd of December, 2011

Activists entering their third month of protest outside St Paul's Cathedral can stay for Christmas after the high court judge hearing the case for their eviction said he would not reach a verdict before the courts reopened on the 11th of January. The counsel for the City of London Corporation had pressed for an immediate decision on an order evicting Occupy London from the churchyard in what is a busy time of year for the cathedral. Occupy London has its own schedule of events over the festive season, including ukulele jamming.

10.56pm – Dan Trench, Northern Line, Southbound

'The next station is… Morden. This train terminates at… Morden.'

A teenage girl is eating wings.

With practised dexterity, she uses her lips and teeth to strip the bones clean. The sound of her music fills the carriage. She wipes her fingers before tapping her phone to repeat the last track. The only other person in the carriage is a tall man wearing a navy suit and polished black brogues. He has a dash of grey through his blond hair.

The man starts to moan. Although fast asleep, he appears to be in some kind of distress. Then, he lets out a big, heavy sob.

'You's a long way from home, man,' she calls over to the sleeping figure. 'I be cryin' too if I woz you.'

As the train slows into the station, the wing-eater gets up to leave. But, instead of alighting from the nearest door, she wanders over to the sleeping, crying man.

'Crybaby,' she whispers. 'City boy's a crybaby.'

She leans down to balance the Chicken Cottage box on the man's knee, but the smell of piss makes her recoil, and she drops the box on the floor. The crybaby has wet himself.

The girl sucks her teeth and shakes her head.

'Fuckin' disgusting, man,' she shouts, as she steps off the train.

'Morden is the final stop. This train terminates here. All change, please. All change.'

11.11pm – 'Jabba' (Nigel Oakheart), Dion Restaurant & Nightclub, St Paul's

The DJ cuts the music.

'Ladies and gentlemen, it's time…'

Conversations stop as people turn to watch David Cameron stagger onto the dance floor. He is holding a bottle of Peroni in one hand and a child's cricket bat in the other. A distinctive red briefcase hangs on a thick green bungee cord. Cameron shows off his one-handed forward defence before holding out the bat and nudging the case.

'Let's see what the Budget has in store for 2012,' announces the DJ.

Nick Clegg is jumping up and down in excitement.

'Come on, Dave, give it some welly!'

Cameron raises the bat above his shoulder and swings. The bat catches a corner of the briefcase. The case spins away from him before the bungee cord snaps it back. He sees it coming and ducks but too late. The case hits him in the face; the bat and beer bottle clatter to the floor; Cameron grabs his forehead and squeals.

'*Fucking moron*,' shouts Ed Miliband. A novelty Christmas tie hangs loose around his neck.

George Osborne runs towards Cameron, carrying a jeroboam of Perrier-Jouët. With a shove from the chancellor, the prime minister falls to the ground. Osborne raises the champagne bottle over the red briefcase and brings it down squarely on the gold-embossed *ERII*. The case explodes, showering the dance floor in papier-mâché, gold coins and Monopoly money.

A cheer goes up around the nightclub. Ed Miliband runs across the floor and slides on his knees through the debris of the pinata, and two Nick Cleggs pile on top of him.

Gareth Eary pulls off his George Osborne mask and breaks into the running man, as the DJ turns up the volume, and people flood back onto the dance floor. The head of corporate finance, still clutching his forehead, is helped up by two of his associates and handed another bottle of Peroni.

The Gresham Street Capital Christmas party is in full swing.

From a corner of the club, Jabba studies all this. But in particular he studies Fiona. As she approaches the bar, he knocks back a double Jack and Coke, then pushes his way through a pack of grads to stand next to her.

Fiona smiles. 'Hi, Nigel.'

He can smell her perfume. Her cheeks are red from dancing. She is so beautiful.

'What can I get you?'

'Oh, thanks, but I'm getting a round.'

'That's OK,' says Jabba. 'Let me get these.'

'Are you sure? That's so kind,' says Fiona, pushing her hair back away from her face. She smiles at Jabba. 'Is it just me or is it hot in here?'

Jabba feels light and alive.

'They… they're real.'

'Sorry?' She leans in to hear him better.

'They *are* real,' says Jabba into her ear.

'What's real?' asks Fiona, her cheek briefly touching his.

'The earrings.'

Fiona looks confused for a moment, then her eyes open wide.

'Secret Santa? The pearl and… diamond?'

Jabba grins and nods.

'They're real?! They're from you?'

Jabba nods again.

'Oh.' Fiona looks confused. She isn't smiling.

'I… it was…' Jabba mumbles and looks down at the bar.

'Was there a mistake?' asks Fiona. 'They're in my bag; let me get them for you.'

'No, no. I bought them… for you.' Jabba looks up at her and wonders if she understands what he's trying to say.

'I bought them for you.'

'You bought them for me?' repeats Fiona, unsure.

The barman leans across.

'You guys OK?'

'Wait,' says Jabba. 'What are we getting?'

Fiona leans across the bar and gives the barman her order.

'And I'll have a JD and Coke, double,' says Jabba.

Once the barman has gone, Jabba and Fiona stand in silence.

'Umm… I'm just popping to the ladies,' says Fiona.

'Sure.' He nods towards her friends. 'I'll bring the drinks over.'

She smiles awkwardly and retreats.

He gives a lonely sigh.

'Hi, Jabba!' says a familiar voice.

'Fuck off, Eary.'

'Merry Christmas, Jabba.'

Jabba turns to face Gareth Eary, who stands a few inches taller than him. He feels the tension rising between his shoulders. Gareth rests his elbow on the bar and flashes a perfect set of unnaturally white teeth. The heavy gold ring on Gareth's little finger shines fiercely under the bar lighting. The top four buttons of his pale-blue shirt are undone, and his bare chest glistens with perspiration.

Jabba grinds his teeth and silently stares at Gareth. Gareth shrugs and waves at the barman.

When his drinks appear, Jabba fishes a card out of his pocket and flashes his tab number. As he walks away, Gareth shouts after him.

'Merry Christmas, Jabba!'

Jabba slowly makes his way towards the group from Accounts. He edges in and offers around the tray.

Jabba rarely speaks to Accounts, but he knows everything about them. He watches everybody. Everything is information: layers of meaning built on hidden correlations.

A graduate is deep in conversation with the manager of the accounts department, who is in his fifties and perennially passed up for promotion. The graduates, whom he managed twenty years ago, are now managing directors.

Jabba chews his straw and looks for Fiona.

Fiona is in the far corner of the dance floor, enjoying the music, happy in her own company. Jabba stops chewing the straw and a smile curls up at the corners of his mouth.

A group of women dance in a circle around their handbags; a group of men stand nearby watching them. A cowgirl wearing a shot-glass bandolier does brisk trade with a bottle of tequila.

When Jabba glances over at Fiona again, she's with someone. She's dancing with Gareth Eary. Jabba's jaw clenches, and a prickly pressure pops in his head.

Gareth leans in to talk to her, and she grabs the back of his head and holds his cheek beside hers. They move together with the music, Gareth's hands pressed into the small of her back. Jabba doesn't want to see this, but he can't stop staring. Gareth says something, and Fiona pulls her head back and looks at him, then brushes her lips against his, as she rests her cheek back against Gareth's.

Fiona steps back from Gareth and starts to walk slowly away from the dance floor, with one hand behind her back. Gareth catches up with her and follows her, half a step behind, his index finger linked with hers. As they skirt around the edge of the dance floor, Gareth looks across and winks at Jabba, before following Fiona up the stairs, through the restaurant and on to the taxi rank outside.

CHAPTER TWO

Thursday the 1st of March, 2012

Greece faces a decisive week in its struggle to avert a default, with the success of the world's largest sovereign debt restructuring poised on a knife-edge. The benchmark thirty-year Greek bond is currently trading at twenty-three cents on the Euro.

6.36am – Gareth Eary, Gymbox, City

The Farrow and Ball colour wheel that's been sitting on his kitchen table does not include the light brown of Maria's skin, which is something between Templeton Pink and Mouse's Back. At work, Gareth thinks about sex throughout the day, but this morning, while he's having sex with Maria, he is preoccupied with the colour of the feature wall in his new flat. Gareth stands over Maria, who is lying on her back on the massage table, eyes closed in concentration.

The decorator had told him not to bother with Farrow and Ball, because it's hard to get a good finish with it and also because it costs twice as much as Dulux, which they'll mix down at the builder's merchants to an identical colour anyway. This all makes perfect sense but is beside the point.

Apart from the muffled dance music from the cardio hall outside, the only sounds in the massage room are the steady rhythm of Gareth's balls slapping against Maria's glutes, and her regular, controlled breathing: in through the nose, out through the mouth, just like when she's doing squats. He studies her firm breasts and the cut definition of her abs.

Maria's bedside manner, like her pubic hair, is lacking. As soon as she has pulled her Lycra shorts back over her G-string, she stands by the door, impatiently tapping the end of her Biro on the yellow clipboard.

'Are you adding that to my training diary?'

'No.'

'But that's *got to be* ten minutes of cardio.'

Maria raises an eyebrow. 'Your heart rate needs to be above 152 for cardio.'

Maria taps the Biro a little more loudly on the clipboard while she scans the room.

'We're going to finish with twist crunches and then some stretching.'

When she is happy that Gareth has composed himself, she unlocks the door and holds it open for him.

There's a blast of sound and activity. Dozens of overweight, balding men wheeze and sweat across rows of running machines and exercise bikes. Scattered amongst them are girls in Lycra, with ponytails and perfect make-up, sipping bottles of water. Two giant screens at the end of the hall show music videos without sound, and in a booth between them, which is suspended from the ceiling, the DJ smashes dance tracks into a high-tempo pulp. Her peroxide-white crew cut and skinny shoulders pop frantically back and forth in time with the music. The oversized electric clock shows that it is not yet 7am.

A huge graffiti-style slogan adds to the calculated edginess.

THE CITY'S UNDERBELLY IS GREEDY,
DECADENT & MORALLY BANKRUPT.
WELCOME HOME.

Maria leads Gareth through the free-weights room. There are no women here, only young men in tight vests, with big shoulders and thin legs, who pump and swagger and slurp on energy drinks. The air is heavy with testosterone and the smell of metal.

'*Aaaagghhh!*' Smash. Smash.

'*Hhhhuuaa!*' Smash.

Power screams, and the crash of weights on the rubber-tiled floor, overpower the music from next door. As they pass through, Gareth eyeballs around the room, instinctively pushing out his chest and lifting his chin. There's a class going on under a large metal CrossFit frame, which fills one corner of the room.

The stretching area is just a corridor between the free-weights room and Studio Two, where a yoga class is underway. There used to be a dedicated stretching area in Hall Three, but it was cleared out to make way for a steel octagon.

Maria passes Gareth a twelve-kilogramme medicine ball, and he starts to do twist crunches in sets of forty. At the end of his fourth set, Gareth's abs are on fire, and he collapses back on the mat. Maria lets him catch his breath before getting him to do a fifth set.

Afterwards, Gareth lies on his back with his left leg in the air while Maria pushes down on the ball of his foot to stretch his hamstring.

'You know, the champagne bar at the top of Tower Forty-Two has the most fantastic view...'

'Gareth, the sex is fun, but you're not my type.'

'Oh...' Gareth stumbles and, unusually, is at a loss for words.

It's only a moment, but the silence stretches on in Gareth's mind. Maria glances at her watch.

'I've got my seven o'clock. Don't forget your hamstring stretches. Same time Tuesday?'

'Tuesday,' replies Gareth.

Maria taps the appointment into her iPhone. 'See ya.'

Gareth watches Maria's peach-perfect, Lycra-clad buttocks slink down the corridor and back through the free-weights room. Her tightly curled hair, dyed a shade or two lighter than its natural colour, is held in a ponytail that falls just below her shoulders. He knows that the protein-swilling meat-heads next door will have paused from smashing metal to stare at her. This kind of thing would normally give Gareth great satisfaction, but today he has a kind of empty feeling.

Because having a positive attitude is an important part of being Gareth Eary, he decides to think instead about his February commission numbers. At Gresham Street, you eat what you kill, which means that half of the £48,000 that Gareth generated in commission last month will go straight into his year-end bonus. Before he joined the City, Gareth had never, ever imagined that making money could be this easy.

Gareth is still lying on the mat, looking up at the carefully exposed architectural pipework, and thinking about the colour of his new feature wall, when the sound of a skipping rope interrupts his reverie.

Whip-snap, whip-snap, whip-snap, whip-snap.

He pulls himself off the mat and follows the sound into Hall Three. In front of a wall-to-wall mirror, next to the boxing ring, a man, tall but slight, is skipping. He bounces from one foot to the other, then runs on the spot before crossing his arms back and forth, always in rhythm, dancing to the metronome beat of the rope.

Whip-snap, whip-snap.

It looks effortless.

On the other side of the ring, a woman with short black hair moves around a red leather punchbag. The bag is suspended on a chain from a metal girder that spans the room. She punches and ducks and moves around the bag, increasing and decreasing her tempo. Her movements are fluid and controlled, but her changes of direction, and the combinations of her punches, are unpredictable. Gareth imagines himself bobbing and weaving around an opponent in the ring; he ducks to avoid a punch and then lands a single knockout right.

The other two people in Hall Three are in the boxing ring, and Gareth recognises one of them. Dan Trench has lost weight: he looks tight, with muscle and sinew. There's also grey, a lot of it, running through his blond hair.

There was a time when Dan and Gareth would drink together every Friday: young men, new to the game, sharing stories about the crazy world that they had become part of. Gareth rarely thinks about those days now.

The other man in the ring is the coach. His nose is squashed against his face. His faded T-shirt and dirty, torn jogging bottoms conspicuous amongst the compression base layers and carefully groomed stubble. Gareth twists the heavy gold signet ring around the little finger of his left hand.

Dan is in the centre of the canvas, bouncing on the toes of his green boxing boots, gloved fists raised, chin tucked tight into his left shoulder, poised. The coach is holding a pair of pads, which he moves as he calls out number sequences.

'One, two; one, two, three; one, one, two, three, two; one, one.'

Dan's response comes in volleys of punches: jab, right, jab, right, hook, jab, jab, right, hook, right and double jab.

'Good. Good. Nice rhythm. Keep covered up. Snap that left hand straight back.'

Gareth had last seen his old friend on one of those great, unplanned Friday nights. Dan always had an energy around him. Maybe it was just that he was comfortable in his own skin. That was almost five years ago.

The clock on the wall buzzes loudly to signal the end of a three-minute round and the start of a one-minute break.

'Change,' shouts the coach.

The woman on the bag moves to take up the skipping rope, while the guy on the rope grabs his gloves and steps into the ring.

As Gareth walks across the hall, he catches Dan's eye and waves. Dan does a double take. They meet by the bag, and Gareth remembers how tall Dan is.

'Long time!'

'How are you?' asks Dan.

'Oh, still at Gresham Street, business is good. Got a new pad in Chelsea.'

'Still living the dream?' asks Dan.

'Still living the dream.'

Dan looks uncomfortable.

'Dan, I heard about what happened. I'm so sorry. I tried calling...'

A furrow grows across Dan's brow. He straightens up to his full height and crosses his arms.

'Twenty seconds,' shouts the coach, who is staring at them.

Gareth looks over at the coach, then back at Dan.

'Dan, we've got to catch up.'

'OK,' replies Dan, unsure.

'Free tomorrow night?' asks Gareth.

'I don't think so...'

'Just for a swift one,' says Gareth.

'A swift one,' says Dan.

'A swift one,' repeats Gareth. 'Let's say five o'clock at The Fine Line. Like old times!'

'Like old times,' repeats Dan, unconvinced.

Gareth puts his hand on Dan's shoulder. Dan's T-shirt is heavy with sweat. The clock buzzes to signal the end of the one-minute break, and the sound of the skipping rope starts up again.

Whip-snap, whip-snap, whip-snap.

Gareth glances back over his shoulder and sees Dan bouncing around the bag, coming in close to throw volleys of punches, then stepping back out of range.

The changing rooms are not yet busy. After taking a shower, Gareth finds a spot in front of the mirror, between an older man drying his chest with a hairdryer and a younger one vigorously slapping talc around his clean-shaven balls. The downlighting flatters Gareth's pecks and triceps and picks out the definition of his abs, but up close the clinical white light also highlights the pores around his nose and the unevenness of his skin.

Gareth's wash bag is made of black calf-leather, with a purple suede lining. Out first is the oil-free, alcohol-free toner, which doesn't dry out his skin. His dabs it on a ball of cotton wool and, as he rubs it gently around his nose, forehead and jaw line, he can feel his face tightening up;

it's a pleasant, fresh feeling. Next comes a small blue bottle of eye cream, which he pumps onto his index finger, then slowly massages into the soft skin around his eyes. Gareth completes the regime with a generous application of moisturiser; it's a thick green gel, with a pleasing texture, and he likes the way it dissolves on his skin.

Before putting on his shirt, Gareth pumps a handful of Molton Brown body lotion from the dispenser on the wall and slathers it over his chest, arms and shoulders. Finally, he fishes a small tin of pomade out of the washbag. He takes a pinch of it and rubs it through his hair before cutting a sharp side parting with his boar bristle brush. He enjoys the sensation of the firm bristles running across his scalp.

On his way out, Gareth sees Maria's 7am warming up on the cross trainer. Gareth gives Maria a wink. A flight of stairs takes him up to street level. There's a sign by the door which wasn't there yesterday.

WHO DO YOU THINK YOU ARE? WHO DO YOU WANT TO BE?

7.52am – Andrew Waite, Green Knight Asset Management, Knightsbridge

A squeal, followed by a roar of laughter, announces Francis Portnoy's arrival. The CEO of Green Knight Asset Management has just made a shocking and lewd comment to the receptionist. Trotting onto the floor, at Portnoy's side, is Augustus.

The bull terrier and his owner share the same heavy brow and pugnacious glare, and they both move with a hurried, rolling gait, which reminds Andrew of a fat child trying to keep up.

Andrew's desk is at the opposite end of the floor to

Portnoy's office, which makes Augustus's morning detour seem all the more calculated. The first time that Augustus pissed on Andrew's desk, the analyst had stood up and shouted and tried to shoo the dog away. But Portnoy's glare across the floor had implied such violence that Andrew was immediately silenced. Andrew's junior position requires him to be philosophical; *at least the floor is carpet-tiled*, he tells himself. Every few weeks, the beige tiles by his desk, stained with dog piss and bleach, are replaced.

Opposite Andrew sits Jude. Despite an Oxbridge first and alarming self-confidence, Jude spends her days booking lunches and buying birthday/anniversary/Christmas presents on behalf of Andrew's boss Peter Mancroft. Something doesn't sit right, but Andrew can't put his finger on what.

Jude's phone rings.

'Good morning, Green Knight Asset Management.'

From the pained expression that draws across her face, Andrew knows that Gareth is on the line.

'Let me save you time and energy by repeating again that, for me to willingly spend one moment in the same room as you, you would have to evolve a personality and expand your horizons beyond the size of your bonus cheque and your next shag.'

Jude looks at Andrew across the desk divider and taps her phone keypad.

His phone rings. 'Brutal,' says Andrew, before picking up the receiver.

Jude shrugs.

After a moment's pause, Gareth is on the line.

'Good morning, squire!'

'Oh, hi, Gareth.'

'Listen, just a quick call about Nobel Ordnance.'

Since Gareth talked Peter into buying Nobel Ordnance six months ago, the shares have halved.

'Yes, Nobel hasn't been our best investment.'

'Andrew, you're absolutely right, I was early on those. Listen, I'm just the broker, there's nothing I can tell you that you guys don't already know, but today's update is good. Revenue's up, margins are soft, but order book is at record levels.'

'I just can't see a catalyst – where's the good news going to come from? Where's the next insurgency? When's the next war?'

'Excellent point, but as you know, sometimes you have to swim against the tide to make money in this market…'

Gareth is still talking, but Andrew has stopped listening. The phone rests on his shoulder. After a few moments, Andrew lifts the receiver back to his ear with a silent sigh.

'…so the shares are at…' Gareth pauses to look at his screen, '…408–411 this morning. Our analyst has them on eleven times next year's earnings, and we just think they're a no-brainer at these levels.'

'Thanks, Gareth.'

Andrew taps on his Bloomberg keyboard and brings up a screen that shows indications of buying and selling interest. It looks like everyone is selling Nobel Ordnance. With the West too broke to start another war, who would buy shares in Nobel Ordnance? Even on eleven times earnings?

The answer arrives in the form of Peter Mancroft, a veteran of three marriages, victim of occasional gout and a man for whom bonus time is a perennial disappointment.

Today, he hobbles across the floor with an ebony-handled walking stick.

'Morning, Jude. Morning, Andrew. What news?'

'Gareth called. Nobel trading statement.'

'Keen on them, is he?'

'He's looking for buyers.'

Peter enjoys delivering monologues about the good old days at Morgan Grenfell. He tells the stories in a familiar way, like Andrew and Jude should know who or what he's talking about. The general theme is that a precocious young Mancroft exercises impeccable judgement to win profit and the esteem of his peers, but close observation has led Andrew to conclude that the stories are made up.

In a small black moleskin diary, Andrew makes a note of every investment decision that Peter makes. Once, when Andrew showed it to Peter to illustrate a point, he called the junior analyst a 'vile little runt', left early for lunch, returned drunk and ignored him for the rest of the week.

Although Peter is a lousy fund manager, thirty-five years in the industry have honed his survival instincts; a portfolio with 120 holdings can hide a lot of mistakes.

Andrew is writing up his notes from yesterday's meeting with Enterprise Inns when he becomes aware of someone standing beside his desk. He looks up to find Richard Newbury, the office octogenarian, limbering up.

'Hello, Richard.'

Newbury leans his wrinkled face in close towards Andrew's. Without his glasses, he's almost blind. The manager of the UK Large Cap Fund smells of ancient decay. A limp crest of white hair lies across his head. Around his collar is a threadbare regimental tie, knotted in a half-Windsor.

'Oh, hello, Andrew. Don't mind me.'

'So... what brings you to this end of the floor?'

'Oh, you know, change of scenery.'

Newbury is wearing comfortable shoes and grey trousers, which sit high around his waist. After some vigorous stretching, he begins to rock back and forth, like a long jumper at the start of their sprint. Although Andrew has watched this ritual many times, he's still fascinated by it. With an unexpected burst of movement, Newbury starts to shuffle down the aisle between the desks. Bizarre as the sight is, no one takes the slightest notice. The floor is almost thirty metres long and Newbury's still picking up speed when, at the very last moment, he sees the wall in front of him and raises his arms to avoid a collision.

Andrew is still looking across the floor at Newbury, now catching his breath, when Peter slams down his phone.

'Another bloody redemption.'

Newbury has been saying that a lot recently.

'Andrew,' says Peter quietly, without looking up.

'Yes?'

'Andrew, come here, please.'

He motions the junior analyst to come in close so that no one can overhear their conversation.

'It's a disaster, a bloody disaster.' Peter is resigned rather than angry. 'Another client's selling out. The cash comes out next week; we need to raise thirty-eight million.'

A few more redemptions like this one, and there will be no money left to manage. Andrew wonders if they will lose their jobs. He wonders how Peter will pay for the mortgage on the place in the Cotswolds, his new wife's new car, three sets of school fees, two sets of maintenance and the basement extension at the townhouse in Chelsea.

'OK, write this down.'

Peter has the portfolio up on his screen and is scrolling through it.

'Domino Printing, Barratt Homes, St James Place…'

Peter rattles off another dozen names.

'Got that?'

'Yeah. Ummm… what do you want me to do with this?'

Peter looks at Andrew like he's just been asked to explain a joke for the second time.

'I want you to *sell them*.'

'All of them?'

'All of them. We need to sell all of those holdings. Give the order to Gareth at Gresham Street. Tell him to sell them at market. Tell him these have got to be settled by next Friday.'

Peter pauses.

'And tell him there's a space in my diary next Thursday for lunch. Nothing French.'

Peter stands up and starts to put his jacket on.

'I'm going out for lunch.'

It's only 11.30am, but, as it's a Friday, Andrew knows that he won't be back.

Leaning on his ebony-handled stick, Peter hobbles off down the floor. As he approaches the final row of desks, he narrowly avoids being knocked down by Richard Newbury.

'Newbury, you bloody idiot!'

Oblivious, the octogenarian shuffles on.

Peter turns down the corridor that leads to the lift and disappears from view.

Andrew picks up the phone to call Gareth, but because he sometimes gets anxious placing orders over the phone, he changes his mind and writes the broker an email instead.

Andrew's desk is piled high with research that he will never read. Amongst the paperwork is a Bloomberg terminal that flickers green and red with live prices, news releases, economic data and messages, and alongside it another screen showing a constant flow of email pop-ups. Hundreds of emails and Bloomberg messages flash across these screens every day, plus thousands of changing data points. Taken as a whole, it paints a constantly changing picture of the world, with countless implications for the investment portfolio. But managing and digesting this flood of information is an impossible task, and, more often than not, Andrew feels like he's drowning in it.

His phone rings. It's an internal number.

'Hello?'

'Andrew, it's Lucia. Has Mr Mancroft left for lunch?'

Lucia speaks with the lilt of her native Poland.

'Oh, hi, Lucia. He has.'

'Good, Mr Portnoy would like to see you in his office.'

'Mr Portnoy? Oh… what about?'

'I have no idea.'

Lucia hangs up, and Andrew sits for a while listening to the dead-line tone. Jude is now looking across the desk divider with interest.

'Was that Lucia?'

'Yeah. Portnoy wants to see me.'

'You? Why does Portnoy want to see *you*?'

Andrew tries to sound cool, but his heart is pounding in his chest.

'I don't know. We've just had another redemption… I think they might be winding up the fund…'

Andrew stands up slowly and straightens his tie. He lifts his jacket off the back of the chair, slides it on and does up the middle button. Andrew's charcoal suit has seen better days. The pockets, which are useful for loose change, credit card receipts, business cards and pint glasses sag like sad puppy ears. Fine fibres from the interlining are coming through the cloth, and he is missing a cuff button.

Pondering his fate, Andrew walks slowly towards Lucia's office, which connects through to Portnoy's.

Lucia's signature style is *Pretty Woman*. Today, she is wearing white stiletto boots and a sheer silk blouse tucked into her shorts.

'Andrew, please sit.'

Lucia knocks twice and opens the CEO's door.

'Andrew Waite is here for you.'

'Send him in.'

Francis Portnoy looks like a tramp. There's a hole in the shoulder of his navy V-neck jumper, the collar of his white polo shirt is dirty and, on his feet, which are resting on the table, is a pair of old squash shoes.

'Sit down,' orders Portnoy, directing Andrew to a leather bucket chair.

'How long have you been with us for?'

'Almost two years, Mr Portnoy.'

'And I understand you're doing this *financial analysis* thing.'

'The Chartered Financial Analyst qualification.'

'Well, Waite, you appear to be in the right place at the right time, because the Board has decided we need to improve the optics for the consultants. These days, no sovereign wealth fund or pension trustee will allocate a penny of capital without sending in the box-ticking fuck-wits.'

Andrew starts to relax a little. Portnoy seems to be paying him a compliment. Andrew looks at Portnoy's shoes. The CEO of Green Knight Asset Management must weigh twenty stone, and Andrew is quite sure that he doesn't play squash.

'How much are we paying you?'

'Sorry?'

'*How much are we paying you?*' Francis spits the words across the table.

'Forty-two K and a twelve-grand bonus last year.'

Francis shakes his head in pity.

'Next month, we are meeting the consultants. These consultants have a mandate from the Abu Dhabi Investment Authority to allocate a billion pounds to UK Mid-Caps. If we give the consultants a good show, there will be more to come. The Arabs will make us fucking rich.'

There's a lustful look in Portnoy's eyes. Andrew wonders how rich Francis Portnoy would have to be to consider himself *fucking rich*. When he floated Green Knight Asset Management on the stock-market, he bagged £120 million for himself and made millionaires of forty-two employees, including Lucia, who bought her parents and her brother adjacent mansions in Wilanów.

Andrew has learnt the two rules of the fund management industry. Firstly, the more money Green Knight manages, the more profit they make, and secondly, the more money Green Knight manages, the worse performance becomes.

'Now, I understand from Peter that you're good at reading accounts and doing discounted cash flows and all that…'

'Yes.'

'Good, because that's what these consultants are interested in. And we can't have you smelling of dog piss, so I've had a word with Augustus and he's agreed to stop urinating on your desk. Isn't that right, Augustus?'

Andrew follows the CEO's gaze across the room. Augustus, who is licking his testicles, looks up at them for a moment and runs his tongue over his nose before turning his attention back to his testicles.

When Andrew turns back round, Portnoy is staring straight at him. Andrew looks down at his hands. Eventually, Portnoy breaks the silence.

'OK, listen. From Monday, Peter Mancroft will no longer be the manager of the UK Mid-Cap Fund.'

Andrew tries to understand what this means. Maybe they're winding up the fund after all.

Portnoy continues. 'From Monday, you will be managing the fund.'

Francis pauses for the news to sink in.

'Well? What do you have to say about that?'

Andrew is stunned. 'Thank you, Mr Portnoy. Thank you for the opportunity.'

'Just don't fuck it up.'

Portnoy turns round to his computer screen and starts to read his emails. Andrew stands up and holds out his hand. The CEO glances up at Andrew, then waves him away.

'Send in Lucia on your way out,' says Portnoy. 'Oh, and by the way, from this month you're on a hundred K basic. Buy yourself a new fucking suit.'

9.44pm – John Gruff, No. 1 Lombard Street, City

The Freshfields' partner is talking to him, but Gruff is distracted. He pushes another piece of Nicorette gum into his mouth and looks across the dining table at the blonde.

There are two-dozen people sat around the table. It's impossible to imagine that all of them have actually been working on the deal. The lawyer is still talking. Gruff can't remember the man's name, or what it is exactly that he does, but he nods slowly to give the impression that he's listening, all the while staring at the blonde, who occasionally catches his gaze.

The decor and service in the private dining room are

perfunctory. Gruff studies the sullen-faced staff clearing the plates. If it were lunchtime they would have a reasonable view of the Bank of England and the Royal Exchange, but at night the picture window just reflects the drab room back at itself.

The investment banker sitting on Gruff's left taps his wine glass with a cheese knife and stands up. Paul Todd talks with the confident ease of a man who believes that he is worth his seven-figure pay cheque. Gruff starts to work out how many nurses that would pay for, then stops, because he doesn't care.

'Today is about a man with a dream. Today is about John Gruff. Through John's force of character and clarity of vision, Albourne Cakes has grown to become the largest food manufacturer in the UK. With the recent acquisition of Warburtons, I'm delighted to announce that the company will be promoted to the FTSE 100 Index at the quarterly review. From next month, John will be the CEO of a FTSE 100 company.'

Paul waits for applause to die down before continuing.

'As Co-Head of Investment Banking at Gessner, it's been my pleasure to work closely with John as we have executed his vision, and I'd like to thank the senior team at Albourne and the deal teams at Gessners and Freshfields for the all-nighters and weekends that they've put in to get these deals over the line. It's been quite a year.'

Paul turns to Gruff. 'John, a few words?'

John Gruff looks around the table and soaks up the applause before standing up.

'Thank you, Paul and the team, for all your work but, actually, the hard part is only just beginning. It falls to me and to Hugh…' Gruff nods across the table at his finance director, '…to prove to our shareholders that those synergies in Paul's spreadsheets actually exist.'

There's a loud snort from the Freshfields lawyer, who is choking on a piece of stilton.

'There are people who think about doing, and there are people who talk about doing, and then there are people who do. Paul and I get things done. And that's what makes Albourne and Gessner a good partnership.'

More applause.

He sits down. Paul stands up again and puts his hand on Gruff's shoulder.

'Well, I guess it just falls to me to propose a toast. To Mr Gruff and his exceedingly good cakes!'

When Paul sits back down, Gruff leans into him.

'Who is that?' he asks, nodding at the blonde at the end of the table.

'That is... Sophie. She's one of the Freshfield associates. She's been angling me to get her a position at Gessner.'

'She's figured out that it's smarter to take a percentage than an hourly rate,' replies Gruff.

'Well, quite.'

Gruff looks at the banker expectantly.

'Of course,' says Paul.

Paul walks down to the far end of the table and returns with the blonde.

'This is Sophie Maxwell, from Freshfields.'

'And from what I hear, future investment banker material,' says Gruff.

'If there's one thing I've learnt, it's that bankers have more fun.' She winks at Paul.

Gruff and Paul both laugh.

'Very confident,' says Gruff.

Gruff offers Paul's seat to Sophie and beckons the waiter. Paul nods to excuse himself.

'Drink?' asks Gruff.

‘Gin and tonic.’

‘A large G&T and a pint of Amaretto, with plenty of ice,’ shouts Gruff across the room.

The waiter hurries over. ‘Sorry, sir, a pint of…?’

‘A pint of *Amaretto*,’ enunciates Gruff.

Gruff turns back to Sophie. ‘Your first deal?’

‘Yeah,’ says Sophie, leaning back in her chair. ‘Not quite as glamorous as I’d imagined. In fact, not remotely glamorous.’

Around the table, a number of people are making to leave, and a kind of queue is gathering behind Gruff’s chair.

‘Excuse me,’ he says to Sophie, ‘don’t go anywhere.’

Gruff works his way through the group of people. ‘Yes, thank you, goodnight,’ he says to each in turn, ignoring any attempts to make conversation. Finally, he gets to Paul, who is talking to Hugh Holmes, Albourne’s new finance director.

‘So, Hugh, just a month in the job and you’re already signing the papers on your first deal! What a riot!’ says the banker.

Hugh shakes his head. ‘It’s a bloody distraction is what it is. And John’s right about those synergies, you know. I can’t see us getting anywhere near those numbers.’

‘Of course, of course,’ says Paul. ‘That would be the First Rule of doing acquisitions. When dealing with investors, thou shalt work backwards from the transaction price to calculate the synergies that justify the deal. Ha, ha! But next time we’ll have your input from the start.’

Hugh shakes his head. ‘The Board are going to think long and hard about any next time.’

‘Come on, Hugh,’ says Gruff, putting his hand on the finance director’s shoulder. ‘You know Paul’s just doing his job. No need to act like he’s just stuck a finger up your arse.’

The waiter arrives with a tray. 'Amaretto, sir.'

'Jesus!' says Hugh, 'is that a pint of Amaretto?'

Gruff takes a gulp from the glass, crunches a mouthful of ice, then calls over Sophie, who is talking to the Freshfields partner.

'Sophie, this is Hugh, our new finance director.'

Hugh nods. 'Sophie, yes, we've exchanged emails.'

'We're going for a nightcap at Bonds,' says Gruff. 'You gentlemen care to join?'

Hugh shakes his head. 'Sorry, train to catch.'

'I thought you were staying in town?'

'I prefer to be home when I can. Two young boys. You know how it is.'

Gruff shakes his head. 'Actually, I don't.'

'I'll keep you company,' offers Paul. 'Just let me sign for this.'

While Hugh gets his coat and Paul goes to settle the bill, Gruff turns to Sophie. 'Bonds is just round the corner… you OK for one?'

'Sure.'

Gruff takes another slug of Amaretto, cracking an ice cube between his teeth.

By the time Paul has found a waiter and settled the bill, the three of them are alone in the private dining room. Gruff and Sophie follow Paul down the spiral staircase and out into the street. It's drizzling. Gruff pulls the collar of his overcoat close around his neck. They walk past the entrance to Abacus, where a small crowd of young men in suits and women in short skirts drag hastily on cigarettes before darting back inside.

Gruff's hand is on the small of Sophie's back. She's tense. The three of them walk down Threadneedle Street, silently contemplating their own agendas.

Inside Bonds, Gruff points Sophie towards a table in the corner, then turns to Paul. He takes the banker's arm and leans in to speak in his ear.

'Don't worry about Hugh. He doesn't get it, and he never will, but he won't be around for long.'

Paul drops the grin that he's been wearing all evening. 'Good. I can't say I enjoy having him piss all over me.'

'I'll make sure his replacement is more... compliant.'

'And also much less compliant,' adds Paul.

They follow Sophie to the table in the corner. Gruff slides into the booth next to Sophie, while Paul sits in the chair facing them.

With his usual grin reinstated, Paul continues. 'So, tell me, John, what's on your to-do list?'

'I want you to do some work on Unilever, Kraft, Nestle, P&G, all the global comps...' replies Gruff. 'I want you to write me a shopping list.'

'I can see you've got things to discuss,' says Sophie, picking up her bag, 'and I should probably be going.'

'No, please stay,' says Paul, standing up. 'John has a proposal I think you'll find very interesting, and I really must be going myself.'

Paul turns to the waiter, who has just arrived. 'So, we'll have a pint of Amaretto. Yes, that's right, a pint of Amaretto, with ice for the gentleman, and let's have a bottle of champagne for the lady.'

Paul pushes a wedge of notes into the waiter's hand. 'Please, take good care of my guests.'

Paul puts his overcoat back on and shakes Sophie's hand, then Gruff's. 'We need him at the analyst's presentation for eight-thirty tomorrow, so please don't let him have too many!' says Paul, winking at Sophie.

After Paul has left, Sophie and Gruff sit in silence for a

moment. Sophie is perched on the edge of the bench with her bag on her knee.

'I told my boyfriend I'll be on the last tube. I really need to go.'

Gruff waves his hand. 'Don't worry, we'll just stay for one. I'll call you a cab.'

Sophie nods but looks unsure.

'You know, I started out where you are now,' says Gruff. 'God, I hated being a lawyer. Grovelling for clients. I hated that. But it was a means to an end.'

Already, the waiter has returned with the drinks.

'And Paul tells me you're looking to move into banking?'

'That's it,' says Sophie, relaxing back into the chair. 'I just finished my training contract. This was the first deal I've been involved in from beginning to end, and watching how the deal team works, I just...'

'You just realised that the lawyers get a shit deal?'

'Yeah.'

Gruff watches Sophie taking a sip of champagne.

'Well, I can help you with that,' says Gruff.

'You can get me a job at Gessner? I'd be so grateful.'

'Paul owes me one. In fact, he owes me plenty. We've been working on deals together for a long time. We work well together, because he understands what I want.'

'I see...' says Sophie.

'Do you?' asks Gruff.

Then, brushing the tip of his finger under Sophie's chin, he asks again, 'Do you understand what I want, Sophie?'

Sophie holds his stare. 'You want... to win.'

'I want to win. And I always do.'

Because she is nervous, Sophie has already finished her glass. Gruff tops her up and slides closer in the booth.

'So, I did an MBA,' says Gruff, 'then moved into a strategy role, which led to a board position. And finally, a large dose of M&A got me to where I am today.'

'I see.'

'But the how is not important; it's the result. Because the ends always justify the means,' continues Gruff.

'The ends always justify the means?' asks Sophie.

'Always. It's a tough industry you're working in. Particularly if you're a woman. But I know a few who've made it all the way. Is that what you want?' asks Gruff.

'Of course.'

'You have the potential,' says Gruff, 'but potential is never enough. You need someone in your corner to open the right doors.'

'Yes, yes,' says Sophie, hanging on Gruff's words.

Gruff can feel her relaxing, becoming pliable, and he thinks, *this is too easy*.

'Well, that's what I can do for you,' says Gruff. 'If you trust me, then that's what I can do for you.'

Gruff takes a twist of Sophie's hair between his fingers and gently pushes it behind her ear.

Sophie looks uncomfortable. Gruff picks the champagne out of the cooler and tops up her glass.

'Do you think I'm good looking?' asks Gruff.

'Yes, I'd say so,' says Sophie.

Gruff has moved his hand down to her knee.

'I always get what I want. Some people find that intimidating. Do you find me intimidating?' asks Gruff, crunching on a piece of ice.

'Why were you staring at me at dinner?' asks Sophie.

Gruff doesn't answer straight away. Instead, he looks into her eyes and pictures what she will look like when he lays her down on the bed in his hotel suite.

'You were the only person in the room that I was interested in.'

'Why?'

'I think you know.'

Gruff leans in towards Sophie, but she leans away.

'Sorry, I've got a boyfriend,' says Sophie.

Gruff laughs. 'Look. This is what people do. This is natural. So relax, this is just about you and me...'

Gruff taps his glass on Sophie's. She watches him drain his drink in one, then, slowly, she raises the champagne flute to her lips and does the same. Gruff leans in again to kiss her, and this time she doesn't stop him.

CHAPTER THREE

Friday the 2nd of March, 2012

Women are joining FTSE 100 boards at such a fast rate that they are likely to exceed a target of 20% of total directors by 2015, an official report will predict today.

7.02am – Jude Delaney-Hall, Hackney, Tower Hamlets

Marianne appears in the doorway looking worried. She's still holding the bin bag that she took out earlier.

'He's there again.'

Jude can't find her swim cap. She glances up at Marianne and nods. Why isn't it in the drawer with her goggles?

'What shall we do?' asks Marianne.

Jude shrugs. 'Welcome to London. That's just how it is.'

She definitely had the swim cap on Wednesday evening when she got back from the Masters session, but what did she do with it?

'Should we give him some food? Should we call the police? I don't know – what is the right thing to do?' implores Marianne.

'We don't know anything about him. If it is even a him. I mean, have you ever seen his face?' asks Jude.

'You think it might be a woman?' Marianne's voice has become louder. 'I kind of imagined it was like an Eastern European guy, like working for cash on building sites, sending money home and sleeping rough. You think it's a woman?'

'Who knows?' replies Jude. 'Maybe it's a trafficked Cambodian sex slave who's hiding from her pimp.'

'Oh, my God! You think he's a trafficked woman!'

'Aha!' Jude finds the swim cap and throws it in her tote bag. 'Come on, let's go.'

Marianne lets out a long sigh. 'I just feel like I should do something.'

Jude stuffs a towel in her Booths Bookshop tote and steers Marianne towards the door.

'Wait,' says Marianne, pulling on a well-loved pair of Pretty Ballerinas. By the door are her work shoes, black block heels with thin straps and patent toes, which she puts in a shoe bag and into her handbag.

Jude stands behind Marianne shaking her head.

'I know you're shaking your head,' says Marianne, 'but it's the uniform. I don't know how you get away with trainers.'

'Nobody cares. And if they do care, I don't care.' Jude shrugs.

Although, meteorologically, the sun has risen, there is no sign of it. The sky is the tone that Marianne calls *London Grey*.

As they leave the main entrance to the block of flats, Jude glances over her shoulder towards the bin room door, which is ajar. She snatches a glimpse of a red sleeping bag. Marianne follows her gaze and shudders.

'Look,' says Jude, 'you've spent your whole life between

a gated community in Cape Town and a boarding school in Kent.'

Marianne shrugs.

'And after all that you've landed in London,' continues Jude.

'I've landed in *Hackney*.'

At the entrance to London Fields is a notice from the Metropolitan Police, asking for witnesses to an incident that occurred in the park the previous weekend. At the corner shop, Jude had overheard that passers-by saw a gun and heard shots being fired.

'What's that all about?' asks Marianne.

'Hmmm. No idea,' replies Jude.

'Anyway, you were saying?'

'Well, in London, the haves and the have-nots live in each other's pockets.'

'Or bin rooms,' adds Marianne.

'Especially in areas that are changing quickly.'

'Gentrifying?'

'Yeah, where property prices are rising, the social mix is changing, and hipster coffee is squeezing out the eel, pie and mash.'

'Eel what?' asks Marianne.

'You never heard of eel, pie and mash?'

'Eel, as in the fish?'

'Yeah.'

'Urgh!' Marianne pulls a face.

'Anyway, what I'm saying is, you've never had to deal with the whole big messy melting pot. And so, now, as an adult, when you come across different segments of society – anyone who's not metropolitan elite – you get all spun out.'

'You mean, when I come across a Cambodian sex slave living in our bin room?' replies Marianne.

'Exactly.'

'But having someone sleeping in your bin room is not normal. Is it?'

'What's normal?' asks Jude. 'Real life is gritty sometimes.'

They walk past a tree surrounded by empty beer cans, pizza boxes and bottles of vodka.

'Where you see grit, I see deprivation,' replies Marianne.

'When you put it like that, I feel bad for dragging you to Hackney. We should have taken the flat on Sloane Street.'

'There's no lido in Chelsea. I'm much happier here.'

Jude laughs. 'I'll remember you said that.'

'And besides, you know how much I love eel pie.'

'It's not eel pie. It's eel, with pie!'

'And mash. Love it. Can't get enough of it!'

At the bus stop, Jude sends a text to '87287' and receives the latest bus times by reply.

'The 55 is here in one minute.'

'OK then,' replies Marianne, 'one-minute debrief on last night.'

'Well, I can confidently say that was my first, last and only try at speed dating.'

'Literally, no one?'

Jude shakes her head.

'Same,' replies Marianne.

'They were all too City Boy for me,' explains Jude. 'How about you?'

'Too immature.'

'What is it about you and older guys?' asks Jude.

'They're just more interesting. They've got life experience and their own opinion on things. Guys our age are mostly just… juvenile,' explains Marianne.

The number 55 pulls in, and Marianne steps into the queue behind a woman wearing a cleaner's bib, holding the hand of a fidgety child in a Spider-Man costume.

'I find old guys a bit sad and decrepit. Like they try too hard to show they still have that youthful braggadocio. I want a man with vigour but in a wholesome way.'

'Wholesome?' Marianne starts to laugh. 'What does that even mean? Like wholemeal bread?'

The bus doors open and people tap the Oyster card reader as they file on.

'I mean, like, not a coke-snorting City Boy.'

'Wholesome? You mean… you mean… you want to meet, like… a lumberjack or something!' Marianne laughs and shakes her head.

'Sure, why not!' shouts Jude as the doors close behind Marianne.

5.17pm – Dan Trench, The Fine Line, Monument, City

Jostling around him, three-deep at the bar, are loud young men, made boisterous by alcohol and the prospect of the weekend. They stand in groups, drinking expensive lager and pretending to listen to one another, while they scan the room for girls.

'…but he didn't realise that he'd replied all, and both of them got sacked…'

'…the video's gone viral. She's the assistant for a broker I know at Lloyds…'

The prospect of seeing Gareth has been hanging over him all day. At some point, he'll have to talk about the accident. The guilt is like a lead weight in the pit of his stomach. A space opens up at the bar and he wedges himself into it.

'Fucksakes,' mutters a voice from over his shoulder.

He turns his head to look at the man, who looks away.

'What was that?' says Dan.

The man looks up.

'You barged in.'

Dan breathes deeply into his chest and slowly straightens up to his full height. The man's pupils narrow down to tiny points. Dan looks at the man's thinning hair and imagines bringing the thick base of a glass bottle down onto his balding crown. He can hear the hollow ring of the hard bottle and the soft thud of the man's skull.

'Is there a problem?' says Dan.

The man grunts and looks away.

Dan orders two bottles of Corona. His phone starts to ring.

'I'm at the bar,' he says.

'Good, good,' replies Gareth, 'I'm holding a spot by the door.'

Dan turns around and sees Gareth standing with his back to the door, idly watching a group of people on the mezzanine floor above. His silk tie is still tight around the collar of his crisp white shirt. Dan nudges his way back through the crowd. Gareth is wearing Oliver Peoples glasses, with round frames that don't suit his face. They lean in to hear each other above the clamour.

'Brings back some memories, this place,' says Gareth.

'Yeah, I'd forgotten about all this,' replies Dan.

He studies the hand-stitched collar of Gareth's suit jacket and his perfectly coiffed hair.

'Is it just me, or did your hair used to be brown?'

Gareth shrugs. 'There's so much to catch up on, I don't even know where to start.'

The weight is gathering in the pit of Dan's stomach. But stronger than the urge to make his excuses and leave is the feeling that he owes Gareth some kind of explanation.

‘Look, I want to say that I’m sorry about dropping off the radar like that. I needed to get away and sort my head out.’

‘I read about what happened. I’m so sorry. I can’t even imagine.’

‘I owe you an explanation.’

‘You don’t owe me anything. It’s just good to see you.’

They stand in silence for a moment, both looking out through the full-height windows at the Friday-night crowd, which has spilled onto the pavement. The City pulses around them, an organism continuously renewing itself, an expression of the dreams and ambition of a million people.

A young man stumbles over. He’s been drinking for some time. From his ungroomed appearance, cheap shoes and ill-fitting suit, Dan can see that he’s not a stockbroker; he doesn’t sell for a living, which means he must be an analyst or a fund manager.

‘Gareth Eeaaaaryyyy,’ says the young man.

‘Oh, hi, Andrew, how are things?’ replies Gareth, turning to introduce Dan to the young man. ‘Dan, this is Andrew Waite; he’s at Green Knight.’

‘Did you know that you have a pint in your pocket?’ says Dan.

Andrew looks down at his jacket pocket and pulls out a glass, which is still half full of beer.

‘I wondered where that had got to.’

‘Actually, Dan used to work at Green Knight too,’ says Gareth.

‘You used to work at Green Knight?’ says Andrew.

‘Columbus Fund,’ explains Dan.

Andrew stares at Dan for a long time, while this piece of information sinks in. Then, a look of realisation spreads across his face.

'You're Dan Trench!'

Dan nods.

'You're Dan Trench!' repeats Andrew, who has taken Dan's hand and is shaking it enthusiastically. 'Hello, Dan Trench, I'm Andrew Waite.'

'Hi,' says Dan, pulling his hand away.

'Good to see you, Andrew, but we've got to dash,' says Gareth, steering Dan towards the door.

A few steps and the two of them are standing on the crowded pavement. There's still a pinch of winter in the air. The last of the sun casts long shadows across the road. An empty glass balances on top of a bollard.

'Dash where?' asks Dan.

'A few new haunts.'

Dan stops and folds his arms. 'I don't know.'

'Why don't you stop being a miserable bastard and let me buy you dinner?'

Dan looks at Gareth and thinks about the fun they used to have.

'And if you don't want to talk about what happened that's fine with me. Honestly.'

'OK,' says Dan.

Gareth waves down a black cab and they settle into the back seat. Soon, they're crawling up King William Street towards Bank.

'Tell me about this boxing,' says Gareth.

'I love it.'

Gareth pulls a face. 'Love getting smacked in the head?'

'Fighting is one of those basic human things. Like eating and fucking.'

'So you actually *fight*?'

'It's called sparring. My first proper fight is in a couple of months. That's what Marc's getting me in shape for.'

'The guy with the boxer's nose?'

'Yeah, that's Marc.'

'What's sparring?' asks Gareth.

'Anyone can turn up and fight. All you need is a gum guard and a pair of gloves. We do a round robin, so everyone fights everyone. You end up fighting all sorts.'

'*Fight Club* for bankers!'

Outside, it's suddenly become dark. A cyclist passes them, his red tail light weaving through the traffic. On Tuesday night, Dan was the last person left in the ring at the end of the night, floating on an adrenaline high. He must have fought nine or ten rounds, and he would have fought more. In the morning, the migraine felt like it was splitting his head apart.

'So, what are you doing with yourself these days?' asks Gareth.

'I'm with City Financial Training.'

'Teaching investment bank grad schemes?'

'Yeah.'

'Rather you than me.'

Somewhere past Bond Street Gareth jumps up from his seat.

'We're here!'

He throws £30 at the driver and ushers Dan out of the cab and down a narrow alleyway.

'Lancashire Court,' Gareth explains, 'where the *hedgies* hang out. And where there are hedge fund managers, there are girls.'

Right on cue, a girl in a short black cocktail dress, with long blonde hair, wearing large pearl drop earrings, walks past.

As they make their way along the alley, Dan notices that the atmosphere is more laid-back than in The Fine Line.

Fewer suits, more chinos. Less lager, more champagne. It's an older crowd, the accents are more polished, and to Gareth's point, there are a lot more women.

They pick their way through the poser tables that line the alleyway, each one just big enough to balance a champagne bucket and a couple of glasses.

Outside Mews of Mayfair, people are listening to the gravelly tones of a middle-aged man with a French accent. Dan notices the man's square jaw and the thick wave of dark hair slicked back over his head. There's something familiar about him. Gareth sees the man too and stops to straighten his tie.

As the man pauses, Gareth steps forwards with his right arm extended.

'Mr Blois! What a pleasure.'

Gareth grabs Mr Blois' hand and pumps it vigorously.

'Gareth Eary, Gresham Street Capital.' Gareth puts his left hand on Mr Blois' arm. 'Don't let me interrupt you, Mr Blois, but you must let me buy you a drink.'

Gareth grins and nods at the rest of the people in the group before slipping between them into Mews of Mayfair. Mr Blois watches Gareth walk away before resuming his story.

'Excuse me,' says Dan, squeezing past the group to follow Gareth.

The bar area is small and dimly lit. The furniture and decor are ironically opulent: a parody of a stately home. A huge chandelier, like a giant piece of costume jewellery, hangs from the low ceiling. Beneath the chandelier, green leather banquette seating is arranged to face out into the room. Gareth walks across the parquet floor and drops himself onto a stool at one end of the bar next to a gold methuselah of champagne.

'Shit, that was Aurelius Blois. He's a fucking rockstar. He manages like twenty billion.'

'He looked familiar,' says Dan.

'Always in GQ, with a different supermodel every time.'

'Good evening, gentlemen,' says the barman, poised like a soldier awaiting orders.

Dan's eye is drawn to the silver pin, which draws together the collar of his white shirt and holds his skinny navy tie in place. The tie matches the colour of his well-pressed apron.

'I'd like a bottle of vintage champagne,' says Gareth.

'Certainly, sir, perhaps the 1985 Krug?'

'Perfect. Send it to that gentleman standing just outside the door.'

'That would be Mr Blois,' suggests the barman.

'Yes, that's him. And give him this too,' says Gareth, pulling out a business card and then throwing his credit card and a £20 note onto the silver tip tray.

The bartender takes the credit card. 'That will be fourteen-hundred, sir. Would you like to open a tab?'

'Jesus!' says Dan. 'Fourteen hundred quid!'

Gareth shrugs.

In one corner of the room are three scruffily dressed men in their fifties. Their voices are clearly audible over the low background murmur. They're drinking whisky and red wine. The loudest one is wearing a flat cap and talking with a mockney accent.

'I did a good bit of business with your old firm today,' says Gareth.

'Who do you speak to?'

'That Peter Mancroft is a broker's dream. He must churn his portfolio once a quarter.'

'Congratulations on having the City's worst fund manager as your best client.'

'The way volumes are going, I'd be screwed without him.'

'Things are that bad?'

'Every week there's another small broker going under. Too many guys like me chasing too little business.'

Gareth orders a bottle of Chateau Lafite, and they fall into easy conversation.

A balding man, wearing an expensive suit, walks into the bar with a woman half his age. She's drunk and giggly. He orders a bottle of white wine, and they settle onto one of the banquettes.

'That'll be you in twenty years,' says Dan.

'God, I hope so,' replies Gareth.

Dan watches the waiting staff glide efficiently from table to table, topping up glasses. By the time they've started on their second bottle, the Ibiza lounge music is getting louder.

'I was just thinking about that time we were sat in The Fine Line and you tried to convince me that what we do, shuffling paper around, is *socially useful*.' Gareth laughs.

'I remember that,' says Dan. 'I said that we facilitate the efficient allocation of capital. We almost had an argument about it.'

'We did have an argument about it. I thought you were joking! But you really believed all that shit.' Gareth laughs again.

'I still do.'

'So, our mutual friend, Mancroft, is doing something socially useful, is he?'

'Mancroft is a cog in a system that supplies capital to

good businesses and withholds it from bad businesses. The system serves a purpose.'

Dan waits what seems a long time for Gareth to respond, but he doesn't.

'Well then, what else is there?' says Dan, feeling frustrated but trying not to sound it. 'Is it just the money?'

'And what if it is just the money?' says Gareth. 'What would be wrong with that?'

From the tone of Gareth's voice, Dan sees that he's struck a nerve. But the alcohol has loosened his tongue, and he can't help pressing his point.

'I'd tell you that you're wasting your life,' says Dan.

Gareth cocks his head to one side and looks thoughtful. He smiles a sad kind of smile.

'The thing is the money's important, but it's not everything. It's also about being someone I was never meant to be. I enjoy playing the part. And I'm good at it.'

'Good at being a stockbroker, or good at playing the part?'

'It's the same thing,' says Gareth. 'I can play any part I want. I choose this part. And I'm fucking good at it.'

A fleck of Gareth's spit lands on Dan's cheek. Gareth turns away and silently drains his glass. Dan watches his chest rise and fall, as his breathing settles back down. Dan feels bad about pushing it.

'Sorry,' says Dan, 'I didn't mean it personally.'

'No, my fault. That's two bottles of red wine and an empty stomach.'

Dan glances down at Gareth's hands. He is twisting a gold signet ring around his little finger.

'Is that for playing the part?' asks Dan.

'Yeah, I guess it is.' Gareth laughs.

Gareth slides the ring off his finger and puts it on the table.

Dan picks it up and holds it under the light. '*Nosce Te Ipsum*, what does that mean?'

'*Nosce Te Ipsum?* I have no idea.'

Dan slides the ring back across the table.

Gareth shakes his head. 'You know, it's funny, I'm paranoid that people might see through me… and now… here I am, seeking out someone who's always seen right through me. I mean, what's that all about?'

Dan shrugs. 'Don't overthink it. You're a good man, Gareth. Let me get some drinks in.'

While Dan orders a round of caipirinhas, Gareth gets up to go to the bathroom. Standing up, he realises how drunk he is.

The gents' is empty, and Gareth takes the nearest urinal. He's thinking about what he said to Dan.

'*Nosce Te Ipsum*,' he says out loud to himself.

'Know thyself,' says a gravelly voice.

Gareth turns to see that it's Aurelius Blois.

CHAPTER FOUR

Saturday the 3rd of March, 2012

Predators are circling Game Group as the UK-listed video games retailer struggles for survival. Interest in Game could mean competition for US peer, Game Stop, which is seen as the most likely buyer of Game's assets. Game's shares fell 64% yesterday after directors expressed 'uncertainty' over the future of the business.

9.57am – Andrew Waite, Bermondsey Street, Southwark

Andrew's hangover is worse than usual. Opening his eyes is painful, but closing them is worse, so he just lies there, in the gloom, staring at the handle of his bedroom door. He remembers Jägerbombs, tequila and champagne. He needs water. He wants to be sick. Better still, he wants to die.

The handle turns, and now his flatmate is standing in the doorway. Angus is dressed, perky and smells fresh from the shower. All things that Andrew is not. Angus also has a plan, and although Andrew knows that it will require a superhuman effort to get out of bed, a plan sounds like a welcome distraction.

Angus points out that, whatever happens, Andrew couldn't possibly feel any worse than he feels right now. This is meant to be motivational, but it also turns out to be untrue. As his feet touch the floor and his body swings into an upright position, nausea rushes through him. He grabs the bin from under his desk to catch a burp of stomach bile.

'Is that all you've got?' asks Angus.

Andrew isn't sure. And then he is. That was a warning shot. His stomach quivers, and then contracts, and now there is vomit streaming from his mouth and from his nose too.

'Hmmm... good,' says Angus, keeping his distance. 'Better out than in.'

When he's finished, Andrew looks up. 'That... feels... better.'

Andrew stands under the shower, with his hand on the wall, pissing into the plughole. His piss smells heavy.

The shower makes him feel a little more human, as does his first lungful of cool spring air. The greasy spoon is just a few doors down. They sit on plastic chairs that are bolted to the floor. Al's Cafe is the last holdout against the gentrification of the street. Angus spreads the *Weekend FT* out across the table. Andrew has his head in his hands. He feels hot. His stomach is churning again.

Angus is talking about a new organic sourdough bread shop in Borough Market. Andrew is concentrating on not being sick. Two huge oval plates arrive. Bacon, black pudding, beans, grilled tomatoes, toast, fried eggs and chips. Andrew looks at the plate and swallows hard. The sight of eggs sets off another wave of nausea.

Andrew addresses the waiter's shoes. 'Please. Bring water.'

The ketchup is in a plastic bottle that looks like a giant tomato. The nozzle is congealed with sauce. Angus gives it a shake and squirts a red trail across his plate.

'Ketchup?' he asks, offering it to Andrew.

Andrew makes a noise that means 'no'. He picks up the fork and pushes it tentatively into a chip, before putting the fork down again. This isn't going to work.

Angus pushes a piece of toast and egg into his mouth, then remembers something and chuckles to himself. 'Oh yeah, I meant to ask, why is there fried chicken all over the hall?'

'I tripped on the IKEA boxes,' says Andrew, staring at the linoleum tabletop. 'I'd rather top myself than build another piece of flat-packed furniture.'

Angus grunts in agreement then asks, 'How was last night?'

'Expensive.'

'Why?'

'Credit-card roulette.'

'Ouch.' Angus sucks on his teeth. 'How much?'

Andrew opens his wallet and slowly pulls out a number of little pieces of paper, before finding the one he's looking for. He studies it before handing it to Angus.

'Three hundred quid,' says Angus. 'Ouch. What about girls?'

'I can't really remember. I was sick on my jacket.'

'Does this finally mean a trip to the drycleaners?' asks Angus.

'Chucked it in the river.'

Angus slaps his hand on the table. 'Love it!'

'Portnoy told me to buy a new suit.'

'Since when does Portnoy care about your wardrobe?'

'Since I became manager of the Mid-Cap Fund.'

'Shit that's massive! But what about your boss, *what's-his-name*?'

'Portnoy gave him the boot. Wants to make things more... professional.'

'*Professional?* But do you actually have any idea what you're doing?'

'No, but I don't think that's necessarily a problem. I don't think many people know what they're doing.'

Angus throws his head back and laughs, and a fleck of black pudding lands on the tabletop.

Andrew wants to tell Angus what a dickhead he is, but talking makes his head feel worse, so instead he closes his eyes and imagines how nice it would feel to be dead. Angus flicks through the sections of the *Weekend FT* and settles on 'How to Spend It'.

'This magazine is so outrageous,' says Angus, as he stuffs forkfuls of chips and bacon into his mouth. 'Look, here's a watch with two mechanical pistons that go up and down. It's fucking ugly and it costs eighty grand. I love this magazine. It's obscene. There's a pair of cufflinks here made from two-thousand-year-old gold coins with Alexander the Great on one side and Zeus on the other...'

Andrew isn't listening. The hangover comes in waves and right now it's taking a superhuman effort not to be sick. The waiter puts a bottle of water in front of him, and he gives a grunt of thanks.

Angus looks up from 'How to Spend It' and studies Andrew for a moment.

'You're in a bad way, aren't you?'

After Angus has finished his breakfast, and Andrew's too, they walk up Bermondsey Street, then take a left turn down St Thomas Street.

Andrew is starting to feel better. He looks up at the

near-completed Shard, which towers over them. 'Don't you just love that building?' he says, admiring the tower's jagged crown, glistening in the spring sunshine.

'I think it sticks out like a sore thumb,' says Angus.

'But that's the point: its boldness, its… unearthliness. On a day like today, against that clear cloudless blue, it looks more part of the sky than the earth. The views from the top are going to be amazing.'

Andrew goes to step off the curb, but Angus quickly pulls him back as a cyclist speeds past inches from Andrew's nose.

'Idiot! Fucking idiot!' screams the cyclist, looking over his shoulder.

'Shit, thanks,' says Andrew to Angus, composing himself. 'I hate cyclists. What a dick.'

They cross the road into Borough Market. Andrew makes straight for Monmouth Coffee, but Angus has spotted some purple sprouting broccoli. He is at pains to explain that this is the first purple sprouting broccoli of the season.

'The stuff from Sainsbury's is better,' says Andrew. 'It comes from Kenya and it's always in season.'

Angus gives him a withering look.

While Angus is in the stall, Andrew stands outside thinking about what Angus said over breakfast about him not having any idea what he's doing. Andrew has always thought of himself as a practical kind of person. Not really the imaginative or creative sort but someone who approaches things in a methodical, logical way.

He is chewing the problem over when Angus returns.

'So, what did *you* get up to last night?' asks Andrew.

'I was in the flat. I had to watch a launch.'

'Satellite launch?'

'Yeah, a weather satellite.'

'How did it go?'

'Fine. It should be in orbit by now,' says Angus, glancing at his watch.

'Oh good. That's good, right?' asks Andrew.

'Well… not for us. We didn't write the insurance on it.'

Andrew looks blank, so Angus continues.

'If there's a problem and the insurance pays out, then the premiums will go up. And then in future every time we underwrite a satellite, we'll make more money.'

'So, if you haven't written it, then you're sitting there hoping the thing's going to explode?' says Andrew.

'Yeah.'

They walk past Posh Banger Brothers. The rich, greasy smell of Cumberland sausages sizzling on the hot plate makes Andrew regret leaving his breakfast to Angus. An inscription on the sign that hangs over the entrance to Borough Market says that the market has been here since 1756.

The queue at Monmouth Coffee stretches along the pavement and round the corner. A barista wearing a black apron walks along the line, taking people's orders and writing their names on paper cups.

'I read this thing the other day,' says Angus, 'the journalist went to a town in Kosovo where there's a whole class of nine- and ten-year-olds called *Tonybler*.'

'What?'

'Seriously, *Tonybler*, or *Bler*. And then one kid who was just called *Tony*. I mean to us Blair is some kind of creepy narcissist, but in Kosovo, he's the man who brought peace to the Balkans. He's a hero…'

'Maybe that'll be Cameron's legacy in Libya.'

'Imagine it. A whole generation named *Juscallmedave*.'

They stand shoulder to shoulder in the slow-moving queue, sniggering.

'Please stop, my head hurts,' says Andrew.

'OK, so what about Boris? What's his legacy?'

'Oh, that's easy. It's got to be the Boris Bike.'

'Even though it was Ken Livingstone's idea.'

'Poor Ken. Must be livid.'

'Or how about Boris as PM?'

'Can you imagine it?'

'Boris and Berlusconi at the G7 doing bunga bunga!'

Andrew starts to laugh before another wave of nausea hits him.

'OK, please, enough. Let's talk about something more sombre before I'm sick again… how's your love life?'

'Actually, the drought may be over,' replies Angus.

'Really?'

'You remember that guy I met—'

'Woah, woah!' interrupts Andrew. 'I didn't ask for details. I was just, you know, making conversation.'

'I know, but you remember that guy I met in Barcelona?'

'Uh-huh.'

'He's in London the weekend after next.'

'I'll make myself scarce.'

'I didn't mean that. But between now and then you do need to help me build my bed.'

When they get near the front of the queue, Angus leans over to browse the counter.

'Can I help you?' asks a girl with long black hair and an American accent.

'Hmmm. Yes. Could I have 250g of the Finca Capetillo.'

The girl takes a scoop from the coffee bin.

'Actually wait…' says Angus, 'is it *organic*?'

Andrew shakes his head and smirks.

'No, it's not,' says the girl, 'but the San Jose La Laguna is organic and it's also from Guatemala. It's shade grown.'

'You hear that, Angus? It's *shade grown*,' says Andrew.

The girl gives Andrew a look that shuts him up.

'Oh fantastic. I'll have that one please,' says Angus.

'How would you like it ground?'

'Espresso please.'

'Oh…' the girl looks concerned, '…well the San Jose is quite a dark roast; if it's for espresso I would really recommend something with a little more fruit, perhaps the Kaffa Forest.'

Angus looks anxious.

'It's organic,' reassures the girl.

'Oh, it's organic.'

'It's from Ethiopia,' says the girl.

'Hmmm… Ethiopia,' Angus thinks carefully about what this means before clarifying, 'the Ethiopian *highlands*?'

'Yes.'

Andrew is smirking again.

'Well, in that case I'll have the Kaffa Forest,' says Angus decisively.

Drinks in hand they cross the road into Borough Market and try to pick their way through the mass of tourists.

'This is slightly less fun than doing laps of Bank tube station at rush hour,' says Andrew.

'We need one of those,' replies Angus, pointing at a pushchair that is being forced through the crowd like a riot truck.

Eventually Angus abandons his search for the new organic sourdough bread shop, and they squeeze their way out of the back of the market and onto Stoney Street. They pass Vinopolis and, turning the corner under the railway bridge, the river Thames opens up in front of them. It's a crisp, clear morning and the low arc of sun burnishes the fronts of the warehouses that line the north bank of the river.

Andrew looks west towards Saint Paul's Cathedral and takes a deep breath.

'God, I love this city. If you can imagine it, someone is doing it somewhere. Whoever you want to be, you can be it here.'

CHAPTER FIVE

Wednesday the 7th of March, 2012

David Cameron has begun a three-day visit to the US to map out an 'endgame' for western intervention in Afghanistan. The prime minister and Barack Obama, US President, will discuss plans to hand over lead combat roles to Afghan forces in mid-2013.

7.24am – Gareth Eary, Gresham Street Capital, City

Every time Gareth steps onto the trading floor, he pictures himself marching into battle. He takes a deep breath, taps his card on the reader, lifts his chin and strides through the security doors. The heels of his shoes clip reassuringly. He reaches his desk, drops into the chair and flicks on his monitors.

'Morning, Jabba.'

Jabba is slurping a can of Diet Coke.

'Fuck off.'

'Bit early in the morning for that, don't you think?'

'Oh, I'm sorry,' says Jabba. 'Good morning… now fuck off.'

Jabba talks to Gareth without looking up from his screen. The remains of breakfast are gathered in the folds of his shirt.

Gareth's boss sits at the desk opposite. Being unerringly professional, fastidiously secretive about her private life and never, ever sleeping with anyone in the City has allowed Jessica to tolerate a long and successful career in an industry full of misogynists.

Jessica finishes talking to Martin before turning to Gareth.

'Gareth, would you mind having Martin on your calls this morning?'

'Yes, I would mind.'

'Come on, Gareth.'

'I'm not a babysitter.'

'But you are the *best*.'

'Oh. Wait. Say that again.'

'You. Are. The. Best. There, I said it. Now, can Martin sit in?'

'Fine, but just this once.'

Gareth's Blackberry starts to ring. *Prek PAINTER* flashes on the screen.

'Hi, Prek, are you at the flat?'

'Yes, sar, I get your note.'

'Yeah, so just to be clear, it's the Elephant's Breath for the bathroom, not the other one.'

'No problem, sar. I get it mixed at Dulux, good price OK?'

'No, Prek. We spoke about this last time. No Dulux. Only Farrow and Ball.'

'But Farrow and Ball much expensive, sar, Dulux same colour, good price, good finish.'

'I appreciate that, Prek, but I want Farrow and Ball, understand? OK?'

'You the boss.'

'Correct.' Gareth tosses his Blackberry on the desk.

Jabba smirks and shakes his head.

'You're a funny one,' says Jabba.

The head of research announces that the morning meeting is about to begin. There's a flurry of activity around the research desk while the analysts take it in turns to give snap updates on their stocks. Gareth jots down the key points and the clients who will want a call. Jabba is staring intently at his screen, but Gareth knows he's taking it all in. Jabba can work two phones and a Bloomberg terminal at the same time as eavesdropping on a conversation half a dozen desks away. He's also very good at his job, which is to execute the client orders that Gareth brings in. And for this reason, Gareth tries to be civil with him.

Pritish, the pharmaceuticals analyst, is next on the mike. He speaks quietly and with an accent. Out of the corner of his eye, Gareth sees Jabba look up from his screen and lean far back in his chair, a satisfied sneer spreading across his face.

'*Hey! Hey!* We can't hear you, *Prit-shit… Prick-shit, speak up!*' shouts Jabba across the room.

Pritish stumbles over his words and stops, red faced. There are a few sniggers, and Jabba looks around the room, grinning. Jessica glares furiously at Jabba.

As soon as the morning meeting is over, Jessica marches purposefully across the floor and into the CEO's office. Gareth and Jabba both watch her through the glass-walled cubicle, angrily making a point. Jabba turns towards Gareth and shrugs: they both know what's coming.

Jessica emerges from the office and marches back to Jabba's desk.

'You, with me, *now*.'

Jabba stares at her, impassively, then slowly reaches down beside his desk and picks up a can of Diet Coke. He opens it, raises the can to his lips and slowly drains it, while Jessica, standing beside his desk with her arms crossed, silently rages. Still staring at Jessica, Jabba stands up and lets out an enormous belch, brushing past her as he strolls slowly towards the CEO's office.

'That man is un-fucking-believable,' announces Jessica before marching back past Jabba, who arrives at the CEO's office a few moments behind her.

Jabba slouches back in a chair and the CEO sits at his desk and nods while Jessica, standing in the middle of the office, gives a lecture.

Emerging from the office, Jabba strolls back to his chair.

'You still here?' says Gareth.

'Final warning,' replies Jabba, staring at his screen.

'I thought you already had your final warning after that scene at the Christmas party?'

Jabba turns to focus on Gareth.

'Listen to me, Eary. I've seen plenty of smug bastards like you come and go. You think someone's handed you a one-way ticket. Well, you're wrong, believe me. I'll still be here, pissing in the water cooler, rubbing people up the wrong way, long after you've gone.'

Jabba sneers until Gareth turns back to his screen.

Gareth's clients will be arriving at their desks around now, so he calls Martin over to talk through his list of morning calls.

While Martin pulls his chair round, Gareth plugs in a second set of headphones.

'OK, top tip for you, Martin. Write this down. Rule 101: you've got to get in with the secretaries. Get through the gatekeeper and the battle is half won.'

His first call is to Epoch Advisors, but as soon as the secretary picks up, Gareth realises his mistake.

'Hello, Gareth,' says the voice on the other end of the line. The tone is curt.

'Ah… hi, hi. How are you? It's been… a while,' replies Gareth.

'Yes, it has.'

'Look, so sorry I've been crap. Just sooo busy at the moment, lots of client stuff going on. You know how it is sometimes, ha!'

'Sure,' replies the secretary.

'I'll message you.'

'Whatever.'

'Umm… is Dominic about?' asks Gareth.

'He's away from his desk. You'll have to call back.'

The line goes dead.

Turning to Martin, Gareth takes his headphones off. 'So…'

In his notebook Martin has written *Rule 101: gatekeeper*, and then the page is blank.

'So, Rule 101,' says Martin.

'Yeah.'

'If I'm honest, it seemed a bit awkward with the secretary,' continues Martin.

'Well observed.'

'I kind of got the impression that you might have…'

'Yeah, I might have.'

There's an awkward silence while Gareth tries to think of something useful to say. Martin absent-mindedly writes *might have* in his notebook.

'OK,' says Gareth. 'OK, so Rule 101, it's tricky, because this is a fine line. So, take this down. Rule 101. You've got to get in with the secretaries, but try not to sleep with them. So, yeah, Rule 101. Do *not* shag the secretaries.'

'I think I can remember that,' says Martin, closing his notebook. 'Useful tip. Thanks.'

Jabba rolls over in his chair and interjects himself between Gareth and Martin.

'Gentlemen. Gentlemen. Next Friday, chance for the boys to get together, let off some steam…' says Jabba.

'Not interested,' replies Gareth.

'I know you're not interested. Wouldn't want you at one of our get-togethers anyway, preening yourself like some kind of nasty *fag*.'

'Look, Jabba. Martin and I have got work to do, and we would appreciate it if you and your horrible little friends would play at pimps elsewhere.'

Jabba slowly turns his chair, pushing it a couple of inches forwards so that Gareth is left staring at the back of his head.

'Don't worry about him,' says Jabba, putting his arm round Martin's shoulders. 'As the new boy I'm sure you're aware how important it is to socialise with your colleagues. Next Friday me and some of the guys are going to have a few beers, then head over to mine. Chip a hundred quid in the pot, we get a couple of girls over, a few drinks and a pinch of *candy*, just a bit of fun, let off some steam…'

Martin nods nervously.

'Good lad,' says Jabba, slapping Martin on the back. 'I'll pop round after lunch for the money.'

Jabba sneers again at Gareth before wheeling himself off further down the desk.

When Jabba has gone, Martin looks at Gareth for explanation.

'Hookers and coke. I'd make my excuses if I were you.'

Martin's eyes widen. The phone starts to ring. Gareth picks up his headset and nods at Martin to join the call.

'Gresham Street, Gareth Eary.'

'Hi, Gareth.'

Flicking the mute button, Gareth whispers to Martin, 'Andrew Waite, Green Knight.'

'Good morning, squire. I was just about to give you a call on Domino's – the pizza that is, not the printing. Note out from our analyst today, he's top-rated on travel and leisure, and he's really pinned his colours to the mast with this one. He thinks that the upgrade momentum is going to run and run. He's upping his target price to 600p. It's a punchy call, but I've got to say, I think he's spot on. Perhaps I can pop over with him some time to talk through the key drivers? Lunch maybe?'

'Yeah, drop me an email,' says Andrew. 'Actually, I called because I see you guys have been doing some volume in Nobel Ordnance.'

'If you've got business in Nobel, you've come to the right place. Buying or selling?' asks Gareth.

'Selling. I have a million to sell at 320p or better,' replies Andrew.

'Right you are, sir. A million shares to sell at 320p or better. And that's all for the UK Mid-Cap Fund?' Gareth is tapping the order into the system as he speaks.

'Correct.'

'Thanks for the order; we'll get the confirmation back to you ASAP.'

Gareth leans back in his chair. 'Order!'

'What's cooking?' asks Jabba as he wheels back past Gareth.

'Selling a million Nobels for Green Knight at 320p.'

After half a dozen calls, Gareth sends Martin out on

the mid-morning coffee run. Business has been swift and, being in a good mood, Gareth has resolved to take Martin under his wing, not least because it can't hurt to win some brownie points with Jessica.

Jessica puts down the phone and looks up at him, shaking her head. 'This market is driving me mad. How are you getting on with Martin?'

'Fine. Not sure he's salesman material though.'

'In the beginning neither were you.'

Gareth's Blackberry starts ringing just as Martin reappears with the coffees. It's a withheld number.

'Gresham Street, Gareth Eary.'

'Hello, Gareth.'

The voice sounds familiar, and Gareth feels the hairs on the back of his neck stand up.

'This is Aurelius Blois, Livermore Capital.'

Gareth's pulse quickens. He pauses and takes a deep breath.

'Mr Blois. Good morning, sir. A pleasure to hear from you. What can I do for you today?'

At the mention of Blois' name, Jessica and Jabba both look up.

'Tell me, Gareth, what's your biggest name? What are you doing most volume in?'

'Well, that would have to be Albourne. That's our biggest name as a house, and here at Gresham Street, I personally see most of our business in ALB.'

'Good.'

Gareth continues, 'And looking ahead, it's moving up into the FTSE 100 Index next month, so I would expect to see volumes increase from here, with a bit of a spike in activity around the month-end as portfolios get repositioned for the Index reshuffle.'

'We will be doing business in ALB, and it sounds like Gresham Street is going to be the place to do it,' replies Blois.

Gareth punches the air.

'That's what I'm here for, sir. As you know, we offer a full-service prime brokerage, research and corporate finance—'

'Yes, yes,' cuts in Blois, 'of course.'

'Perhaps I can pop over to your office today with the paperwork. We can iron out the commission rates and the other details, and we can get you up and running ASAP,' replies Gareth.

'Very good, my secretary will fix up a time.'

Aurelius hangs up and Gareth looks at his Blackberry for a moment before casually placing it on the table. Jessica and Jabba are both staring at him.

Then Gareth springs to his feet and gives Jessica a high-five over the divider.

'*Aurelius-Fucking-Blois!*'

Even Jabba gets out of his chair to slap Gareth on the shoulder. Having Blois as a client is going to be good for everyone's bonus.

'Who is Aurelius Blois?' asks Martin.

8.19am – Aurelius Blois, The Townhouse, Mayfair

Aurelius Blois puts the phone down next to his Piaget. He props himself up into a more comfortable position, then reaches under the sheet to scratch his balls. He flicks the bed spread with his foot to knock the torn foil of a condom wrapper onto the floor, then holds his flaccid penis in his fist with a grunt of satisfaction.

Aurelius likes to start each morning thinking about how he is going to win. It sets him up nicely for the day. Being a winner is a self-fulfilling thing. Aurelius is creative, and he has a flexible approach to things that other people lack. Also, he pays for the best legal advice.

Aurelius admires himself in the mirrored wall of the suite. He sits up straight, takes a deep breath and pushes his shoulders back. He flexes his pectoral muscles and smooths his long dark hair back over his head. *What a fine physique you have*, thinks Aurelius. *You are fifty-two, and you still look this fucking great.*

Feeling pleased with himself for so many reasons, Aurelius grabs his penis again.

Through the adjoining lounge, he hears the bathroom door open, and a moment later a dark-haired, fair-skinned woman pads confidently into the room, sliding a finger down her G-string.

Aurelius watches the woman as she moves up from the foot of the bed towards him.

'I believe that you have perfect tits,' says Aurelius.

'I do.'

'How old are you?'

'Twenty-eight.'

While the girl kisses his chest, Aurelius looks thoughtfully at her side profile in the mirror. He runs his eye from her heel, along the back of her calf, up her thigh, around her bum and down the arch of her back.

Underneath the sheets Aurelius can feel himself starting to get hard.

'Ah, what do you do to me, Ursula!' says Aurelius, lifting her chin in his hand. 'I would love to fuck the day away, but there are many things I must do today to keep the plates spinning.'

The woman straightens up, kisses Aurelius on the lips, slides herself off the edge of the bed and picks her bra off the chaise longue.

'Do you know who I am?' asks Aurelius.

The woman is putting on her bra. 'You're Aurelius Blois. I know you from the *FT*. You're a hedge fund manager.'

'Yes, yes,' says Aurelius, pleased. 'And what else?'

'Your firm is Livermore Capital.'

'And, Ursula, do you think I fuck good?'

'Yeah.'

Aurelius grabs his slightly hard penis in satisfaction. This twenty-eight-year-old with perfect tits thinks he fucks good, and that pleases him very much indeed.

'Are you interested in *finance*, Ursula?'

'Sure, that was my specialism.'

'Your specialism?'

'At business school.'

'You studied finance at business school?'

'My thesis was on a behavioural interpretation of the history of financial markets.'

Aurelius starts to say something but then stops and becomes thoughtful.

Ursula is dressed now and making for the door.

'Wait.' Aurelius sits up in bed and leans forwards earnestly. 'Wait. Can I run something past you?'

'Sure,' says Ursula, stepping back across the room and dropping her handbag at the foot of the bed.

'The truth is I don't… there aren't many people who I can run things past.'

'Sure.'

'First, I have to ask. You don't work for the FSA, do you?' asks Aurelius.

'You're asking if I work for the Financial Services Authority?'

Ursula starts to laugh, and Aurelius laughs too.

'Sorry, I have to ask.'

'No, I don't work for the FSA.'

'Good. So, here's the thing. I can borrow money against the shares that I own.'

'Securities lending?'

'Exactly. And with that money from the banks, I can go out and buy more shares, to boost my returns.'

'Leverage. Risky.'

'It's only risky if you buy the wrong shares. If you buy the right shares, then you double your returns.'

'OK.'

'Here's the clever bit. When you buy shares, you don't pay for them right away. You can wait until the end of the settlement period, which is usually three days later.'

'Like three days' credit?'

'Exactly. And with the right broker, you can get extended settlement. Five days, ten days, maybe more.'

'OK, so you can get these shares, use them as security for leverage and only pay for them ten days later. And when the time comes to pay, I guess you've already sold the shares and got the cash, so you can just do the same thing all over again.'

'Yes, yes, that's right. Shit, would you like a job?'

'Thank you, but I have a job,' replies Ursula. 'So you need to find a share that is easy to trade, so you can keep rolling the position over.'

'Yes, that's very important. And also to find a broker who is quite *flexible*.'

'Makes sense.'

'Thanks, Ursula. It's helpful for me to talk it through with you.'

'Sure.' Ursula is dressed. At the door of the hotel room she turns. 'I have a question.'

'Sure.'

'Your firm is called Livermore Capital after Jesse Livermore?'

'Exactly. The greatest speculator of all time.'

'I see. But I thought that in the end he lost all of his money and killed himself.'

CHAPTER SIX

Thursday the 8th of March, 2012

Arbuthnot Banking Group reported a £10.2 million loss and a gloomy prognosis for the small broking sector, which has undergone a wave of consolidation in the past year as stockbrokers struggle amid a weak market for capital-raising and falling trading commissions.

8.04am – Dan Trench, Northern Line, London Underground

It's already 8am, which means that the starched white shirts and hand-made shoes passed through here some time ago. Dan shuffles up behind the polyester sheen of an ill-fitting jacket and surveys the carriage. Not a working cuff or six-figure swagger in sight.

At each stop there's an ebb and flow. A bald head impressed with a mean, red face pokes through the carriage door.

'Excuse me! Excuse me! Can you move up please. *Move up*.'

Shuffle shuffle, shuffle shuffle.

Dan studies the other commuters, sitting with their heads buried in copies of *Metro*, listening to music and playing on their phones. Every individual inhabits a world that exists only for them. Dan imagines the tunnel flooding with water. Forty metres below the surface, in this claustrophobic coffin, how would all of these people react? How would they face the certainty of death? In those final moments, clawing at each other in desperation, they would finally see how they spend their lives surrounded by other people and yet are completely alone.

Dan pulls *The Economist* out of his coat pocket and opens it at the obituary.

At Bank he shuffles towards the door. Shuffle shuffle. Past the angry, bald head. Shuffle shuffle. Off the train. The flow of bodies takes him off the platform and onto the escalator. A sticker on the rubber handrail reads *We are the 99%*.

Above ground, Dan makes for the coffee shop, and after ordering, he joins the people standing around the bar waiting for their names to be called.

'…sixteen sells and two buys, and he doesn't have a single model. He just swans around like a Rothschild while people carry bags for him…'

'…the courts cancelled their licence and the shares fell forty per cent, then the chairman issued a statement saying it's not a licence, it's a statute. The courts can't touch them, so the shares are back up…'

A fixed-gear bike is mounted on the wall and laid out on the shelf beneath what appears to be a chemistry lab. A barista sporting an ironic moustache calls out Dan's name while pouring a swan-motif in his flat white.

It's a short walk to the offices of City Financial Training, and Dan arrives to a mood of unrest. Some of today's course materials have not arrived, one of the projectors has exploded and both photocopiers are broken. Colin dances around a lifeless machine, like an angry imp, shaking his fists.

'Does nothing fucking work in this place!'

He pulls open the back of one of the photocopiers and finely concertinaed paper spews out.

'Fuck it!'

Dan is by the coat stand, hanging up his jacket. 'Morning, all.'

There are a few distracted replies, but most of the lecturers are immersed in last-minute prep for their 9am classes. In a glass cubicle in the corner of the room, Jackie is on the phone. Jackie was brought in by the new private equity owners to 'sweat the asset'. It's thanks to her that each lecturer will soon be a generalist, teaching across every course.

As Dan settles behind his computer, Rakesh, sitting at the desk opposite, looks up.

'Have you seen today's insider dealing case? Seven of them trading on information from the print room.'

Rakesh, who teaches regulation and compliance, subscribes to daily email updates from the FSA. For him, the distinction between market abuse and market manipulation is of existential significance.

'It looks like the FSA is finally growing some teeth,' he adds, passing the article over to Dan.

Colin, who has grown tired of shouting at the photocopier, notices the paper coffee cup on Dan's desk.

'What is it with you and that posh, wanky coffee?'

'Good morning, Colin,' replies Dan.

'Have you seen this new syllabus?' continues Colin, waving a textbook in Dan's face. 'I'd rather teach creationism than teach this crap.'

Colin is still hovering by Dan's desk. 'What you up to today anyway? No teaching?'

'Grad training at Gessner Bank,' explains Dan.

At 9am there's an exodus and it falls quiet in the tutor office. The only person not teaching today is Rakesh, who is engrossed in the current edition of *Financial Regulatory Briefing*.

Dan grabs his laptop and teaching notes and leaves the building, heading down an alleyway which brings him out at the back of Gessner's offices.

The boardroom on the ninth floor is full of well-tailored twenty-somethings, parrying egos. The accents are international, the diction polished at business school. They pause when Dan walks in, then carry on chatting as he sets up his laptop. At 9.30am, Dan claps his hands to get the class's attention.

'Ladies and gentlemen!' he shouts above the chatter. 'My name's Dan Trench, and I'll be running your training today.'

He pauses a moment while the noise dies down.

'We're going to spend the day looking at financial maths, but before we get into that, let's go round the table and you can each tell me a little about what you do.'

As the grads give their names, Dan jots them down on a piece of paper. Marianne speaks with a dash of South African, and there's something about her that Dan is instantly attracted to. It's not an obvious, perfectly made-up prettiness. It's something else, something *womanly* that he only noticed about her when she started talking.

Dan spends the morning explaining the maths that goes into valuing bonds, shares and options. It takes a little time to get into his flow, but soon Dan is on autopilot, clicking through the slide pack with the familiarity of habit. At one point it occurs to him that he's been staring at Marianne, and he wonders if it's been obvious to anyone else.

During the break he browses the *FT*, while the grads organise a run down to the coffee shop. Later in the morning he sets the class some exercises, which gives him a chance to finish reading the *FT* and also to scan through his emails and check on how his share portfolio is doing.

Dan often finds himself watching the clock while he's teaching, counting down the minutes to the next break, so he's pleasantly surprised when he glances at his watch and sees that it's almost 1pm. The prospect of lunch prompts much discussion amongst the graduates. Umbrellas, in particular, are debated and decided against. Eventually Blackberrys and Mulberry handbags are gathered, cashmere coats buttoned up and the group makes its way out to the lifts.

Dan waits for the last of them to leave before heading down to the lobby. Outside, he wanders the old alleyways around Cornhill until he finds the spot he's looking for: a bench which looks out over a neat square of grass. Although the day dips low over the rooftops at this time of year, this tiny south-facing churchyard still catches the sun. He shares his lunch with a pigeon. It hobbles awkwardly on the stump of a missing foot, pecking at crumbs. Occasionally its head cocks to one side and tiny, expressionless eyes peer up at him.

Sometimes Dan feels like he doesn't actually exist. He has the physical presence of a real person, and he eats and breathes and interacts just like everyone else, but this is only the outward appearance of existence. Inside he is just an observer, watching himself going through the motions of living without any connection to the world around him.

Dan's thoughts are interrupted by the click of leather shoes on flagstones. A man in a navy suit, clutching a blue insurance broker's bundle bound with an elastic band, hurries past, his face flush from lunchtime drinking.

Back in the boardroom an immaculate blonde is gliding around the table on vertiginous heels, replacing the cups and saucers. Fresh flasks of hot water and coffee arrive, and small bottles of still and sparkling water are arranged at each place setting. The class returns in dribs and drabs. Noticing that one of the students is walking up to speak to him, Dan glances down at a list of names.

'Oh, hi… Amit. How are you enjoying the course?'

'It's mostly business school recap,' replies Amit, 'but what I wanted to ask is – one of the guys looked you up – is it true that you used to run the Columbus Fund?'

'Yes.'

'Shit, man. So, are you, like, running a hedge fund now or something?'

'No.'

'So, this teaching is, like, *all* you do?'

'Yeah, this is it,' replies Dan.

'Hmmm. Interesting career change… do you mind me asking why?'

'Actually, I do.'

Amit stares at Dan for a moment, then shrugs and goes back to his seat.

Dan begins again soon after 2pm. The stragglers grin apologetically as they drift in.

'This afternoon we're going to talk about risk. So, tell me, in an investment context, what is risk?'

'Risk is downside,' replies one student.

'Losing money,' offers another.

'So risk is to do with losing money?'

There is general nodding around the table.

'Amit, what does Modern Portfolio Theory have to say about risk? How do we measure it?'

Amit shrugs.

'Well, MPT tells us that risk is a function of the *volatility* of your returns, usually the correlation of that volatility with some kind of benchmark or index. If you do ten per cent when the market does five, sure, you're happy you've outperformed, but your risk might have actually have gone up. So risk isn't just losing money but also making more money than you had expected to make. Risk includes downside *and upside* volatility.'

Although Dan feels that he is making an important distinction, the class is tranquilised with boredom, except for Amit who is shaking his head.

'So, if the market does five and my portfolio does ten, you're saying that's a bad thing?'

'I'm saying that, depending on the correlations, the data may show that your portfolio has become riskier.'

A pair of glasses are removed and cleaned. Someone else crosses their arms. Suffocating indifference hangs in the air. Dan glances out through the glass wall at dark clouds announcing rain.

'Here's another example. If we believe a share is worth 90p, then it's going to be a good investment at 60p and an even better investment at 50p. Common sense says that the shares are *less* risky at 50p than at 60p or 90p. But the way we calculate investment risk means that if they fall to 50p then the shares have become *riskier*.'

Around the boardroom table Blackberrys are discretely clicked. The last few drops are wrung from a flask of coffee. Ovine eyes stare at the projector screen. Dan looks at the graduate sitting closest to him. He imagines bringing his laptop crashing down into the young man's face, leaving a bloody mess of teeth and broken plastic and a mangled pair of tortoiseshell glasses.

Dan walks over to the back of the room and studies the streaks of rain that are running down the glass wall. He wonders how long he can stand there before the class realises that he's stopped talking. Dan studies the room behind him in reflection. He imagines launching one of the black leather and chrome boardroom chairs through the glass pane, a shower of shimmering crystals raining down onto the street.

Nine floors below, umbrellas sway and pirouette between the puddles. A cycle courier snakes through the slow-moving traffic. Two figures scurry out of a black cab. Across the City a million people keep the wheels of this great machine turning. A chaos of noise and activity feeding off itself.

He glances at Marianne. Her jumper is too big. She catches him looking at her and smiles. The class is meant to finish at 5.30pm, but by 5pm the grads have lost interest and so has Dan.

A few stick around at the end to ask questions. When the rest are gone, Amit sidles up.

'Dan, I'm interested in becoming a fund manager. Managing money is more the career for me than investment banking. What's it like being a fund manager? What do I need to do to move across to the buy side?'

'Being a good fund manager is about personality as much as brains. You need to be in control of your emotions, because the market will fill you with confidence at the top and make you doubt yourself at the bottom.'

'Sure. What else?' Amit is unimpressed. 'I mean, what was it like running the Columbus Fund?'

'Mostly it was quite boring.'

'Boring!' snorts Amit. 'How could it have been *boring*?!'

Amit is shaking his head. Dan hasn't said any of the things that he wanted to hear.

'Well, good luck with everything,' says Amit as he leaves.

Dan is alone and the room is quiet. He lets out a long sigh of relief and undoes his top button. He's packing away his laptop when Marianne pushes open the door.

As she walks across the room, Dan notices that she's lost the oversized jumper. Her white shirt shows off her figure and also her bra. And her hair, which is a light golden-brown, also looks different. She walks right up to him, a little too close. He takes half a step back.

'Hi… Marianne. How can I help you?'

He can smell perfume and mint on her breath. She's trying to look confident, but Dan can see that she's nervous.

'Can I buy you a drink?'

CHAPTER SEVEN

Friday the 9th of March, 2012

Dominique Strauss-Kahn, the disgraced former head of the International Monetary Fund, was placed under investigation yesterday for alleged involvement in a prostitution ring based in the French city of Lille. Eight other people, including senior police and business figures in Lille with links to Mr Strauss-Kahn, have been arrested or placed under investigation, suspected of running a brothel out of the city's Carlton Hotel.

4.47pm – Gareth Eary, Cock & Woolpack, Finch Lane, City

Two young men are smoking in the lane. One of them is telling a story, jabbing a finger at his friend and then pointing away into the distance at an imaginary colleague or client. He gets to the punchline and they both curl up in laughter. The suits look cheap, but the watches are expensive; one of them is definitely a Panerai Luminor, the other is a bit harder to make out, but it could be a Hublot. Gareth chuckles to himself at the idea of wearing an eight-thousand-pound watch with a three-hundred-pound suit. Watching them through the window of the Cock & Woolpack, he remembers exactly what it was like, that moment you feel you've made it: earning more money than your parents ever had in a whole lifetime of grind and toil.

The men each take a last draw on their cigarettes before stubbing them out in the brass ashtray on the wall outside the door of the pub. As they walk away down Finch Lane, one straightens his tie, while the other says something that makes them both start laughing again.

It's 4.45pm and the pub is deserted, apart from a woman sat alone at one of the poser tables opposite the bar. Gareth had smiled at her while he was waiting for his drinks, and she had smiled shyly back. Her black tote is Fendi.

He's chosen a spot that gives her a good view of his profile. He stands with his shoulders a little back and chin slightly lifted. The chin thing is always tricky: it's about finding the angle that is just the right balance of *alpha* and *approachable*. Lift the chin too high and the effect is rather haughty but not enough and you fail to project the right level of confidence. It's something that Gareth's spent a lot of time working on. For this profile view he'd also like to be wearing his glasses, but it's too late now and it would only invite a flood of invective from Jabba when he eventually returns from the toilet.

Gareth takes a sip of Spitfire and wonders how the conversation with Jabba is going to go. He's chosen this pub because none of their colleagues will venture this far from Gresham Street. A man sees Gareth through the window and waves, but Gareth is in his own thoughts and doesn't notice the man until he is walking away, and

Gareth recognises that it's his tailor, who works out of a small shop in the next lane.

After what seems like a very long time, Jabba reappears. Squinting at Gareth through heavy eyelids, he finishes the double Jack Daniel's and Coke in one. He puts down the empty glass, sniffs and blinks his eyes, which look a little watery.

'Another one?' asks Gareth.

'Yeah.'

When Gareth returns Jabba is playing with his phone.

'Save a trip to the bar,' says Gareth, sliding over two double Jack Daniel's and Coke.

Jabba places his phone, screen facing down, on a bar mat next to the drinks.

'So,' says Jabba.

'So... you want to know what this is about.'

Jabba curls his top lip to show a row of small discoloured teeth. 'I know what this is about.'

'What do you mean?'

'I mean that, unlike you, I don't spend the day drifting around with my head up my arse.'

'Right,' says Gareth, taking a deep breath and reminding himself that he needs Jabba on his side.

'*This* is about Aurelius Blois,' says Jabba.

'How do you know that?'

'Because something about that guy doesn't smell right.'

Gareth shakes his head and laughs. 'He runs one of the biggest hedge funds in the City; he manages money for every family office in Mayfair and probably every sovereign wealth fund too. He's *brilliant*. The man is a *genius*.'

Jabba checks his phone, then puts it back down on the beer mat.

‘What do you need from me?’

Gareth knows that his usual blend of flattery and self-deprecation isn’t going to work.

‘Look, Blois is going to make a huge difference to your bonus and mine. So, I think we’re going to be on the same page with this…’

Gareth pauses, but Jabba remains silent.

‘Blois needs to stretch out the settlement period on his trades, so rather than T+3, he can settle in, say, ten days.’

Jabba looks at Gareth silently. Gareth imagines cogs whirring in Jabba’s brain, calculating the move that will give him the greatest advantage.

‘Look, this is zero risk. In exchange for extending a few days, we’re going to get *so much* business. It’s just a *no-brainer*,’ adds Gareth.

‘So, you need me to warehouse the stock without compliance catching on,’ says Jabba.

‘Yeah. I need you to park it in your trading book.’

Jabba shakes his head. ‘Park it in my trading book? It’s a fucking stupid idea. You know I can’t do that.’

‘Look, we both know that management don’t give a shit as long as you’re making money,’ replies Gareth.

Jabba is playing with his phone again.

‘You become a hero – I get it – but what’s in it for me?’

Gareth laughs. ‘Ummm… like… putting an extra zero on the end of your bonus?’

Jabba slowly shakes his head.

‘You don’t get it, do you, Eary? What I’m saying is why should *I* help *you*?’ Jabba pushes his finger hard into Gareth’s chest. ‘*You* are a jumped-up little prick who thinks he’s got it all worked out with those stupid *fucking* glasses and that whole bizarre pinky-ring thing. I mean, what the fuck?’

Jabba stops talking and juts his head forwards into Gareth's face, like a tortoise snapping at an inquisitive finger. Gareth's nose fills with the sugary smell of Jack Daniel's and Coke, cut with the sour tinge of Jabba's breath.

'Let me tell you, Eary – I *know* you. Yeah? I see *right through* you. And you haven't got a fucking clue. So let me ask you the question again. *Why should I help you?*'

This is going much worse than Gareth expected. But he knows that Jabba's playing with him, trying to knock him off balance, and he knows that he's just got to take it because too much is at stake to tell Jabba to go *fuck himself*, which is what Gareth would really like to do right now. So Gareth tries to act cool, as if Jabba's comment about the pinky ring isn't completely messing with his head.

'Tell me, Jabba, how do I make this sweet for you?'

Jabba finishes his drink, then looks out of the window, and for a long time neither of them say anything.

Eventually, Gareth breaks the silence. 'A cut of my commission?'

Jabba sneers, 'That would be too easy.'

'Then what?'

Jabba looks out of the window again without replying.

Gareth tries to think what Jabba could possibly be after.

'Look, Jabba, either we're doing this or we're not. I don't care enough about this deal to play your little games.'

'Now, now,' Jabba is shaking his head, 'we both know that's not true. You've spent ten years scraping and fawning, trying to catch a whale like this, and now you've got him in your sights there's literally *nothing* you wouldn't do.'

Gareth follows Jabba's gaze out of the window. It's just turned 5pm and suddenly the lane is crawling with commuters.

‘All of these people,’ says Jabba, ‘sitting at their computer screens, watching the clock tick down to five. Desperate to spend ninety minutes travelling back to some miserable commuter town for a night in front of the TV eating an M&S ready meal.’

Gareth can’t resist. ‘And what’s your favourite M&S ready meal, Jabba?’

Jabba ignores him. ‘If I’m going to help out with your little scheme, you’re going to do something for me.’

‘What?’

‘You’re going to come down off your high horse and get involved in my Friday night get-togethers.’

‘Your hooker parties?’

‘Yeah.’

‘You want me to join your Friday Club, and in exchange you’ll sort out this warehousing for me?’

‘There’s a little more to it than that.’

‘I thought there might be.’

‘You’re going to show up at mine next Friday, at eight o’clock prompt, with a bag of candy and a couple of girls.’

‘Are you fucking joking?’

Jabba is enjoying himself. ‘And then on your CV, underneath *Master of the Universe*, you’ll be able to add *pimp* and *drug dealer*.’ Jabba is rubbing his hands.

Gareth shakes his head. ‘Look, Jabba, you don’t need me to do that. Let’s be grown-up about this. Seriously.’

‘That’s my price,’ says Jabba, picking up his phone and putting it in his pocket.

‘Wait,’ says Gareth as Jabba stands up.

‘There’s nothing more to discuss.’

Gareth watches Jabba walk out of the pub and into the tide of people.

6.51pm – Marianne Bleekman, Rocket Bar and Restaurant, Adam's Court, City

From across the courtyard, through the glass doors, Marianne can see Dan at the bar, standing a head taller than anyone else. She stops for a moment and takes a deep breath. Her tummy is tumbling with nerves and excitement. It's not going to take much for her to fall heavily, hopelessly, deliciously for Dan Trench. She felt it the moment he walked into the boardroom at Gessner, and she feels it again now. The Blackberry in her pocket buzzes.

At the bar. What can I get you?

GTx she messages back.

Stepping into the bar, she watches Dan glance down at his phone and then lean over to the barman. She wonders what he will smell like. She wonders what he will taste like. The moment she lets go of the branch, the fast waters will take her.

She takes another deep breath, then pushes her way through the crowd to the bar. She comes up behind Dan and squeezes his forearm.

'Hi, Dan.'

'Oh, hi.' He leans down and kisses her cheek. He is hot and slightly sweaty.

'Sorry, I've just come from the gym,' he explains. 'Just a quick session. I do something every day or else I go a bit mad.'

'You work out every day?'

'Yeah.'

Marianne reaches up and grabs his bicep through his shirt. She puts her hand to her mouth.

'Mmmm. You *do* work out every day.'

Dan's red cheeks turn a shade darker.

He hands her a G&T and guides her through the bar. They find an unoccupied corner of a poser table to rest their drinks.

'So.'

'So,' says Marianne.

'Strong move.'

'Strong move?'

'Yeah, asking me out for a drink. Strong move! Was it the Efficient Market Hypothesis or the discounted cashflow or—'

'Shut up!' Marianne grabs the back of Dan's neck and pulls him down and kisses him.

'Wow. Like I said. Strong move.'

Marianne feels her face go flush. 'Sometimes it's easier to just be a bit impulsive. That felt good. Right?'

'That felt great. And kind of takes the pressure off. I was feeling quite nervous.'

On the table behind them a tall red-haired man returns from the bar with a tray of Jägerbombs, to whoops of delight from his friends. It looks like an office night out. Two girls push the shots away and shake their heads. The red-haired man knocks back his Jägerbomb, and then the two that are going spare, before howling into the air and thrusting his crotch at another colleague.

'So, what made you ask me out?' continues Dan.

'Well, it wasn't the course. You were so boring!'

They both laugh.

'No way! Was it that bad? Seriously?'

'Yeah. It was really bad. You started off OK, but after lunch you just kind of tailed off. I mean, you couldn't have been less enthusiastic if you were dead.'

'I had no idea it was so bad.'

'And what was that thing in the afternoon where you just stopped mid-sentence and started staring out the window?'

'Oh yeah, that. I honestly didn't think anyone was actually *listening*.'

Marianne puts her hand over her mouth to try and stop herself laughing, but the harder she tries the worse it gets. She suddenly lets out a snort, which sets Dan off, and they both laugh until there are tears in their eyes.

'Seriously it was awful.'

'Shit,' says Dan, shaking his head. 'I really had no idea.'

'And then there was that thing where you were kind of just ignoring everyone else in the room apart from me...'

'Oh no. I was worried I might have been doing that. Was it really obvious?'

'Yeah. Super obvious.'

'That's bad. Sorry about that. It must have come across as kind of... urgh, pervy.'

'Actually, I really liked it. It made me go a bit tingly.'

'*Tingly?*'

'Tingly.'

'You didn't put *that* on the feedback form, did you?'

'Oh, don't worry about the feedback. You had a bit of a fan club going on actually. If I hadn't got there first, I'm pretty sure Amit would have asked you out!'

'Oh yeah, Amit Patel, MBA.'

'He's been raving all week about this *Columbus Fund*. Like you were some big deal who threw it all away.'

'Well, not exactly... that's not exactly what happened.'

They both turn to look at the office night out that's in full flow on the table behind them. The red-haired man's shirt is now unbuttoned to his navel, and he is thrusting his crotch in manic delight as two of his friends down their pints.

The man who finishes first slams his empty glass on the table, then gets high-fives all round, before resting both his hands on the table to compose himself. Suddenly he pulls himself away and runs for the toilet to a round of applause from his colleagues.

'So, tell me about you. I want to know everything. Why London, why investment banking?'

'The truth is, Dan, I don't really have a plan. My father... he's always been totally driven, he's the one with the plan, for himself, for the family, for me... Durham, economics, London, Gessner... and so I've always just kind of gone along with it. It's like inertia. And also, I haven't come up with an alternative. And until I do, it's good to know I'm following *a* plan, at least, even if it's not *my* plan.'

'Sounds like your dad's got expectations.'

'Yeah, there have always been lots of expectations.'

'Expectations are the context in which we build our lives. Sometimes before a stock can outperform, expectations need to be rebased. Share price performance isn't about how the company is doing in any *absolute* sense; it's about what's happening *relative* to expectations. Reset the expectations and the stock can really fly. It's the same with people. Being happy is all about expectations.'

'I'm not sure I follow,' says Marianne.

'OK, two people, both wake up one morning and discover that they are worth ten million quid. Does that ten million quid make them equally happy? No. Actually it makes one of them feel like the king of the world, and it makes the other one feel suicidal. Why? Because yesterday one of them was homeless with a few pennies to her name, and the other one was a billionaire. Being happy is all about expectations.'

'And so is share-price performance?'

'Exactly.'

Marianne beckons to Dan to lean close. She puts her lips next to his ear.

'Dan,' Marianne whispers, 'your chat is so bad. At the moment I give it a two or three out of ten. I really fancy you, but if you ever become less cute, your chat is going to have to seriously improve.'

'Jesus,' says Dan.

'Expectations investing. That is not sexy chat.'

'You don't hold back, do you?'

Marianne shrugs.

'OK, change of subject. Let's get deep and meaningful. What do you *want*, Marianne? What do you want from life?'

'I can tell you, but it will terrify you. Genuinely. You will be afraid.'

'Try me.'

'What I want is to completely and utterly give myself so someone. I want to be totally and inescapably in love.'

Dan nods.

'You seem relaxed,' continues Marianne.

'I once went on a date, a first date, where my date spent the whole evening talking about all the babies we were going to have and what their names were. *That* was terrifying,' he explains. 'But you? You don't scare me at all.'

'Most guys don't get it.'

'I totally get it. I've been in love. I was engaged. It was the most wonderful thing.'

'You were engaged to be married?' Marianne feels her stomach tighten up.

'Yeah. Look, I'm… I'm thirty-five. It would be weirder if I'd never been… at that point in my life, wouldn't it?'

Marianne thinks about it before replying. 'I guess you're probably right. Most of the guys I date have never been in a serious relationship. Like *engaged* serious. You know?'

'I come with baggage.'

'I didn't mean it like that.'

'It's true though.'

'So, what happened?'

'What happened?'

'To the engagement. What happened?'

Dan goes quiet and looks down at the palms of his hands for a moment, before looking back up at Marianne.

'Let's not kill the Friday feeling. I'll tell you everything another time. I promise.'

CHAPTER EIGHT

Wednesday the 14th of March, 2012

David Cameron has tried to dispel Labour claims that he is 'out of touch' by defending his love of Cornish pasties. 'I am a pasty eater myself,' announced the prime minister during a press conference on the Olympic Games. 'I love a hot pasty.' Mr Cameron said he had last eaten a pasty from the West Cornwall Pasty Company at Leeds railway station, but it later emerged that there had been no outlet there since 2007.

11am – Jude Delaney-Hall, Strand, Charing Cross

Despite the miserly windows, the views across the river are exceptional. While the publisher talks, Jude ticks off the landmarks: Oxo Tower, National Theatre, London Eye.

'...of course, I'm thinking TV, or even film. I mean this would work very well on screen.'

'Absolutely right,' declares Jude's agent, Patrick, in a nasal Sloane patois. 'This is the zeitgeist *right now*. Burn the *bankers*! Burn the *wankers*! Readers can't get enough of it.'

'Patrick, this book has got nothing to do with burning bankers,' snaps Jude.

'The dialogue is sharp,' continues the publisher, 'but there's too much jargon. You're going to lose the reader. A confused reader is not emoting.'

Patrick strokes his Liberty print cravat.

'I think you mean empathising,' replies Jude.

The publisher frowns.

Patrick winks at Jude from behind his thick-rimmed, once-fashionable spectacles. On a table in the corner behind him are two small boxes labelled *AUTHOR'S COPY* in black marker.

'Every industry has jargon,' continues Jude. 'Understanding it is the entry price. You can have finance for dummies, or you can have realistic dialogue. But you can't have both.'

'OK, let's step through it,' says the publisher. 'Start with the *short selling* storyline. Is it the short selling that's illegal, or is it the insider trading? Or both? It's not clear.'

'Insider trading is *illegal*. Short selling is *legal*. Short selling just means you are profiting from when something falls in price, rather than profiting from when it rises in price. Usually, it involves borrowing a share and selling it, then buying it back later, hopefully at a lower price, when the time comes to return it.'

'And does this short selling happen a lot?' asks Patrick.

'It's common at hedge funds. That's what the "hedge" part of hedge fund means. They offset some of the risk on their long positions by going short on other positions.'

'I have no idea what "offset" means, but the whole thing sounds both complicated *and* pointless,' says the publisher. 'The "long" and the "short" just cancel each other out. Surely?'

‘So, imagine there’s an oil company that has some problems that are going to affect the share price,’ explains Jude. ‘You want to short it because you think the shares will fall in value, but there’s a risk that the oil price will go up, which will lift the shares of *all* oil companies.’

‘Ah. So, you short the dud and buy a good one. Then if all oil companies go up, you’re still OK?’ replies the publisher.

‘Exactly. You’ve hedged your sector risk and, in theory, just isolated the company-specific risk.’

‘That sounds very clever,’ says the publisher.

‘Very clever,’ agrees Patrick.

‘And what about insider information?’ asks the publisher.

‘Insider information is non-public, price-sensitive information,’ explains Jude.

‘Non-public and price sensitive? But surely that’s how all bankers make money!’ guffaws Patrick.

Jude sighs. ‘Look, this is not just a book about *bankers*; it’s a cast of fund managers, stockbrokers and corporate CEOs. You have *read* the book… haven’t you, Patrick?’

Patrick gives a little cough, then looks down at his cravat.

Jude turns back to the publisher. ‘I’m not saying Patrick’s completely wrong. But, in principle, if you have inside information, you mustn’t trade on it.’

‘And does insider trading happen often?’

‘Well, about half of the time when one company takes over another company, the share price moves up before the deal is made public.’

‘So, it’s pretty obvious? The insider trading?’

‘Yeah.’

‘And what happens to these people who do it?’

‘Usually nothing.’

‘They get away with it?’

‘The bankers always get away with it!’ exclaims Patrick.

‘Well, there’s probably one or two insider trading prosecutions a year.’

‘And there might be hundreds of instances of insider trading?’ asks the publisher.

‘No one knows. Probably thousands,’ explains Jude.

‘Thousands. OK. And apart from takeovers, what other insider trading is there?’

‘Well, if the management of a company can see that things are going better, or worse, than the market is expecting, they can make money by buying, or short selling, their own company’s shares.’

The publisher shakes her head. ‘But that’s so obvious: they’re bound to get caught.’

‘They’d have to do it through an unrelated party, or an offshore company, so that it can’t be traced back to them.’

The publisher looks down at her notes. ‘And what about *accounting manipulation*? That’s just *cooking the books*?’

‘Yes, if the CEO can make things look better than they actually are, by massaging the numbers, then their bonus will be bigger.’

‘And massaging the numbers, that’s illegal, presumably?’

‘Well, it depends.’

‘It depends?! How can cooking the books *not* be illegal?’ replies the publisher.

‘Without getting too technical, there’s a difference between accounting *shenanigans* and outright fraud,’ continues Jude.

‘Ooohh *shenanigans*,’ exclaims Patrick. ‘That reminds me of when poor dear Torquail was sent down from Oxford.’

The publisher looks at him coolly before turning back to Jude. 'Lastly, you need to find a way to help the reader to understand all of these different roles. Like, what *is* the difference between a hedge fund manager and an investment banker?'

'Fair point,' says Jude. 'Investment bankers work for the companies. They help the companies acquire other companies and raise money from investors to do those acquisitions. They get paid fees for helping their clients complete deals. A stockbroker feeds a fund manager with bits of information about companies and tries to get the fund manager to leave them an order to buy or sell the company's shares. They get a little bit of commission whenever the fund manager leaves them an order. The fund manager invests money on behalf of pension funds, sovereign wealth funds and private individuals. They get paid a percentage of the funds that they manage.'

'And a hedge fund manager?' asks the agent.

'Just a glamorous version of an ordinary fund manager.'

'And when you say *the Arabs*...'

'That's the Middle Eastern sovereign wealth funds. ADIA for Abu Dhabi Investment Authority, KIA for Kuwait, or the Saudis. These are the biggest investors in the world. Everybody wants them as a client.'

'Oil money!' says Patrick.

'It's all very interesting,' says the publisher, 'you just need to find a way to work it into the narrative, to keep the reader *empathising*.'

'Very good!' says Patrick.

'Look, Jude,' continues the publisher, 'I know you and Patrick have spoken, but just to reiterate, you have *got to* fictionalise it. I mean, the legal team are going to have kittens with all the names in here. The people you name here… these people are in the newspapers every day. Some of them *own* the newspapers. It's just not possible. Legally, not possible. Not for us, anyway. Maybe some mad indie imprint with a death wish. But not this house.'

Jude is quiet. She knows the publisher is right, but that doesn't make it any easier to swallow.

Patrick breaks the silence by clapping his hands on the table. 'Before we wrap up, can we talk about the sex?'

The publisher shakes her head. 'What sex?'

Patrick guffaws. 'Exactly! You need to get some sex into this manuscript, Judith! Stop being such a bloody prude!'

'Oh, Patrick, you *silly man*!' exclaims the publisher.

'Don't worry, darling, you're not my type!' shouts Patrick, flashing a very British set of teeth.

The publisher becomes shrill. 'Patrick! Patrick!'

Jude stands up. 'Shall I leave you to it then?'

'Oh, Judith, don't be like that,' says Patrick. 'Always so serious, darling.'

'I do actually need to get back to work.'

Patrick shrugs. 'Suit yourself. But how is dear old Arty, by the way?'

Jude sighs. 'Papa is his usual *light-hearted* self.'

'Do be gentle on Arty,' replies Patrick. 'He takes on a lot. And he always means well.'

'I will pass on your regards,' says Jude.

As she closes the door behind her, the pair start up again.

'…no, Patrick, no!'

7.32pm – Gareth Eary, Mews of Mayfair, Lancashire Court, Mayfair

It's only been a week, but a lot has changed since Gareth was last here.

'Table for two: Eary.'

'Of course, sir, I have your reservation here. Would you like to wait for your friend at the bar, or shall I take you straight to the table?'

'Table, please. *Aurelius Blois* will be joining me,' adds Gareth. He likes how those words make him feel.

'Mr Blois? We have his usual table, sir.'

Gareth lifts his chin a little. 'Please, lead the way.'

Gareth orders the Chateau Lafite and a few moments later Aurelius arrives.

'Mr Blois.'

Aurelius steps forwards, past Gareth's extended hand, and gives the broker a hug followed by a vigorous slap on the back.

'You know last time we were here, I thought you were playing a joke. I saw you and I thought you were someone else, I thought *that's Winterbottom pretending to be a broker from Gresham Street, what kind of joke is he playing?* but then it was only when the champagne arrived with your business card that I understood that you were… you. I was confused about who you really were. *Nosce Te Ipsum!* Ha! Ha!'

Gareth laughs, although Aurelius's joke sits uncomfortably.

Aurelius has a large mouth, and when he grins, Gareth fancies that he can see every one of the Frenchman's teeth. He catches Gareth staring and opens his mouth wide as if for a dental examination.

'You probably noticed that I have four extra teeth. Actually, they come in useful sometimes.'

'Four extra teeth? I didn't know that was possible.'

'I got double wisdom teeth. That's when I knew it was my destiny to become a hedge fund manager.'

Gareth isn't sure if Aurelius is making a joke.

'But anyway… we were talking about Gerard Winterbottom. You know who I mean, of course,' says Aurelius.

'Oh yeah, Gerard and I go way back,' says Gareth.

'Of course.'

'So… you do business with Gerard?' asks Gareth, trying to sound casual.

'We used to do a lot with Numis. I was Gerard's best client. But no. We no longer do any business with them. Not a penny. And you know why?'

'They had a problem with your booking and settlement requirements?' replies Gareth.

'The real issue, the difference between us and the Winterbottoms of this world, is *vision*. Being able to grasp the big picture. The moment I explained our new booking and settlement requirements to Winterbottom, I got a letter from his compliance department closing my account. *Closing my account.* I mean, the ingratitude of that man.' Aurelius pauses and takes a long breath.

The sommelier has been hovering at a discrete distance and now offers Gareth the Chateau Lafite.

'Perhaps you'd like to taste,' offers Gareth.

Aurelius takes his time, twirling the glass, nosing and examining the wine. He looks at the sommelier. He tastes the wine then nods.

'It's fine.'

'Thank you, sir.'

The sommelier pours, offers a half-nod, half-bow, and leaves.

'Would you like to look at the menu?' asks Gareth.

'Please, you do that; I will have my usual. Now where were we…'

'You were talking about Gerard.'

'Exactly, because when I ask you to do business for me, it's no good to say, I don't know how to do that, let me ask compliance about this, let me get this signed off first, I need the paperwork for that. Do you understand? I don't do business like that. When I see the opportunity, I need you to grab it for me.'

'I understand. The booking and settlement arrangements are in hand.'

'Your dealer is on board with the arrangements?'

'We have an... understanding.'

'That's what I want to hear.' Aurelius leans in and beckons Gareth to do the same. 'OK, so here's the play. ALB.'

'ALB. We do a lot of business with Green Knight in that one,' replies Gareth.

'Sure, I know the register.'

'They have some in the Mid-Cap Fund, but it's mostly the Columbus Fund.'

'OK, interesting.' Aurelius nods. 'So, the good news for you, Gareth, is that, soon, Green Knight will only be the second-biggest holder, because a handful of other entities with no connection to Livermore Capital, or to each other, will collectively be the biggest holders. But only you and I will know that.'

'You want the trades booked through separate entities, always below the three per cent disclosure threshold?'

'Correct. When the time comes to settle, our lawyers in London will let you know the legal entity. It will be different each time.'

'And Livermore stays below the radar and off the shareholder register.'

'Precisely. We'll start on Monday with forty million at VWAP, over the next three, four weeks, whatever you think is sensible given the liquidity.'

'I just need you to drop me a line or a call in the morning and we can get the ball rolling.'

A frown starts to gather between Aurelius's eyes.

'This is what I mean, Gareth, about initiative, about vision. You are not thinking, you are just quoting passages from the compliance handbook.'

'Oh, it's nothing like that… it's just in case… there's any confusion. We need a record that an order has been placed.'

'Otherwise?'

'Otherwise if… something… you know.'

'No, Gareth, I do not know "if something". Either you are questioning my integrity, or you are not.'

Aurelius opens his eyes wide and gives the impression of a disappointed parent waiting for an apology.

Aurelius continues, 'Maybe the maths will provide clarity. So, forty million ALB, that's say… thirty-five million pounds of business in month one. That annualises to almost a million pounds in commission. That would make me your firm's biggest client by an order of magnitude. Am I right?'

The waiter appears. 'Will you be having something to start, sir?'

'Not for me,' says Aurelius. 'I will just have the usual, please.'

'I'm sorry, sir, I'm new here…'

'You're new here?'

'Yes, sir.'

'Well… welcome to Mews of Mayfair, I am Aurelius Blois.'

'Thank you, sir.'

'This is my usual table, and my usual order consists of one Côte de boeuf, no sides, served blue. If there is anything else you need to know, you can ask the maître d'.'

'Yes, sir...' The waiter hesitates. 'Sir, the Côte de boeuf, you understand that is for two people?'

'I understand that precisely.'

'Very good, sir...' The waiter is still hesitating. 'The Côte de boeuf, sir... the chef recommends... that it be cooked medium to well done, sir.'

'What's your name?'

'My name is Giacomo.'

'You are from Italy, Giacomo, and you are new here.'

'Yes, sir.'

'Well let me explain this thing, Giacomo, because you are new. This restaurant has a very fine chef, and he knows how to cook a fantastique Côte de boeuf. I'm sure you know this already. Now I understand that you and the chef are concerned that, served blue, the fat will not have time to render, and I will miss the flavour.'

'Yes, sir.'

'But here's my secret, Giacomo. I don't eat the Côte du boeuf for its flavour. I eat it because, tonight, when I lie in bed with a beautiful woman, the Côte de boeuf, cooked blue, with no sides, will make me firm and virile like a bull.'

'Yes, sir.'

'Like a young, horny bull.'

'Yes, sir.'

'Say it, Giacomo, so I know you will remember it.'

'Like a young, horny bull, sir.'

'Very good.'

'Thank you, sir.'

CHAPTER NINE

Friday the 16th of March, 2012

Retail analysts reacted with weary resignation as Clinton Cards went into administration yesterday. 'There is no real surprise on that front,' said one. The greetings card chain had long grappled with high rents and increased competition. 'They had a failing business model and a huge pile of debt.'

5.07pm – Dan Trench, Gymbox, City

Descending the steel stairs, the sound of techno and smell of lemongrass cleaner rise up to greet him. And as Dan steps onto the polished concrete of the basement floor, he feels calm.

He changes slowly, purposefully, focused in the moment. 'Fight Club' is in Hall Three but not for half an hour, so first he finds a quiet spot in the corner of the free-weights room. He has beaten the after-work rush, and the room is almost empty.

Dan likes to visualise before he steps into the ring. He runs through combinations, footwork, blocks, counterpunches. His concentration is broken by a voice.

'Hello? Hello? Mate?'

Dan looks at the short muscular man standing in front of him in rugby shorts and a navy stringer.

'Mate, would you mind?'

The man points at the bench press. Dan adds up the stack: 120kg.

'Spot me? Would you mind?'

Dan grunts.

He stands behind the bench as the man bangs out reps in a slow, steady rhythm. Dan counts in his head. At nine, the man starts to slow down.

'Three more, three more,' says the man.

At eleven, the man's arms start to shake and Dan steps close up to the bench and places his hands under the bar, feeling the weight across his palms.

'Last… one,' gasps the man.

Dan looks down at the man's bulging red face. Upside down and distorted by effort, it takes on an abstract appearance. Dan imagines turning his palms down onto the bar and pushing. He imagines the look of confusion and then fear in the man's eyes as he pushes the bar onto his neck. He imagines the man's scream drowned out by the bang of techno music and the increasing pressure on his throat. Dan casts a glance around the empty room.

'Mate!'

Dan looks down at the man, who is struggling to get the bar off his chest.

'Spot me!' There is urgency in the man's voice.

Dan nods and takes more of the weight on his palms. Together they squeeze the bar up and drop it back onto the rack. The man breathes out and sits up on the bench.

'Ummm… cheers… mate,' he says, eyeing Dan cautiously.

A small crowd has gathered around the boxing ring in Hall Three. There's always plenty of interest in 'Fight Club', but mostly people are just there to watch.

'OK, you know the rules,' shouts the coach. 'Everyone fights everyone, round robin, who's up first?'

Dan knows all of the regulars, their styles and weaknesses.

'OK. Right, are you guys fighting?' The coach points to three blokes who've strolled over from the bags.

The three blokes shake their heads.

'OK, well *step back*. Step back from the ring please. Come on, anyone who's not fighting please step back from the ring.'

The coach turns to the five guys standing on his side of the ring.

'OK, so it's the regulars... anyone else?'

The coach looks round at the rest of the people standing round the ring.

'Fine. Next time, eh, guys? And if you'd like any coaching, come and see me afterwards.'

The coach turns back to the regulars.

'OK, Rich and... Grigor. Go.'

Rich is tall and thin and keeps his elbows high, like a kickboxer. He fights defensively. Grigor is short and squat like a wrestler and loves to brawl.

Rich and Grigor climb through the ropes and into the ring.

'Three minutes. First minute, jab only. Grigor, you're a southpaw, aren't you?'

'Yeah.'

'OK, should be interesting. Rich, come here. Let me see that chin strap.'

Rich is a graduate on the institutional sales desk at Fidelity.

‘OK, that’s better.’

The coach turns to Dan and the other pair waiting by the ring.

‘You guys, stay warm. Skipping, three minutes.’

Dan grabs a rope and moves round so that he has a good view of the ring. All eyes are on the round timer.

Ding, ding.

Whip-snap, whip-snap.

In the ring, Grigor is struggling to get close enough to Rich to use his jab. Rich dances around Grigor, popping him with fast, light punches. Both boxers try to find a rhythm while they wait for the coach to call the first minute. Grigor, frustrated, hustles inside with a hook to the body.

‘Hey! Jab only!’ shouts the coach.

Grigor puts his hands up apologetically. Grigor is an IT consultant with two teenage children.

‘OK, that’s one minute.’

Grigor knocks his fists together enthusiastically and rushes Rich into the corner of the ring. He throws a hook to the body and grimaces as he catches his thumb on Rich’s elbow. Rich throws a straight right to the head and Grigor takes a step back, momentarily stunned.

‘Break,’ shouts the coach, leaning over the rope at the side of the ring. ‘OK, Grigor?’

Grigor nods.

‘*Fight.*’

Dan is skipping, but his mind is in the ring. First, he is Grigor, trying to get inside, and then he is Rich, using the jab to keep the IT consultant frustrated and at a safe distance. When the round is over the coach calls the fighters over to the side and gives them each a few tips.

‘Grigor. Slip the jab, slip the jab.’

The coach is moving his shoulders as he shifts his weight from one foot to the other.

'Slip, slip, step, and you're inside. Left hook to the body. Bang.'

Grigor copies the coach.

'Got it?' asks the coach.

'Thanks,' says Grigor.

'Rich. I know you can do a one-two, but let's add a hook. Let's try a jab, right, hook, right.' The coach runs through the combo in slow motion. 'Yeah?'

'Sure,' says Rich.

The coach does it again, faster, 'one, two, three, two', then looks at Rich. 'Come on.'

Rich copies the combo.

'Good. OK. Rich, you stay and… Dan, you're in.'

Dan steps up onto the side of the ring and holds the rope for Grigor, then steps in himself. He takes his gum guard out of his pocket and pops it into his mouth. The coach helps Dan with his gloves, then holds him for a moment, gripping the back of Dan's neck. The coach is tall and stands eye to eye with Dan. He leans in and talks quietly into Dan's ear.

'Just remember that the guys are here for friendly sparring, yeah? Don't be a dick, OK?'

'OK.'

'Seriously, last week I was this close.'

The coach taps a knuckle on Dan's chin.

Dan nods.

Rich is shadow boxing while he waits for the bell. He doesn't enjoy sparring with Dan. No one does.

Dan walks into the middle of the ring and stands quite still, watching the timer. He feels his heart rate increasing, and the sound of the bell sends a ripple of energy through his body. He reaches a hand out to tap gloves with Rich.

Dan and Rich trade jabs for the first minute of the round. But after that, Dan's power and wider range of shots quickly give him the upper hand. Dan relaxes into a rhythm and soon has Rich on the rope trying to cover up.

'Break!' shouts the coach. 'OK, Rich?'

Rich nods.

'Come here,' says the coach, waving Rich over.

The coach says something into Rich's ear.

Rich nods.

'You got that?' asks the coach.

Rich looks at Dan, then back at the coach. 'Yeah.'

'Good. OK, *fight*.'

Dan comes at Rich with a jab, but instead of blocking, Rich slips the punch and counters with a right cross that comes in over Dan's extended left arm and bangs him straight between the eyes.

For a split-second Dan is somewhere else, then instinct kicks in and he throws a jab, right, uppercut combo. The uppercut connects cleanly with Rich's chin and snaps his head back. Dan watches Rich stumbling back in slow motion, right arm reaching out to break the fall. There's an exhale of breath around the ring, but Dan doesn't hear it. And he doesn't hear the coach shouting 'break' as he throws another right that accelerates Rich's head onto the canvas.

There's excited shouting from around the ring. Suddenly the coach is through the ropes, pinning Dan's arms to his sides and pushing him back against the ropes.

'Out of the ring!' screams the coach in Dan's face. 'Get out of the ring! *Now!*'

Dan shakes off the coach's grip, and the coach responds by putting one hand up around Dan's neck. Dan knocks the coach's arm out of the way, then lunges forwards and brings his head down hard onto the coach's nose.

Immediately there is blood everywhere. Dan can taste it in his mouth, and he realises what he's done.

'Shit.'

Now four more Lycra-clad trainers are in the ring, pushing Dan through the ropes. His feet barely touch the floor as he is carried up the steel stairs and past the front desk before being thrown out on the street. He is still wearing his head guard and gloves.

Lombard Street is busy with the evening rush. People step around him, bump into him, nudge past him; he's in the way. His T-shirt is heavy with sweat, and with the adrenaline wearing off, he feels the chill. People are staring at his vest. He looks down at the fresh crimson patches.

A hand squeezes his shoulder in a familiar way. It's his personal trainer, Marc.

'I could see that coming,' says Marc.

'I can't believe I did that,' says Dan.

'He never liked you. And you have a problem with… well… you have a problem. I could see that coming.'

'I should go and apologise.'

Marc shakes his head. 'You step back in that gym, and you'll be lucky to come out alive.'

'No,' says Dan, shaking his head. 'You think?'

'Seriously,' replies Marc.

'Fuck.'

'You really busted his nose. Everyone's going crazy in there.'

'You saw it?'

'Yeah, I saw it. He was trying to wind you up. I guess it worked. I could see it coming. I mean that was a bloody stupid thing you did, but I could see it coming.'

'Shit.'

'Look. I'll go back in and collect your stuff. Put on a fresh top. We'll get a pint. We'll have a chat and work out what to do.'

Dan looks at the floor and nods, then looks back up at Marc. 'I need this. I need to fight, otherwise... otherwise... I don't know. But I just need it.' Dan holds his arm out towards the entrance to the gym. 'I need it.'

'I know,' says Marc. 'I know.'

CHAPTER TEN

THREE YEARS EARLIER

Sunday the 30th of August, 2009

6.28am – Dan Trench, Snowdonia, North Wales

The hire car is all shiny-new and smells of plastic. Dan and Sarah are on the A5, heading south. Jack Johnson is playing on the radio. As they turn the corner into the Ogwen Valley, Tryfan's distinctive shape appears, silhouetted against the sunrise.

'Yes!' says Dan. 'Look at that. I'm pumped.'

He puts his hand on Sarah's knee. 'So, how about Milestone Buttress? Or we could do Suicide Wall.'

'Suicide Wall will be damp,' says Sarah.

'OK, the Buttress then, before it gets busy,' says Dan.

On their left is the lake. Gravel crunches under the wheels as Dan pulls into a narrow layby. It's early and the road is empty.

Dan grabs the rucksacks. and they lay out their kit in the boot of the car. A rack of hexes, a couple racks of nuts, a few cams, quickdraws, carabiners, slings, harnesses, helmets.

He picks up two pairs of ropes. 'Forties or sixties?'

'Sixty,' says Sarah. 'Just in case.'

Dan picks up three racks of nuts and looks at Sarah.

'We don't need to bring all of this stuff, do we?'

Sarah looks at him and shakes her head. 'You're not at the climbing wall you know! This is what trad climbing is all about.'

'Yeah, but I'm just a bit more *alpinist*, you know.'

'Trust me, Dan, what seems like a good idea in the car park when you're full of coffee and bacon sandwiches quickly becomes a bad idea when you're stuck halfway up the crag with the wrong gear.'

Before they set off, Dan takes off his smock and stuffs it into the top of his rucksack. 'It's going to be a gorgeous day, and I can't think of anyone I'd rather spend it with!' He gives Sarah a squeeze as they walk side by side up the steep path.

At the bottom of the crag, Sarah pulls out a well-thumbed guidebook. 'Start with something gentle? Rowan Route?'

Dan pulls a face. 'Come on! Let's live a little!'

'Direct?' suggests Sarah.

'I heard the finish on Super Direct is amazing,' says Dan.

Sarah laughs. 'The finish on Super Direct is… memorable.'

'Well, I'm up for it.'

'OK. Well, you can lead the last pitch then.'

Dan takes Sarah's hand and pulls her towards him. He wraps his arms around her and holds her tight.

'I'm so happy we're getting married,' says Dan.

'I love you,' says Sarah.

Sarah studies the guidebook as Dan puts on his climbing shoes. When he's laced up, she points out the line.

'The first pitch is about twenty-five metres. Finishes at the ledge.'

'Cool.'

Sarah checks his knots, and Dan checks her belay plate. The sun is shining on the crag on the opposite side of the valley. The sky above is pure blue.

'What a day,' says Dan.

'When you're ready,' says Sarah, pulling out an armful of rope. 'And remember, red rope on the right, green on the left.'

'Red is right,' says Dan looking down at the two knots on his harness.

Dan brushes the toes of his climbing shoes on his trouser legs and steps up onto the rock. He smears his shoes against the rock to feel the grip.

'Love a good bit of granite.'

'Rhyolite,' corrects Sarah.

'Alright, smart-arse.'

A few metres above the ground Dan places a small nut in the crack and clips in.

'Good to get the first clip in,' says Sarah.

'Beautiful,' says Dan, as he carries on up the pitch.

CHAPTER ELEVEN

Monday the 19th of March, 2012

Fred Goodwin, former CEO of the Royal Bank of Scotland, has been stripped of his knighthood. Under Mr Goodwin's leadership, the bank took excessive risks in the years preceding the financial crisis, leading to a £45 billion bailout by taxpayers. Previously, only convicted criminals have had knighthoods taken away.

10.33am – Martin Fowey, Paternoster Square, St Paul's

Friday night flashes through his head like a fistful of blurry Polaroids. He feels shame at being part of it but also thrilled by this glimpse into another world. Jabba's voice rings in his ears. *Girls and candy.*

Gareth is late. Martin wonders if he's waiting in the right place.

He looks down at the well-scrubbed flagstones beneath his feet. He can just make out what's left of stencilled letters sprayed in red paint. *Capitalism Isn't Working.*

Then Gareth strolls right past him.

'Gareth.'

But Gareth carries on walking.

'Gareth!' Martin takes a few strides and taps Gareth's arm.

Gareth spins around. But it's not Gareth. The details are familiar: the hair, the cut of the suit. Martin glances at the hand clasping the cup of coffee, and even the pinky ring looks the same. But it's not Gareth.

Before Martin can apologise, Gareth calls from a couple of steps away, 'Martin, sorry I'm late...'

When Gareth notices who Martin is standing with, his expression changes.

Martin glances at Gareth and then at the doppelgänger. But the doppelgänger is more convincing. Somehow the shade of Gareth's hair isn't quite right, and the doppelgänger's suit looks worn in all the right places.

Gareth's tone is uneven. 'I see you've met Gerard.'

Gerard looks at Gareth blankly.

'Gareth... Eary,' says Gareth, grinning awkwardly.

'Of course, Gareth Eary, from...'

'Gresham Street.'

'Gresham Street. Of course. How are you, Gareth? Sorry, total mind blank there for a moment.'

Gareth is smiling and bobbing his head like a nodding dog.

Gerard frowns. 'Nice, uh, glasses.'

'Oh thanks, yeah, they're Oliver...'

'...Peoples – Gregory Pecks. Yeah, I've got a pair just the same actually. Only mine are horn and those look like tortoiseshell.'

Gareth stops nodding. 'Horn? I didn't realise.'

'Sorry?'

Gareth looks lost. 'Tortoiseshell and horn.'

Gerard glances at Martin, who shrugs.

'Right, chaps, nice to see you both, must dash.'

Gerard spins on his heel and paces away from them at a quick march.

'Was that Winterbottom?' asks Martin when Gerard is out of earshot.

'Hmmm?'

'Was that Gerard Winterbottom?'

'That? Oh, yes,' replies Gareth, looking off thoughtfully in Gerard's direction.

'Everything OK, Gareth?'

'Hmmm.' Gareth snaps out of his reverie. 'Yes, let's go.'

As they walk in silence down Paternoster Row, Martin tries to think of something to say.

'I always wanted to ask, why is Nigel called Jabba?'

'Hmmm?' replies Gareth.

'Nigel's nickname... why Jabba?'

Gareth frowns. 'Jabba... you know... Jabba the Hut.'

'Jabba the *Hut*?'

'Yeah, you know, the fat worm who tries to eat Princess Leia,' replies Gareth.

'What?!'

'Seriously?' replies Gareth, looking closely at Martin. 'Oh, never mind.'

Standing at the end of the lane, outside Itsu, is a woman about Martin's age with short dark hair, combat boots and a red crop top under an oversized black jacket. On the placard she's holding is a stylised graphic of a charging bull restrained by many thin, red cords. Above the image are the words *The Beginning Is Near*.

'We are the ninety-nine,' she says softly as they pass.

'Well, that was kind of funny,' says Martin.

'What?' replies Gareth.

'Finally meeting your... rival... Winterbottom. I almost feel like I know him, you talk about him so much.'

'I do?'

'Yeah. All the time.' Then Martin wonders if he's treading on delicate ground. 'I mean, not all the time, but… I hear his name mentioned on the desk now and then. It was good to put a face to a name.'

'Sure.'

'It's funny because when he walked past, I thought he was you!'

Gareth looks up. 'Oh, really!'

'Yeah.'

'That's fantastic!'

'Fantastic? Why?'

'Oh, did I say that? I don't mean *fantastic*. I mean… I meant that's funny…'

'Yeah.'

Gareth is looking at Martin expectantly. 'So… in what way?'

'Umm… what, *in what way*?'

'In what way did you think he was me?'

'Oh. I guess a certain manner, a certain kind of suit, pair of shoes… just lots of little things. I guess it's an Eton, Oxford, Army thing, right?'

'Eton, Oxford, Army thing?'

'You know him from Eton and Oxford, and you were in the Guards together, right?'

'Oh, that. Yeah, yeah.'

'Yeah. Just a certain type. You know… I mean, of course not that you're a *type*, but… you know what I mean.'

'Yeah, yeah.'

They wait at the lights, then cross the road onto Cheapside. Martin can see that Gareth's mind is wandering again.

'How was your meeting?' asks Martin.

'Very good, very good indeed. Livermore Capital... just got the account-opening papers signed.'

'Livermore Capital... oh, isn't that...'

Gareth nods. 'Yeah, that's Aurelius Blois.'

'Great.'

'Yeah, yeah,' replies Gareth, still thinking about something else.

Then Martin decides to just come out with it. 'Can we talk about Friday night?'

They've just crossed over onto the north side of Cheapside, and Gareth looks over his shoulder, then stops and pulls Martin into the alleyway. The sign above Gareth's head reads *Gutter Lane*. Martin now has his full attention.

'Look, I'm glad you brought that up,' replies Gareth. 'I wasn't... I didn't expect to see you there.'

'I didn't plan to be. You were right: I should have steered clear. But we were out for a swift one after work and Jabba caught me after a few pints, and I just thought, *what the hell*, and we all rolled out of the bar and caught cabs to his place and that's when you arrived...'

'Yeah.'

'You arrived and that's when I realised what I'd got myself into and I felt embarrassed about being there but also confused, because I didn't think you were into that stuff.'

Gareth sucks his teeth. 'It didn't look good.'

'And after you left, Jabba said you did a bit of dealing and pimping on the side... which was a joke, right?'

'Yeah. I guess it was.'

'I'm sorry to bring it up, but I just feel really... fucked up about the whole night. The whole thing was wrong, but there's no one else I can talk to about it. There's no one who would understand.'

Gareth is looking at the pavement and twisting the gold ring round his little finger. He looks up and down the lane, and then at Martin.

'Look, I owed Jabba a favour. That's the only reason I was there. And if there's one piece of advice I can give you, it's to steer clear of Jabba. Stay on the right side of him if you can, but keep your distance… I kind of got myself in a situation with Jabba where I owed him a favour. I didn't want to be there any more than you did. But it's done. Let's just forget about it and move on, OK?'

'OK,' says Martin.

Gareth lets out a deep breath and puts his hand on Martin's shoulder. 'And you're OK?'

'Thanks. Yeah, I'm OK.'

'You've got it off your chest?'

'I guess so.'

'Chalk it up as a life experience. It's one of those things. It happened. Move on. Yeah?'

'Yeah. Thanks, Gareth.'

'Come on,' says Gareth, turning up the cut-through which will bring them out onto Gresham Street.

They walk in silence for a moment. Martin can sense that Gareth wants to say something else. Something important.

'Do you think it's meaningful?' asks Gareth.

'What's meaningful?'

'I mean, do you think it's a meaningful difference?'

'Sorry, you've lost me.'

'Between tortoiseshell and horn.'

6.13pm – Dan Trench, TKO Gym, Canning Town

The first thing Dan notices is the smell. Not a bad smell, but distinctive. Kind of musty but cut with turpentine, or maybe bleach.

The music stops and there's a low crackle from the Tannoy.

'Please do *not* leave *any* valuables in the changing room. We have a *thief* in the gym. Rest assured that when we catch the *cunt* we're going to *break his fuckin' legs*!'

A cheer goes up around the hall.

'Thank you.'

The Tannoy cuts out and the music comes back on.

Dan stands just inside the main door, looking for Marc.

On the far side of the hall there are three boxing rings and a collection of punchbags hanging from a frame made of scaffolding poles. Hungry young men shadow box in one of the rings.

'*Ah, ah… ah, ah, ah…*'

The sound and movement are fast and aggressive.

On the near side of the hall is an empty space, where people skip and shadow box in front of a series of full-length mirrors. In the corner next to Dan is a line of ageing exercise bikes and rowing machines, a weights bench and a rusting stack of dumbbells. A man and a woman stand next to an open door marked *Office*.

Dan makes his way across the hall towards them.

'So, who's training them tonight then?' says the man.

As Dan approaches, the pair stop talking and turn to look at him.

'Hi… is Marc around?' asks Dan.

'Whadya want, mate?' The man, tall and wide, with a short neck and thick forearms, looks Dan up and down through heavy eyelids.

'Whadya want? No spinning classes here, mate.' The man snorts. He has small, cauliflower ears.

The woman smiles at Dan in a motherly way.

'Don't worry about him, darling. He's just a cunt.'

'Who's a cunt then?' replies the man with cauliflower ears.

'I'm Dan.'

'Hi, Dan.' The woman offers her hand and Dan shakes it. 'Nice to meet you. I'm Blix, and this is Mick.'

Dan holds his hand out to Mick, who ignores him and turns back to Blix to continue his conversation.

'So, who's training them tonight then?' asks Mick.

'Marc's training them tonight,' replies Blix. 'I don't need you tonight because there are only gonna be a few of them. I need you next week.'

'Well, I'm busy tonight, aren' I.'

'That's what I'm saying. *I don't need you tonight.*'

'Well, that's lucky, init.'

Mick stares at Blix for a moment, then turns and strolls across the hall, swinging his shoulders as he moves, like a status dog spoiling for a fight. Approaching the ring, he starts to bark instructions at the young men who are shadow boxing.

Blix rolls her eyes and turns to Dan.

'How you doin', darling? You fancy some boxin', do ya?'

'Yes.'

Blix nods at the projector screen above their heads, which is showing a fight.

'That's our champ.'

'Who?'

'Him fighting, that's our champ. That's his title fight last month. We got a few up-an'-coming fighters at our gym. JJ's here today. He's turning pro.'

'Is Marc around?'

'He's taking group training. You here for Fight Night?'

'What's Fight Night?' asks Dan.

'Fight Night,' says Blix.

'What's Fight Night?' asks Dan.

'Fight Night,' says Blix.

Dan pauses for a moment, wondering how to rephrase the question.

'Sorry, what *is* Fight Night?'

Blix points at a poster on the office wall.

'Fight Night.'

Under the heading *Bad Boy Promotions FIGHT NIGHT* is a montage of young men with serious faces in boxing stances. Various ticket prices are listed down the side. Along the bottom it says *Friday the 1*st *of June, Troxy, Commercial Road, London.*

'Fight Night,' says Dan.

Blix points across the hall at a door marked *Men.* 'Get changed in there. But don't leave anythin' in the changing room; bring your bag and leave it here.'

She points at the row of benches along the wall behind her.

Inside the changing room the walls are covered in patches of thick black mould. At one end of the long, narrow room are benches and clothes hooks, and at the other end is a single shower, a pair of urinals and a toilet. There's a dip in the middle of the room which has collected an inch-deep puddle of water and piss.

Standing at the urinal, a drop of water lands on Dan's head. He looks up at the high ceiling which is black with mould and glistening with condensation. Another drop lands on the floor beside his foot.

'Shithole,' says Dan out loud.

When Dan emerges, half a dozen people are standing around Blix.

Some look the part in silky knee-length Lonsdale shorts, boxing vests and boots. A couple are dressed more like Dan, who is wearing an old T-shirt, gym shorts and running shoes. There are tattooed necks, legs and forearms.

A middle-aged, heavy-set man with shoulder-length dreadlocks is bouncing from foot to foot, rolling his shoulders.

'If you can dance, you can box,' he says to no one in particular. 'If you can dance, you can box.'

Dan stands beside a short, stocky man, young but prematurely balding, who is wearing a boxing vest.

'You do much sparring?' asks Dan.

'Every night.'

'You spar *every* night?'

'Can't get enough of it.'

Marc emerges from the office.

'*Listen up, gentlemen*. Let's warm up.'

Dan catches Marc's eye and the coach nods back at him.

'JJ, you know the drill,' says Marc.

JJ moves with lightness and rhythm. His uniform, like Marc's, is a dirty mismatched tracksuit top and bottoms, paired with old Adidas boxing boots.

JJ begins jogging round the hall and alternating between throwing air punches, swinging his arms or dipping down to touch the floor with one hand, then the other. The rest of the group, there are now a dozen or so in all, file in behind him.

'Alright, boss,' says Marc as Dan jogs past.

After jogging round the hall for five minutes there's a relay race which involves push-ups and flipping a truck tyre from one end of the hall to the other.

When the warm-up's over, Marc gets the group up into one of the rings.

First, he walks round each person, checking their stance. 'Front foot one o'clock, back foot two o'clock, half a metre apart.'

'When you move forwards you move your front foot first; when you move backwards you move your back foot first; when you move right you move your right foot first and… you get the picture. Off you go.'

Dan skips forwards and backwards, right and left.

Marc moves round the crowded ring giving tips: 'Small steps, small steps; keep your hands up.'

After a couple of rounds of movement, Marc introduces the jab.

'The jab is your most important punch.' Marc demonstrates, flicking out his left hand and bringing it back to his chin. 'When you snap the jab, make sure you turn your fist.' Marc demonstrates a few more times. 'You can and should double up your jabs. Double jab to the head; jab, jab. Jab to the head, jab to the body; jab, jab. Now your turn.'

After three rounds of shadow boxing, Marc tells two people to stay in one ring and everyone else to move across to the other.

'Yous lot are shadow boxing while you wait your turn to spar,' he explains. 'Each pair does two rounds of sparring, then the next two get in. Got it?'

Marc points at Dan and the balding young man whom he was chatting to earlier.

'You two are in next. Head guards on and get ready.'

Dan nods at the guy that he's been paired up with.

'I'm Dan.'

'Billy.'

Marc tells the pair in the ring to touch gloves. Dan and Billy watch in silence as the boxers begin dancing round each other. Unsure, they hover out of range, tentatively throwing single jabs.

From the corner of the ring, Marc gives advice.

'Keep your right hand up – remember *hold the phone*.'

'If the jab lands, then you're in range, so use it!'

In the second round the boxers are more relaxed, getting within range behind their guards, throwing combinations of punches, then stepping back or rolling off to one side.

'They're looking good,' says Dan.

Then one of the boxers charges forwards, swinging wildly.

'*Stop*,' shouts Marc. 'Come here.'

Marc waits for the boxer to come across to his side of the ring.

'Less of that. Stop fighting, start boxing. Work the jab.'

Marc throws a pair of double-jabs to illustrate his point. 'Jab, jab. Jab, jab.'

The boxer nods and, back in the middle of the ring, the pair touch gloves and start again. Circling and jabbing. A few moments later Marc shouts 'time' to bring the second two-minute round to an end.

As the first pair jump down, Dan pops his gum shield in, tightens the Velcro on his gloves and steps into the ring behind Billy. He can sense that Billy is nervous, and knowing this makes him feel more relaxed. As soon as they're in the ring, Marc tells them to 'touch gloves' to start the first round.

Billy's face has tightened up, and his pupils have shrunk to tiny points.

Staying light on his toes, bouncing slowly round to his right, Dan stays cautiously out of range. He throws a jab which Billy slips, countering with a right cross. Dan's guard is low, and the punch hits him on the forehead. The strike isn't painful, but it sends a shot of adrenaline through Dan and, as Billy steps back, he rushes forwards with a double jab that Billy blocks, followed by a left hook which strikes Billy sweetly below the ribs. Billy responds with a left hook that grazes Dan's head as he ducks out of the way.

Billy comes forwards into the middle of the ring and Dan throws another jab. Billy's counter-jab comes in over his guard and lands on the bridge of his nose, which stings and makes his eyes water.

'If you throw uncovered jabs,' shouts Marc, 'you're gonna get hit.'

For the rest of the round, Dan peers warily at Billy from behind his guard, nursing his sore nose. He's relieved when Marc shouts, '*Time*.'

Marc calls him over. 'How's it going?'

'Bit rougher than Gymbox.'

'Yep. Enjoying it?'

'I am.'

'It's not one of those nice City-boy gyms like you're used to.'

Dan thinks about the inch of piss on the changing-room floor and grins.

Marc glances at the clock. 'So, quickly, when you throw the jab you gotta use your guard.' Marc illustrates by bringing his right hand up to cover his face. 'Throw uncovered jabs like what you're doing and you're just gonna get hit.'

Dan nods.

'OK?' says Marc.

'OK.'

Marc glances up at the clock. 'Start on two.'

Billy and Dan both stand and stare at the clock, and as the hand comes round to two, they lean in and touch gloves.

In the second round, knowing that he has the upper hand, Billy comes forward confidently. Having pushed Dan into a corner, Billy lunges with a jab, overcommitting and coming off balance when Dan ducks. His fist snatches at the air above Dan's head. Dan taps Billy in the ribs as he skips around him and back into space in the middle of the ring. Billy turns and comes forwards again, throwing a flurry of straight shots which Dan blocks easily. He is soon back against the ropes, and as Billy feints a jab, Dan ducks and tries to move round to the right again. But this time Billy is waiting for him.

Dan doesn't see the punch. There is no pain. For a moment there is no sensation at all. He just stands there with his guard down and his mind blank. Then Billy hits him a second time, square in the face, and instinct kicks in, bringing his arms up to cover his head.

The room is spinning and his legs feel weak. Billy has backed off a few paces.

'*Time*,' shouts Marc.

Dan's legs are wobbly as he steps down and so, before joining the others shadow boxing, he steadies himself for a moment against the side of the ring. He pulls off his gloves, then fumbles with the buckle on his head guard; the buckle is small, and his hands are shaking. Next, he takes out his gum guard and notices that his lower lip is swollen. He licks the sweet, rich taste of blood from his lips. He runs his fingers along his nose, which is tender to the touch. Dan smiles. He is completely and vividly alive.

CHAPTER TWELVE

Thursday the 22nd of March, 2012

G4S has lost over £500 million in market value since it admitted it could not fulfil its obligation to supply 10,400 security guards for the London 2012 Olympic Games. The 'Olympishambles' is only the latest in a series of high-profile slip-ups committed by the firm. Last October G4S guards misplaced the keys at Birmingham prison; prisoners were locked in their cells for nearly twenty-four hours. In August the firm fired two employees who fitted an electronic tag to a man's prosthetic leg, which he proceeded to remove in order to break a court-imposed curfew.

7.30pm – Dan Trench, PLC Awards Dinner, Old Billingsgate Fish Market, Lower Thames Street

With a nod, five waiters place ten plates of beef wellington on the table.

Gareth leans across and puts his hand on Dan's shoulder. 'I know this isn't your scene. I really appreciate you being here.'

Dan is filling in last-minute, but he only agreed to come because he knows that Marianne will be here. Table seventeen.

Dan looks through the categories: 'Best Strategy', 'Best Management Team', 'Entrepreneur of the Year', the list goes on and on.

'Do you guys do short recommendations?' asks Dan.

'What's your short?' replies Gareth.

'Sell the winners.'

'You *sell* the companies that win an award?'

'I've back-tested it. When expectations are so high, it's virtually impossible not to fuck up.'

Gareth shakes his head and laughs. 'You're such an awkward, contrarian bastard.'

'It's just mean reversion. For a while you just happened to be in the right place at the right time.'

Dan looks across the hall, trying to make out the table numbers. The old Victorian fish market has been given a *Moulin Rouge* twist. Before dinner there were burlesque dancers and circus acts performing on the river-front promenade outside.

Jessica turns to Dan and points at the order of events card. 'I've seen him before. Awful.'

He follows her finger down to the after-dinner comedian. 'Oh yeah, he *is* awful.'

'So, how is life after the City?'

'Oh, you know, it's nice to have the time to focus on other things.'

'I'm sure… say, have you met Andrew Waite?' says Jessica, turning to Andrew who is sitting on her left. Andrew's bow tie tells a story of struggle and defeat.

'Yes, we've met.'

Andrew has put away a lot of house red and looks

unlikely to make it to dessert. There's a stain running down the arm of his dinner jacket.

Andrew leans over Jessica to speak to Dan. 'Dan, my man! I could do with some advice…'

After the main course is cleared, Jessica swaps places with Andrew. Dan can see that she is keen to put herself between the pissed young fund manager and the person sitting on the other side of him, who is an important client.

'How's the fund doing?' asks Dan.

'That's what I wanted to talk to you about,' replies Andrew.

'How can I help?'

'The thing is… well the thing is… I've got no idea what I'm doing.'

'The good news is that you couldn't possibly do a worse job than Mancroft.'

'I'd like to pick your brains about how you ran the Columbus Fund. Your framework… for making decisions…'

'You want to talk process,' says Dan.

'Process…' Andrew nods.

Dan hands Andrew a business card. 'Give me a call.'

Andrew stares at Dan, then at Dan's card, then back at Dan. 'Thank you, Dan Trench. You are a legend.'

Gareth is flirting with a waitress. As she leans in to speak to him, his hand slides down her back. He whispers something and she laughs and puts her hand on the back of his chair. Gareth has just given her a business card when his phone rings. He points at his phone apologetically. As she leaves Gareth grabs her hand and winks.

Gareth answers the phone. 'How are you getting on… no, that's perfect, dinner's almost finished… I'll come out and get you… two minutes.'

He slips the phone back into his pocket.

'Who was that?' asks Dan.

'Hot date,' says Gareth.

Dan laughs out loud. 'You're a rogue, Eary. It will catch up with you one day.'

'Well, until it does…' Gareth stands up and squeezes Dan's shoulder, then picks his way between the tables towards the main entrance.

'Where's he going?' asks Andrew, watching Gareth disappear into the crowd.

'Client,' explains Dan.

While the guests tuck into a trio of crème brûlée, sticky toffee pudding and clotted-cream ice cream, the host comes up onto the stage to begin the award ceremony.

'Excuse me,' says Dan, standing up.

He circles anticlockwise round the hall, examining the table numbers. He spots table seventeen. His heart is beating hard in his chest. He scans each seat. He scans a second time. And a third. But she's not there. Dan's shoulders drop.

With a long sigh he steps back to lean against a pillar and, standing there in the shadows, a familiar feeling of emptiness descends on him. He looks round the room full of people drinking and laughing. They all seem so far away.

'Hello,' says a voice from behind the pillar.

There are butterflies in his stomach as he turns round. 'Hi…'

'What are you doing here?' asks Marianne.

'I was… actually… looking for you.'

Marianne takes a step towards him. The ripples of her dress shimmer. Dan recognises the smell of her perfume. He wants to sink his face into her hair, which hangs in loose curls over her soft, pale shoulders.

'I've been thinking about you,' says Dan.

'I got that impression from all the messages. Clearly not one of those *wait five days* kind of guys.'

'I'm not cool enough for that.'

'No, you're not.'

Marianne is standing up close now. Dan reaches out and takes her hand.

Suddenly there's someone standing in between the two of them.

'*Dan Trench legend!*' shouts Andrew.

Andrew steadies himself, with one arm over Dan's shoulder.

'Andrew, be a good chap and piss off,' says Dan firmly.

Andrew carries on talking but, catching something in Dan's eye, stops himself. He removes his arm and stumbles off towards the bar.

'Sorry about that,' says Dan.

Marianne pulls Dan in towards her and bites his lip.

'Let's get out of here.'

CHAPTER THIRTEEN

Tuesday the 27th of March 2012

The news that the UK Financial Services Authority will prosecute Ian Hannam, the world's most prominent mining banker, over allegations that he shared inside information, has sparked debate about the opaque rules around market abuse. Unusual price moments, which can indicate insider trading activity, precede around 30% of UK mergers and acquisitions, a figure the FSA is aiming to reduce.

12.12pm – Aurelius Blois, Blanc Brasserie, City

Aurelius enjoys the sensation of hunger. When his stomach is empty, he feels sharper and sees things more clearly. Sometimes Aurelius thinks that he would have made an excellent hunter-gatherer, because being a hedge fund manager is also about living on your instincts.

The restaurant is another of those white tablecloth, brass fittings, smart, bland places that exist so that people like Gareth have somewhere to take clients for lunch. *Bland Brasserie*, says Aurelius to himself, laughing out loud. It's a good one.

Aurelius spots Gareth through the full-height window. The broker is sat in the middle of the main dining area at one of the tightly packed tables for two. Otherwise, the restaurant is empty.

There is an earnestness about Gareth that reminds Aurelius of a chipmunk. The broker squeezes out from behind the table so that he can stand to shake Aurelius's hand, but Aurelius beckons him to sit back down, so they end up shaking hands with Gareth half crouched over the table.

'I hope you don't mind eating a little early,' says Aurelius.

'Early suits me just fine.'

As he sits down, Aurelius considers the broker's well-tailored navy suit and silk tie. The tortoiseshell glasses don't quite seem to fit, which is to say that Gareth wears them a little awkwardly.

'You should have laser-eye,' says Aurelius.

Gareth looks blank for a moment.

'Ah yes, I forget I'm wearing them sometimes,' replies Gareth, touching his glasses. 'You've had laser-eye?'

Aurelius shakes his head. 'Never. twenty-twenty. Perfect.'

'Lucky for some.' Gareth laughs and picks up the wine list. 'I've seen a very nice bottle of white.'

'Not for me. You will think I'm not very French, but I don't drink at lunchtime, and I don't like long lunches. I like to stay sharp.'

'Of course,' says Gareth, motioning to a waitress who is hovering by the kitchen counter, 'what will you have?'

'Water. Sparkling,' says Aurelius to the waitress.

Aurelius studies the waitress's pronounced cheek and jaw bones: severe but not unattractive.

'Same,' adds Gareth.

'And we will order too,' says Aurelius.

'Right-o,' says Gareth, scanning the menu.

'Would you like to see the specials board?' asks the waitress.

'Sure,' replies Gareth.

She returns a moment later with a large blackboard.

Aurelius turns back to the waitress. 'I'll have two beef burgers; please make sure that they are rare.'

'Two main courses of the beef burger?'

'Yes.'

'Both at the same time?'

'Yes. Rare.'

'Two rare beef burgers,' says the waitress, jotting the order down on her pad.

'And I'll have the Dover sole,' says Gareth.

'Of course. And a bottle of sparkling water. Anything else? Any sides?'

Gareth looks at Aurelius, who shakes his head.

A waiter comes with a bottle of sparkling water and while he fills their glasses, Gareth makes small talk. While Gareth talks, Aurelius studies the polished brass railing behind his head.

Aurelius interrupts Gareth mid-sentence. 'One thing, Gareth… I'm getting the contract notes; everything is rolling over as it should. As far as we're concerned, the extended settlement is working. How is the arrangement going for you? Is it running smoothly at your end?'

'We're seeing plenty of flow and my dealer is taking care of the extended settlement. It's all going well.'

'And the moment you have any concerns you will tell me.'

'Of course.'

'Because if the liquidity dries up in ALB, we can find another stock. What we're doing here can work with any stock.'

'Interesting,' says Gareth.

'So, if you see anything unusual in ALB, anything at all, I need to know.'

'Of course…'

Aurelius can see that Gareth wants to say something else. 'Of course, but?'

'Oh, but nothing. I was just wondering, because I know it's going to come up sooner or later – my boss is rather… fastidious about this kind of thing; it's her job to be I guess…'

'Yes?'

'Would it be a terrible inconvenience if you could call on the recorded line instead of my mobile? There's no problem; it's just to keep Jessica happy.' While he talks, Gareth squirms uncomfortably in his chair. 'It's just to… umm… tick the box, you know. Ha!'

'I think you know the answer to that already,' replies Aurelius.

'Of course. I just had to ask, you know.'

'Let's not speak about this again.'

'Of course.'

The restaurant has suddenly started to fill up, which means it must be 12.30pm. Two portly men are shown to the table next to them. One of them apologises to Aurelius and Gareth as he pushes himself through the gap between the two tables.

'Let's just hope you don't need to get up for a piss,' replies Aurelius.

Aurelius looks over at the larger tables by the window.

'Next time, we'll sit there. This, this is like sitting in a pig pen. A pig pen for bankers!' Aurelius laughs at his own joke. It's a good one.

The waitress arrives with their food. She places Gareth's Dover sole down first, then the first of Aurelius's burgers, but on the cramped little table, she struggles to find space to put down Aurelius's second plate.

'No problem,' says Aurelius. He takes the plate, picks up the beef patty with his fork and hands her back the rest of the meal.

'Rare?' he asks, examining the piece of meat.

'Yes.'

Aurelius motions for the waitress to wait, while he tackles the plate in front of him, discarding the brioche, chips and salad, placing the beef patty on his side plate on top of the first and handing her back the dish.

After cutting through each patty, inspecting it and finding it satisfactory, he looks up at Gareth, who is watching him.

'Would you like anything else to go with that? Some sides?'

Aurelius shakes his head. 'Full stomach, empty mind.'

'Of course,' says Gareth, sliding his fork into the Dover sole. 'Bon appetite!'

Aurelius watches Gareth pushing food into his mouth and wonders what would happen to all of the people in the restaurant if civilisation ended. Likely they would die of starvation, unable to feed themselves, or perhaps with the onset of winter they would die of cold. Society would probably invert, with the waitresses and the cleaners and the security guards taking over and the investment bankers and brokers and fund managers becoming some kind of weak, subservient underclass. Except for Aurelius Blois, of course, who would continue to live on his instincts.

CHAPTER FOURTEEN

Thursday the 5th of April, 2012

Jamie Dimon, Chief Executive of JP Morgan, yesterday told analysts that rumours of growing losses suffered by Bruno Iksil, a trader at the US investment bank's London branch, dubbed the London Whale, were 'a tempest in a teapot'. The Wall Street Journal had previously reported that a number of hedge funds and traders, including some working at other branches of JP Morgan, had taken bets against Iksil's credit-default swap positions.

6.17pm – Dan Trench, TKO Gym, Canning Town

'Listen up!' shouts Mick. 'Now remember your number. One, two, three. One, two, three…'

Mick walks around the hall tapping everyone on the shoulder as he calls their number.

'Ones with me, twos with JJ, threes with Marc. Everyone, glove up.'

There's a scrum around the kit bags. Gum guards, gloves and head guards appear; hands are rewrapped.

Blix stands by the office door. 'Make sure you see me about tickets before you leave tonight.'

Dan is in Mick's group. He's the first up the step and through the ropes. He moves around the canvas, rolling his shoulders, visualising jabs and rights.

'*Wait*,' shouts Mick. 'How come there are seven in this group and five in that group? What fuck can't count to three?'

He stares impatiently at the group.

'Look, six in this ring, six in that ring. Six plus six. It's not fuckin' difficult.'

Once the group has sorted itself out, Mick explains the drill.

'On the bell it's two minutes of shadow boxing. You need to get used to two minutes' work, one minute's rest.'

Mick rests his large forearms on the ropes and looks at the clock.

'On the bell... *go*!'

Six figures spring into action, each moving with a different rhythm, shuffling and turning as they throw punches and then skip out of reach of imaginary opponents.

'*Ah, ah, ah*.' One boxer moves forwards in a fast, aggressive flurry.

'*Tsh, tsh... tsh, tsh... tsh, tsh*.' Another executes their punches with careful precision.

Dan ignores everyone else and focuses on his own combinations. The movements flow easily. Months of training, ducking, slipping and throwing punches at the pads has committed the drills to muscle memory.

After a couple of rounds, they switch to pad work.

Mick brings Billy forwards to demonstrate a combination: left, right, roll, right, hook.

‘One, two, roll, two, three,’ calls Mick.

Billy works through the moves, slowly at first, then faster the second time. Mick holds up the pads for a third time and now Billy’s movements are sharp and precise, arms snapping back after each punch.

‘Not much wrong with that,’ says Mick.

Dan and Billy get paired up and Billy takes the pads first.

‘Two minutes, on the clock…’ says Mick. ‘Go!’

Dan tries the combination, but Billy is holding the pads too far apart, making Dan overrotate and throwing him off balance. Dan imagines the shock on Billy’s face as a right hand flies between the pads and into his nose.

‘Together,’ says Dan, pushing Billy’s hands closer together.

Billy’s face tightens up, like it does when they’re sparring, and he returns to his old pose with the pads wide apart.

Dan laughs to himself.

‘OK.’

He moves his feet back into stance and bounces on his toes. Left, snap; right, snap; on the roll Dan shuffles his feet forwards, then drives his right hand forwards between the pads, *bang* into Billy’s face; then hook into the side of Billy’s head.

Billy looks at Dan, stunned for a moment, then rips off the pads and charges at him, swinging his arms wildly.

‘*Oi!*’ shouts Mick. ‘*Oi!*’

Suddenly people are pushing Billy and Dan back into the ropes on opposite sides of the ring.

Billy is screaming in rage.

Mick comes up behind Billy, reaches over the ropes and wraps a forearm round his chest.

'*Enough!*'

With one arm across Billy's chest, Mick picks him up and drags him over the rope, then drops him on the floor beside the ring.

'In the office. *Now*,' shouts Mick, then turns to Marc and waves an arm at Dan. 'You sort that one out.'

'Fuck,' says Dan under his breath.

Now Marc is standing beside the ring.

'Outside,' says Marc.

Dan follows Marc out of the main door and into the stairway.

Dan's never seen Marc angry before. 'What was that?' asks Marc.

'I'm sorry,' says Dan. 'I just—'

'What you do in this gym is on me. You understand?' says Marc.

Dan nods.

'This is *my* office. Ten in the morning till ten at night. Guys like JJ, this is their livelihood and mine. This shit,' Marc waves back at the gym, 'pays the bills, but this is not why I'm here. You understand?'

Dan nods.

'You got something going on… I can see that, and I want to help, but I need you to be all working up there,' says Marc, tapping a finger on Dan's head guard. 'Understand?'

'Yeah.'

'This is my world and what you do here is on me. You fuck around again, that's it.'

'I'm sorry, Marc.'

'Don't misunderstand me,' says Marc, pushing past him and through the door back into the gym.

CHAPTER FIFTEEN

Wednesday the 18th of April, 2012

Boris Johnson, London Mayor, yesterday used a rugby analogy to admit he would like to 'have a crack' at being Prime Minister. 'Obviously if the ball came loose at the back of the ruck – which it won't – it would be a great, great thing to have a crack at.' David Cameron, Prime Minister, laughed at suggestions that Johnson could replace him. Their rivalry goes back to their years at Eton College where Johnson was two years ahead of Cameron. Speaking about his school years, Johnson recalls, 'I do remember Dave. Someone said to me "That's Cameron Minor", and there was this tiny chap. I dimly remember it.'

8.49am – Dan Trench, City Financial Training, London Wall, City

Dan drops the rucksack and running shoes by his desk. He wipes his brow, which is damp. He's hot and his shirt is sticking to his back. The wall clock, which is always a few minutes fast, reads 8.52am.

Rakesh marches into the office with his teaching notes under his arm, tosses his coat on the back of his chair, opens the notes, finds his place and continues reading.

At the back of the room, the photocopier sits open with the toner cartridge lying on the floor. Colin is on his knees, trying to grip the edge of a sheet of paper which has been chewed up inside the machine.

'Why?' groans Colin. 'Why, why, why!'

Dan looks up from his emails. 'What are you teaching, Rakesh?'

Rakesh is buried in his notes.

'Hey, Rakesh, what have you got today?' repeats Dan.

'Derivatives course, first time… I mean look at this,' says Rakesh, holding up his hands, 'I'm the compliance guy; what do I know about *valuing swaptions*?!'

'Fuck it!' shouts Colin, kicking the toner cartridge across the floor. 'This is what happens when the accountants take over!' He looks pointedly at the glass cubicle at the opposite end of the office.

Rakesh shares a wry smile with Dan.

Dan turns round. 'Hey, Colin, come here, this'll cheer you up.'

'What!' snaps Colin.

'Seriously, come and see this email,' says Dan.

'Are we being offered redundancy? Have they legalised euthanasia?' replies Colin.

'No, look at this one. I think it's a strong contender for email of the week… this guy wants to know how to convert 0.8 into a percentage.'

'Bullshit.'

'Honestly, look,' says Dan.

Colin walks across the room and leans over Dan's shoulder to read the email. 'Jesus Christ!'

'*Harold Noblet, Associate Director*,' reads Colin, 'and I bet he makes a hundred K.'

Dan laughs. 'And the rest.'

Rakesh glances up at the wall clock, closes his file and starts rummaging through his drawer. 'Anyone seen my tie?'

He finds it under the lever arch file and rushes out of the tutor office.

Nine o'clock passes and it becomes quiet in the tutor office. Dan is trying to find the right tone of gentle mockery for his reply to Harold Noblet. He sends the email, then rereads it and wishes he hadn't.

A reminder pops up that he's meeting Andrew Waite at Taylor Street Baristas in forty minutes. There's not enough time to make a start on prep for his evening class, so he picks up the *FT* instead. On the front page of the 'Companies and Markets' section is a piece about Deutsche Bank and the Libor scandal, which he leaves on Rakesh's desk. He reads about mergers and closures amongst small stockbroking firms and job losses in the City and wonders how Gareth and Gresham Street are doing. But during all of this he's also thinking about Marianne, and so eventually he gives up trying to read the paper and starts to write her an email.

Jackie, the managing director, pokes her head out of the glass cubicle at the front of the room.

'I'm going out for coffee. Who wants one?'

Dan is trying to find the right mix of witty and urbane, while also keeping it light and casual so as not to give the impression he's spent twenty minutes agonising over it. He notices that someone is standing behind him and turns round to see Jackie running a hand through her blonde bob.

'Coffee?' she asks.

He notices her nude nail polish and the two heavy gold rings on her right hand.

Dan glances at his watch. 'Actually I'm just heading out. I'll walk with you.'

He turns off his screen and grabs his phone and wallet.

'No jacket?' asks Jackie, as they leave the tutor office.

Dan shakes his head. 'Still hot from running into work.'

'Training for something?'

'Yeah, actually, training for a fight.'

Jackie raises an eyebrow. 'What kind of fight?'

'A boxing match,' says Dan, holding the lift door for her.

'Why do you want to fight?'

'I enjoy the…' Dan chooses his words carefully, '…the physicality of it.'

Jackie looks unconvinced. 'By *physicality*, you mean violence?'

Dan follows her out of the lift into the lobby. They stop on the steps outside the entrance. Dan enjoys the cool breeze blowing through his shirt.

'Where are you heading?' asks Jackie.

'Taylor Street.'

'Oh good, me too.'

They walk in silence for a while. Dan is still thinking about his unfinished email to Marianne when his phone vibrates, but it's just a message from Andrew.

A double-decker bus is driving towards them up Moorgate. Dan looks at the driver. The bus is within touching distance. For a moment he imagines stepping out in front of it. He feels the impact of his head on the windscreen; no pain, just a loud bang and the feeling of moving through the air, and then a sensation along the length of his body as he hits the tarmac, and then silence. The bus passes.

'Have you done many of these private equity buyouts?' asks Dan.

'Too many.' Jackie laughs. 'Healthcare, industrials, financial services. Cut costs, focus on cash flow, improve operations… it's never quite that simple, of course. Every time it's a different business, with different issues, different people, different culture.'

'And how's City Financial shaping up?' asks Dan, knowing he won't get a proper answer.

'Like I said, it's never simple.'

The queue at Taylor Street reaches almost to the front door and Dan feels bad about leaving Jackie to wait in it while he goes to join Andrew at a table in the window.

Andrew stands up to shake Dan's hand. 'I really appreciate you making the time.'

'No problem,' says Dan, taking a seat.

A waitress appears at the table. 'Two flat whites?'

'I ordered,' explains Andrew, then he pulls a piece of paper out of his Moleskine and hands it to Dan.

'I found this when I was clearing Mancroft's desk.'

It's a photo of an advertising billboard. On the billboard, Dan and Peter Mancroft are stood with their arms crossed, looking rather severe against a background that could be the Milky Way and a headline which reads *STAR MANAGERS OUTPERFORM*. On the pavement in front of the billboard, Dan and Peter Mancroft are stood in the same pose, except that Dan has an embarrassed grimace on his face and Mancroft looks a foot shorter.

Dan studies the photo. 'Portnoy used to take the whole team out round London on a double-decker bus to look at these billboards. Mancroft and I were the grey hairs of experience and the dynamism of youth, or something like that. How did you find working with him?'

'Mancroft? All I learnt from Mancroft was the best places to go for lunch.'

'And how was the portfolio when you took over?'

'Fine. We just tracked along with the benchmark.'

'With enough holdings to bury the odd mistake?'

'About 120,' replies Andrew.

'If you're going to be wrong, then don't be bold. Mancroft may not have known much about investing, but he was smart about career risk.'

Andrew looks thoughtful.

'OK,' continues Dan. 'Did you bring the accounts?'

Andrew picks up a large glossy book that's sitting on the bench beside him and hands it to Dan.

'*Albourne PLC, Annual Report and Accounts, 2011*,' reads Dan from the cover. 'Why Albourne?'

'Meeting them next Thursday.'

'John Gruff?'

'Yeah. Mancroft and I met him a couple of times last year. He was raising money for acquisitions,' explains Andrew.

'That sounds about right,' says Dan. 'He's an egomaniac. You invested?'

'We are. It's done quite well for us, actually.'

'And thoughts on the accounts?' asks Dan.

'Well… I've never actually read them. I read the broker research.'

Dan shakes his head. 'Brokers have their own agenda, and it's not necessarily the same as yours.'

Dan flicks through the *Report and Accounts* and stops at page eighty-two, the 'Consolidated Balance Sheet'. He hands it to Andrew. 'Let's start here. Thoughts on the balance sheet?'

Dan sits back, drinks his coffee and watches Andrew running down the table of numbers.

'Well, the property, plant and equipment has doubled to six hundred million and the *goodwill* has gone up four-fold to one point eight billion because of… the acquisitions,' says Andrew.

'Good. So every time Gruff buys a company, he pays a fat premium for the assets and that premium appears here as goodwill, right?' says Dan.

'So, you think Gruff has overpaid for these acquisitions?'

'That's my hunch, but how would you prove it?'

'I guess *ask the broker* isn't an option.'

'No, it's not,' says Dan. 'You need to work out the returns that these acquisitions are generating and see if it all stacks up. Take the Warburtons deal for example: from what I can tell, it's been a well-run business, lean cost base – probably too lean, which could be a problem further down the line – and that pricing power is very much with the customers, the supermarkets, so margins are only going one way.'

Andrew is scribbling furiously in his Moleskine.

Dan sits back and pours two glasses of water.

'OK,' says Andrew, looking up.

'The key thing to remember when you meet with Gruff is to focus on the facts and not allow yourself to be drawn in by the personality or the story.'

'That's kind of obvious, isn't it?' says Andrew.

'Well, put it this way, who does Gruff remind you of?'

Andrew laughs. 'I guess he could be George Clooney's angry twin.'

‘Right, so he looks like George Clooney. He’s a bit abrupt maybe, but he can be charming too, and you walk out of the meeting thinking he *must* be a good CEO. You walk out of that meeting, and you *want* to buy his story, before you’ve looked at the financials, the business model, competitive environment, the valuation, et cetera. Sure, you do all that too, but in the back of your mind the decision’s already been made.’

Andrew starts to disagree, but Dan doesn’t hear, because he’s just seen Marianne walk past the window.

‘Sorry, got to dash. Thanks for the coffee.’

Before Andrew can reply, Dan is out of the door. It’s cold outside.

‘Marianne!’

She turns round and smiles and walks back towards him. As soon as he sees her smile, Dan feels a lightness come over him. He wants to hold her and kiss her.

‘Hey you,’ says Marianne.

‘Monday night… wow,’ says Dan, his throat suddenly feeling dry.

‘Me too.’

Marianne is moving closer to him now, until her hip brushes against the back of his hand, which is in his pocket. Dan takes his hand out of his pocket and holds her wrist, and for what feels like a long time, neither of them say anything. He can feel his heart beating in his chest, and he can see Marianne’s chest rising and falling with her breath. Then she’s kissing him, and in that moment, nothing else exists.

CHAPTER SIXTEEN

Friday the 20th of April, 2012

Seymour Pierce, one of the leading small-cap brokers by client numbers, is in talks with three foreign financial institutions about an injection of new capital, as it seeks to secure its position in the increasingly competitive broking sector.

1.58pm – John Gruff, Gessner Bank, Threadneedle Street, City

John Gruff leans back in the Eames office chair, picks a piece of Nicorette gum out of his mouth and pushes it onto the white porcelain saucer next to his coffee. He glances away from the view of St Paul's Cathedral and over at Paul Todd and the consumer goods analyst, who are sat at the far end of the table. Laid out in front of them are thick piles of management accounts.

Gruff gives a long, bored sigh. Neither of the men at the far end of the table look up.

In Gruff's hand is a deck with the Warburtons and Albourne logos on the front. Beneath the logos are the words *Acquisition. Integration. Synergy.*

'Well?' says Gruff, throwing the deck across the table. 'This is what the numbers are meant to say. How hard can it be to join up the dots?'

Paul looks up. The consumer goods analyst continues tapping away on a laptop.

'Well?' asks Gruff again.

'Sorry, one moment,' replies Paul.

Gruff shakes his head and pulls out his Blackberry.

Paul looks hard at the laptop screen, then stands up.

'I think... I think...'

'Well, I'm delighted to hear that. Well done. Clever boy,' replies Gruff.

Paul puts his hands up. 'Look, John, we've got our best man on the job, but Abhik is just going to need a bit more time to unpick this.'

Gruff chucks down his Blackberry. The sound of it skittering across the table makes Abhik look up.

'I don't care if you've worked out the answer to three decimal places or if the sensitivity analysis has conditional formatting. All I need to know is how much shit we're in and what you're going to do to get us out of it.'

'Of course.' Paul nods. 'We can give you the headline numbers, right, Abhik?'

In all the time that Gruff has been sat in the boardroom, Abhik hasn't said a word.

'Yes,' says Abhik.

'He talks!' says Gruff.

'What's the earnings miss? Roughly?' asks Paul.

'Very roughly, it's a twenty per cent miss at the operating level,' explains Abhik. 'Then after the debt service, that turns into a forty-something per cent earnings-per-share miss.'

Gruff feels a hit of adrenaline.

'*Four zero?* Forty? Forty per cent?' asks Paul.

The consumer goods analyst nods.

'Are you sure?' asks Paul.

'Plus or minus a couple of per cent.'

'Holy shit,' says Paul.

'OK,' says Gruff, matter-of-factly. 'What's the plan?'

Abhik shifts uncomfortably in his chair.

'*What is the plan?*' spits Gruff.

'OK, so I'm not saying that this is what you *should* do,' explains Abhik. 'This is just, you know, technically, what you *could* do to get from the number you've got to the number you want.'

Gruff stares silently at the consumer goods analyst.

'OK,' continues Abhik, 'so we've got a couple of million of restructuring provision from the last acquisition left on the balance sheet… for a rainy day… which is what this is. So we can bury a chunk in that. Then there's a couple of multi-year contracts with some accrued income and a bit of *flex* in terms of sales we can pull forward from next year, which might be another million on the bottom line. I'm also thinking… you might, just might, be able to capitalise some of that interest charge if we can show that a portion of the debt is directly against the line expansion project. But that's only going to be, maybe, a quarter million tops, and the auditors will probably push back on that.'

'OK, but we're still a long way off,' says Gruff.

'Yeah…' Abhik turns back to the laptop.

Paul steps in. 'So, broadly, I think a lot of the additional costs are going to have to go into other *exceptional* items. Abhik and I will work out exactly what those items should be and how we can craft a narrative around it. Then we'll add a bit of distraction: we'll pull together some three-year margin, growth and cashflow targets which are credible but ambitious enough to get investors excited. We know what the number needs to be to keep the market happy and to meet your share option vesting targets, and we will make sure that happens.'

'OK. And what about cash?' asks Gruff.

Paul smiles. 'Cash is my specialty. I know a very good factoring firm who will buy your receivables. We can make the year-end cash number practically whatever you want it to be. Cash is actually the easiest number to fix.'

'Factoring?' replies Gruff. 'But won't the shareholders smell a rat?'

'The beauty of factoring is that you don't need to disclose it,' explains Paul.

'Not in the notes?' asks Gruff.

'Nowhere. Not a whisper.'

For the first time that day, Gruff smiles.

'Good. *This* is what I pay you for.'

'The missing piece of the jigsaw is your new finance director. When will he be gracing us with his presence?'

'He won't.'

'O-k-a-y…' says Paul slowly, 'but he's… on board with the plan, right?'

Gruff is silent.

Paul shakes his head. 'Look, John, for *any* of this to work, Hugh needs to be one hundred per cent on board with it. We can provide the numbers, but it's *his* name on the accounts. Without him we've got nothing.'

'Leave it with me,' replies Gruff.

CHAPTER SEVENTEEN

Monday the 23rd of April, 2012

Ocado, the online grocer founded by three former Goldman Sachs bankers, has given investors a rough ride since its 2010 IPO. Challenges faced by the company have been coming thick and fast with ongoing warehouse issues, a £2.4 million full-year loss and a share price languishing well below the 180p IPO level. In a trading statement yesterday, Ocado announced its third profit warning in as many months.

5.38am – Dan Trench, Clapham Common, South London

Dan pulls the door closed behind him and strides out into the darkness. The cold air fills his lungs and sharpens his senses. He crosses into the park over an empty road. In the early morning the ground underfoot makes a satisfying crunch. He recognises the people that he passes by their dogs, the owners hovering expectantly by the squatting canines, small black bags in hand. Who is the master here?

Dan runs into work whenever he can. While he runs, his mind drifts. He rarely remembers exactly what he's been thinking about, but he's always left with a sense of calm and focus, ready to start the day. It's twenty-five minutes to the river, and as he turns the corner, the Thames opens up in front of him and the wind begins to bite. Dawn has crept up, darkness has given way to greyness, but there is no sign of the sun.

Rain begins to fall. At first, it's like a mist in the air, then gradually it becomes a heavy shower. But the icy dampness doesn't bother him; he focuses on it and savours the sense of being alive. Big Ben shows that it is not quite 6.30am as he runs past down the opposite bank. The riverside is busy now with runners, walkers and the occasional cyclist. Sometimes when Dan comes up behind another runner, their pace changes. Sometimes the difference is only just perceptible, and Dan pulls easily past. Other times the runner will kick, and Dan will do likewise. He will run faster and faster until his lungs feel like they are going to explode and his legs become jelly.

The stretch of South Bank around the London Eye is thick with commuters, and groups of tourists are also starting to appear. Already, a man is selling roasted chestnuts from a small metal cart. People pass with their umbrellas up and heads down, leaning into the rain. In a dry corner under Blackfriars Bridge a homeless man lies curled up in a green sleeping bag on collapsed cardboard boxes. A trickle of water is seeping into the corner of the cardboard. Someone has left a Pret sandwich.

Dan is thinking about Marianne. The minty heat of her breath, her voice, the softness of her skin. He begins to speed up, and when he reaches the end of the Millennium Bridge, with St Paul's rising up to fill his view, he is flying.

Suddenly, he sees Sarah on the pavement ahead.

There is a sickening weight in Dan's stomach. Sarah is on her Blackberry; her face is turned away. Dan's legs feel unsteady. He wants to throw himself on the ground at her feet, to beg her forgiveness, to make everything OK. Then she turns and looks in Dan's direction, and he sees that it's not Sarah. Just another woman with a ponytail in a trench coat.

A man carrying a leather case turns unexpectedly into his path and Dan knocks into his shoulder with full force. The man stumbles with the force of the blow but stays on his feet.

'Dickhead!' shouts the man.

Those are the first words that anyone has spoken to him today.

Dan is running past a construction site on Throgmorton Street when a door in the blue hoarding is flung open in front of him and a swarthy, slightly built man wearing heavy boots falls through the doorway to Dan's feet, followed by a larger man wearing a hard hat and fluorescent bib. As the man on the floor gets up, the other man strikes him on the back of the head, knocking him back down onto the street.

'Hey, stop that,' shouts Dan.

'You little *rat*. I'm going to fuck you up, you little rat,' shouts the larger man, punching the smaller man in the back of the head again.

Dan feels a kick of adrenaline. 'Stop that,' he shouts again, but even as he says it, he realises that he doesn't want to stop them; he wants to join them. He glances round at the small crowd that has gathered, mostly young men in suits, voyeurs, standing a safe distance back. The larger man has the other by his overalls and is dragging him to his feet, then spins and slams him against the blue hoarding. Dan can't hold himself back any longer. He steps forwards and grabs the larger man's shoulder.

'That's enough.'

There is fury in the man's eyes. He spits his words. 'Who the *fuck* are you?'

He tries to pull himself back from Dan's grip, but Dan holds him firm.

'Who the *fuck* do you think you are?' screams the man again, his voice an octave higher and crackling with anger. Dan gives him a sneer, which has the intended effect.

The man throws his hard hat on the ground, then grabs Dan by the neck of his Helly Hansen base layer. Dan feels the snap of stitching as the man tightens his grip. Dan watches as the man raises his left hand above his head like a hammer and, just as the fist reaches an apex, Dan snaps a left hook into the man's ear and twists out of his grip. The man is stunned for a moment, then turns to look at Dan. He frowns and gently rubs his ear. The fury has gone now, replaced with grim determination. He studies Dan for a moment, then lowers his shoulder and charges. Dan skips to one side and smacks his fist into the man's ear again as he rushes past. The man lets out a sharp wail and grabs his right ear, steadying himself against the hoarding. The banner above his head reads *Responsible Construction*. He rubs the side of his head on the shoulder of his fluorescent bib, leaving a thick crimson smear. Breathing heavily now, he turns again to face Dan, this time shuffling cautiously forwards with his guard up in a loose boxer's stance.

Moving back into range, the man swings at Dan's head with his right hand, but Dan steps forwards, avoiding the punch, and buries his forehead into the man's nose.

The man pulls back and crashes against the hoarding, clutching his face.

'*My nose, my fucking nose*.' There is blood running down his hands.

There is an intake of breath from the crowd. Dan stands watching the man. He looks in the man's eyes and sees that the fight is gone from him, and for a moment, Dan feels sorry for him. Then he turns to carry on his way. People step back.

'Hey, what's going on?'

'He just bust the builder's nose.'

'What?'

'That guy in the running kit. He just bust the builder's nose.'

'No way, what happened?'

'I don't know, I just saw him headbutt the guy.'

'Hey, isn't that Dan Trench?'

'Can't be.'

'Shit. He's an animal.'

CHAPTER EIGHTEEN

THREE YEARS EARLIER

Sunday the 30th of August, 2009

Dan Trench, Snowdonia, North Wales

Dan is in his flow. His feet and fingertips move deliberately and effortlessly between the cracks and edges; he carefully shifts his balance as he works his way along the line. Sarah is now out of sight beneath the slope of the slab. He stops for a moment to study the route ahead, but something doesn't seem right. He looks back down the way he's come, and it dawns on him that the line he should be on is out to the left.

The climb down looks nasty. He looks across the rock face towards the correct line. The features are sparse, but if he trusts his shoes on the slab it should be OK.

'Fuck it,' he says under his breath.

Dan takes a step out onto a dimple in the rock and stretches his left hand up and across onto an edge. He takes a deep breath, then shifts his weight onto his left foot. Now he is committed.

As Dan makes the traverse, one of the ropes trailing below him becomes stuck behind a flake of rock. Taking the rope in his right hand, Dan tries to flick it over the flake, but the rope is too tight.

'Slack on red!' he shouts down to Sarah.

A muffled reply comes from below.

Dan tries a second time and now the rope whips over the flake and swings back across the slab until it hangs vertically below him again. Dan glances down to check that it's running smoothly and immediately sees that something's not right. A feeling of dread falls over him.

Flicking the rope has dislodged his last piece of protection; the nut and the quickdraw that was clipped into it have disappeared down the rope.

Dan glances back down the route. He pictures the next piece of protection: a hex that he had wedged behind a flake of rock six or seven metres down. Even when he placed the gear, he wasn't particularly happy with it. Seven metres of rope gives a fourteen-metre fall… plus some stretch… the chances of the flake taking that kind of fall are… zero. And if that gives way… he tries not to think about it, but if the hex gives way he'll be grounding out. Twenty-five maybe? What are the chances of surviving a twenty-five-metre fall? Which part of his body would hit the ground first?

Dan's confidence evaporates; his left leg starts to shake. His fingers push deeper into the crack. He moves his left foot, trying to find a better purchase.

'Shit,' he whispers to himself. 'What am I doing? I'm such a dick. I don't want to die.'

He wonders if he should shout down to Sarah. But what would she do? There's nothing she can do.

'Keep it together,' Dan says out loud.

This is all in my head, Dan tells himself. *I just need to get a grip, and everything will be OK.*

Dan closes his eyes and takes a deep breath. He focuses on his breathing and tries to block out everything else. After a few moments he opens his eyes and looks at the traverse towards the next line. He tries to relax as he works through the moves in his head.

'These are easy moves,' Dan tells himself. 'Just relax and trust your shoes.'

Dan's forearms are rock solid. If he doesn't relax, they will start to cramp up. He takes his left hand out of the crack and shakes it off, then stretches out to curl his fingers over a small ledge. It's a little less positive than he'd like, but it's a good hold. His foot finds a sharp flake that bites the rubber on the toe of his shoes. He switches feet, then he carefully shuffles his hands along the ledge until he meets the line that he should have been on all along.

Beside his head is a new-ish-looking bolt. Dan snaps a quickdraw into it then reaches down between his legs to grab the red rope. As he clips it in, a wave of relief washes over him.

'Take on red!'

He feels the red rope go tight. There is a good placement to his left. He quickly puts in a second piece of protection and clips in with green.

'Take on green!'

Now the green rope goes tight.

'Have you got me?'

He feels himself being pulled into the slab under the tension of the rope.

He relaxes his hands and legs so that his knees rest against the rock, and his full body weight is now going through his harness and into the ropes. Suddenly he feels exhausted. He needs some food. He needs sugar.

Somewhere above him is the ledge which marks the end of the first pitch. It's out of sight but he knows it's not far. He slides his foot into the crack which will take him up to the end of the pitch. Dan takes the weight back onto his feet.

'Climbing!' he shouts.

The ropes go slack.

The end of the pitch is closer than he thought and in a few minutes he's set up his anchor and is bringing Sarah up behind him. Sarah makes short work of it and soon he can see her coming up the line that he should have been on all along.

Sarah is grinning as she hauls herself up onto the ledge beside Dan.

'Piece of cake?' asks Dan as he clips her into the anchor.

'What happened to you?' asks Sarah. 'I thought you were having a nap halfway up.'

'I had a… moment. Actually, I took the wrong line and ended up on a tasty traverse.'

'You probably don't want to know this, but your third bit of gear popped out.'

'I saw it go. It made me feel quite unhappy,' says Dan.

He puts his arm round Sarah, and they sit with their legs dangling over the ledge, enjoying the view and each other's company.

Sarah reaches into her smock and produces two Mars bars. 'Breakfast?'

'Lifesaver,' says Dan, ripping off the wrapper and putting a whole bar into his mouth. He grins at her through chocolatey teeth. 'Thanks.'

'You had a bit of a wobble, didn't you?' says Sarah.

'Yeah.'

'There's an alternate route for the final pitch if you want to do something less punchy.'

'See how I feel when we get there. I don't like…'

Sarah finishes his sentence, '…giving up… yeah, I know.'

Sarah leads the second pitch effortlessly. Soon she's set up her anchor and is belaying Dan up behind her. Every couple of metres Sarah has put in some gear. Dan admires her placements; each one is perfect. She puts in two bits of gear on a section where he would have just put in one. He reflects on his near-death experience this morning and sees that he needs to embrace the gear placement. By the time he gets to the top, Dan is feeling confident. He's got his mojo back. Or maybe it's just the sugar. Either way, he's up for it.

CHAPTER NINETEEN

Wednesday the 25th of April, 2012

The UK economy has entered a 'double-dip' recession, after shrinking by 0.2% in the first three months of 2012. A sharp fall in construction output was behind the surprise contraction, the Office for National Statistics said. The UK economy was last in recession in 2009.

10.33am – Andrew Waite, Green Knight Asset Management, Knightsbridge

Lucia's email instructed that all meetings are cancelled, and everyone will be sat at their desks when the consultants arrive. The more people there are in the office the quieter it is, and today a monastic silence hangs over the floor. Except for that infuriating squeaking.

Squeak, squeak.

From the kitchen back to his desk. Another ten more paces to go. Andrew feels his cheeks turning red.

Squeak, squeak.

The sound echoes across the floor. Almost there. Five paces have never seemed so far.

Squeak, squeak.

He reaches his desk with a sigh of relief.

'New shoes?' asks Jude, without looking up.

He touches his jacket lapel. 'New suit too, actually… and new business card.'

Engrossed in her work, Jude doesn't respond.

'Jude?'

'Yes?' replies Jude, still typing.

'Why do you do this job? You could be doing anything. You must be bored stupid.'

Jude chuckles to herself, then looks up.

'I *appear* to work at Green Knight Asset Management, but really I'm just a figment of your collective imagination.'

On Monday Andrew found a page that Jude had left on the printer behind his desk.

'So…'

Jude is still typing.

'So, this book… what's it about?'

Jude looks at Andrew and leans back in her chair.

'You finally worked it out.'

'You left a page on the printer,' explains Andrew.

'It only took you seven months,' replies Jude.

'What's it about?'

'It's a novel. Completely fictional. Any similarities with this batshit crazy place are purely coincidental.'

'God, you're writing about Green Knight!'

'For legal reasons, no, absolutely not. That's not what I'm writing about.'

'Wow. Can I read it?' asks Andrew.

'Of course. When you buy a copy, I'll sign it.'

With that, Jude turns back to her keyboard.

Andrew looks at his watch. The consultants have been in the boardroom with Portnoy and Tony Dye, the head of research, for almost an hour. Will they come out here, or will they call him in there? He wants it to start so that it can be over.

There's a valuation model up on his screen. Will they want him to go through a model, or will they want to talk about the market outlook, or investment process, or something else? He has no idea. Being on his feet calms his nerves, but the squeak of his new shoes stresses him out, so he just sits there, looking at the screen and at his watch and flicking through the notes scribbled in his black Moleskine.

Andrew watches Lucia marching across the floor. Then his phone starts to ring. It's Gareth. But as he takes the receiver, the boardroom door opens. Portnoy pokes his head out and catches Andrew's eye across the room.

Andrew hangs up. This is it. He takes a deep breath. He picks up his trading diary and a pen.

Squeak, squeak.

Andrew walks across the office to the boardroom.

Squeak, squeak.

The boardroom table is spread with presentations and cups of coffee. A plate of biscuits sits to one side, untouched. Tony Dye is saying something about 'sector rotation'. Portnoy, who has swapped his dirty V-neck jumper for a starched white shirt and Hermes tie, looks bored.

Andrew waits near the door until Tony has finished talking, then walks round the table to the nearest of the two consultants.

'Andrew Waite, pleasure to meet you.'

'James Francis, Mercers, and this is my colleague…'

'Sonita.'

Andrew shakes hands with them each in turn and exchanges cards. He walks back round the table to take a seat beside Portnoy.

Squeak, squeak.

Portnoy seems amused. 'New shoes?'

Now that he's in the boardroom, Andrew is feeling a little more relaxed. It helps that the consultants don't look much older than him. He arranges the trading diary and pen and the two business cards neatly on the table in front of him.

'So, Andrew,' says Sonita, looking through her notes, 'you've been running the fund for…'

'Four weeks,' replies Andrew.

Portnoy sits up in his chair and releases a low growl.

'Andrew has been *lead* manager for four weeks, but he's co-managed the Mid-Cap Fund for the last… twelve months.' Portnoy looks at the consultants and then at Tony, who nods emphatically.

'And it's only because of Andrew's…' Portnoy pauses for the right word, '…Andrew's *EXCEPTIONAL* talent, his *exceptional* eye for picking stocks, that we've decided to give him full responsibility for the portfolio.'

'So, Andrew, how long will it take for your management of the portfolio to feed through into the performance numbers?'

Andrew glances at Portnoy before answering. Portnoy's glare says, 'Don't you dare fuck this up.'

'I'm focused on value, which often means betting against the momentum at first. That's made the performance a little… volatile… in the short-term as I've repositioned the portfolio but… with that now largely complete… we are perfectly positioned…'

The consultants are scribbling in their matching Black 'n' Red wire-bound notebooks. Andrew looks over at Portnoy, who nods at him to continue.

'…and as you know, it takes time for any investment thesis to play out, which is why I find that the best performance from a holding often comes only in its second or third year in the portfolio.'

Andrew's left hand rests on the black Moleskine, as if this might help him to remember the words written in it.

'And would you mind telling us a bit more about what you look for in a stock?' asks Sonita.

'The principle is quite simple really: I'm looking to buy good businesses at bargain prices.'

'Sure. Could you elaborate?'

It seems too easy. Could it really be this easy? Andrew asks himself as he reels off his reply.

'Well, in essence I'm looking for cash-generative growth companies with dominant positions in niche markets, backed by high barriers to entry, a strong management team, conservative revenue recognition and a fit-for-purpose balance sheet...'

The consultants are both nodding. Even Portnoy seems interested in what Andrew has to say.

'And valuation?'

'Finding cheap stocks is easy, but avoiding valuation traps is hard. Most cheap stocks are cheap for a reason, so my job is to understand what the market has priced in and to find opportunities where the market has overreacted to events or where our investment thesis is not reflected in the valuation.'

'Sure, but what about specifics?' says the other consultant.

Andrew nods, warming to the topic. 'We use all of the usual relative valuation metrics, or course, but where we differ from most other buy-side firms is that we also maintain a DCF model on every holding.'

'You have a DCF for every holding?' says Sonita.

'Yes.'

‘Well, I think the best thing to do at this stage is to dive right in and you can run us through some of your models.’

Portnoy gives a grunt of approval.

‘Of course,’ says Andrew. ‘We could pull up a couple of chairs at my desk.’

Portnoy grunts again.

‘Sounds good,’ says Sonita, nodding at her colleague.

Tony Dye stands up. ‘Why don’t I give you a quick tour of the floor while Andrew sets up?’

After some more nodding and agreement, the consultants thank Portnoy for his time before following Tony out of the boardroom. As Andrew makes to leave, Portnoy takes his arm.

‘Well done. And nice suit.’

8.24pm – Marianne Bleekman, La Relais de Venis, Throgmorton Street, City

Marianne feels cold as she steps through the revolving doors and onto Threadneedle Street. She hugs her arms across her chest. Her hands are clammy. She had been looking forward to tonight, but anticipation turned to dread at about 3.30pm when Faisal sent her a video, then leant in close and told her not to watch it at her desk.

La Relais is a two-minute walk from her office and there’s always a queue. The menu is salad, steak, chips, and that’s it. Less choice is a winning formula.

She’s early. Dan will be on his way back from the boxing gym. She thinks about his firm body and feels a tingle of anticipation. She imagines his hands round her waist, and then a moment later he is standing behind her with his hands round her waist. He turns her round and pulls her close, her face in his chest and his head in the hair on her shoulder.

'I've missed you,' he whispers.

Marianne breathes in his cologne and feels the heat of his body, fresh from the shower. His body is pressed tight against hers. She closes her eyes and remembers the feeling of his weight on top of her, inside her.

She pulls herself away, blushing.

'Two?' asks the waiter.

'Yeah, two.'

'Come with me, please.'

He shows them to a table. Marianne slides onto the banquette and Dan takes the bentwood chair opposite.

'Have you been here before?' asks the waiter.

'Yes,' says Dan.

'And how would you like your steak cooked?'

'Rare for me please.'

'Medium,' says Marianne.

He scribbles their orders on the paper tablecloth and leaves them with the wine list.

Marianne looks at Dan and wonders if she could just forget about the video. Not mention it. Not spoil what would be a wonderful evening. But deep down she knows that she has to have this conversation. And she has to have it now.

'I'm crazy about you,' says Marianne.

'And I'm crazy about you, too.'

'But I hardly know anything about you. And whenever we start to talk about the big stuff, you close up.'

'I know,' says Dan, looking down at the table and folding his arms across his chest.

'Look… there's something we've got to talk about. Today someone showed me this video. It's been going round. It's a video of you.'

Dan glances up at her, then back down at the table.

'Ah.'

Marianne watches him silently.

'Is that the video someone took in the street with the builders… when I was breaking up a fight… with the builders fighting… and I step in?' Dan stumbles over the words.

'That's not what I saw in the video. You're beating up a man in the street. In the middle of the street, surrounded by people on their way to work… I thought it had to be someone else, but it's you, isn't it?'

'I don't think the video shows the whole thing because there was a smaller guy getting attacked and I stepped in to break it up… I was just running into work and a fight broke out in front of me and I had to do something. The video makes it look worse than it was.'

Marianne shakes her head. 'The more I've thought about it… the more it makes sense. All of these pieces that were floating around just fell into place. Boxing isn't just a hobby like mountain biking or golf. You need the violence.'

Dan looks at his hands for a long time before looking up and answering. 'You're right. I don't think about it quite like that but, in a sense, you're right. I… I… I do find a kind of peace when I'm boxing that I don't find anywhere else.'

'Why do you need it, Dan? Where does that come from? Let me in, whatever it is, share it with me. Let me help you.'

'It's stuff that I haven't… worked through yet. I need to make peace with it. I need to make peace with myself.'

'Are you talking about your ex?' asks Marianne.

'Sarah,' replies Dan.

'Stop holding me at a distance. Let me in, Dan. Tell me about Sarah.'

'I'll try. What do you want to know?'

'Well, when did it end?'

Dan puts his hands over his face and lets out a long, controlled breath.

'I haven't seen her for almost three years.'

'Why did it end? What happened? You were engaged and happy and you thought you had it all worked out. Then what changed?'

Dan lowers his hands. Deep glistening wells have gathered in the corners of his eyes. Then he blinks, and tears roll down his face.

'I'm sorry,' continues Dan. 'I can't talk about it.'

Marianne reaches out with open hands across the table, but Dan leans back, his arms folded tight across his chest.

'Three years is a long time to keep a knot in your heart, Dan. Please. Let me help you. Let me in. Talk it through with me.'

'God, I miss her so much.'

The longing in Dan's voice makes Marianne uncomfortable. She desperately wants to stop the conversation, but there's something she has to know.

'Do you… do you still…?'

But as soon as she starts to ask the question she stops, because she can't bear to hear the answer.

'Yes.'

'No. Please don't say that.'

'I still love her. I would do anything to be with her. It's like what you said on our first date about giving yourself completely and utterly to someone. How can that be undone?'

Marianne is trying to understand how things have unravelled so fast and so far.

'But what does that mean? For us?'

'I don't know. I'm sorry. I need to work this out myself. I'm not ready to talk about it. I need to find peace before I can give myself. Before I can give myself to you, Marianne.'

'I don't understand. Dan. What's going on?'

'Marianne you are an amazing, wonderful person...'

'Please, no. Dan... Dan... I... I love you.'

Desperate, wasted words.

Dan stands up.

'Wait.'

'I'm so sorry,' says Dan.

Dan turns and slowly walks out of the restaurant without looking back.

Marianne feels completely numb, but she knows that soon the numbness will pass, and pain and sadness will take her.

CHAPTER TWENTY

Saturday the 28th of April, 2012

The Treasury intends to privatise the Royal Mail via an IPO in the second half of 2013. Analysts expect that the Royal Mail could be worth £3–£4 billion in what would be Britain's largest privatisation since the 1990s. From Monday the cost of a first-class stamp will rise from 46p to 60p.

10.42am – Gareth Eary, stately home, Surrey

The Hedge for Good invitation was hand-delivered to the office on an otherwise uneventful Thursday afternoon in March. The chat on Bloomberg Messenger had blown up earlier in the day as the first invites had landed, and Gareth had an inkling that this might be his year. To his knowledge, no one at Gresham Street had ever attended. Jessica was pleased for him but clearly jealous. Even Jabba had asked to see the handwritten, gilt-edged invitation.

After the initial thrill, the anxiety started. Firstly, the invitation said *Carriages at 11pm*, which was kind of like being an evening-only guest at a wedding. Gareth tried to be philosophical about this. And nobody else needed to know that he wasn't a full weekend guest.

Logistics was the second issue. Gareth pictured the *GQ* photographer snapping him stepping out of an Aston Martin – a DB5 in British racing green, or even a DB9 would fit the bill – but after a few phone calls it became clear that every luxury car rental and private hire service in Surrey had been fully booked for months.

When the day finally arrives, Gareth has plenty of time to reflect on all this from the back of a Skoda Fabia estate. After a twenty-minute stand-off at Guildford train station, while he hopes that something (anything) else would pull up, Gareth capitulates. At first, he resolves to hop out at the top of the drive, but then it starts to rain, and there is nothing for it but to stoically meet his fate.

Outside, a forlorn-looking doorman stands under a gold umbrella. Gareth throws the driver £40 and tells him to keep the change, hoping that he will pull away promptly. But the driver is in no hurry and instead sits on the drive with his window down, admiring the Jacobean Revival frontage in between puffs on his fag.

From the entrance hall Gareth catches the harmony of a string quartet coming from beyond the inner doors. Between him and the Party of the Year is an energetic young lady with a clipboard, a svelte waiter with a tray of champagne, and four handy-looking fellows, each stationed in front of a Doric column. Gareth admires their faux combat uniforms and decides that the smock would work well in navy, in a less aggressive fit, as a kind of Sunday morning on-my-way-to-brunch throw-on.

'Hello, I'm Minty, can we help you with your bags?'

'I'm travelling light,' replies Gareth.

‘May I have your name please, sir?’

‘Eary, Gareth Eary.’

Minty draws her finger down the list and nods. ‘I see that you’re with us for the day, Mr Eary.’

There is something in her tone that implies his lack of a full weekend invite is a crushing personal indictment.

‘On behalf of Aurelius Blois, it’s my pleasure to welcome you to the Hedge for Good fundraising weekend.’ Minty hands Gareth a small glossy pamphlet. ‘This is the itinerary for the weekend and a plan of the house. The charity auction will take place after dinner.’

‘Thanks, Minty. There’s just one thing.’ Gareth leans in to whisper in her ear. ‘When do you get off?’

Minty blushes. Gareth pushes a business card into her hand.

The waiter steps forwards. ‘Champagne, sir?’

As Gareth takes a glass, the entrance hall doors swing open. Before stepping through, Gareth pauses for a moment to recognise this moment as a milestone that he will look back on in years to come.

The entrance hall leads directly into the atrium, framed by a giant open fireplace on one side and a sweeping staircase on the other. Light floods into the room from a glass dome in the ceiling. There are only a handful of people in the atrium, mostly waiting staff, striding purposefully across the space which joins the various reception rooms.

Gareth follows the sound of Vivaldi into the ballroom. In the middle of the room, in an area enclosed by a black velvet rope barrier, dances a ballerina in a gold leotard. Gareth studies the guests who stand around, chatting over the string quartet. He is looking for the money. He isn’t interested in chatting to salesmen, brokers, investment bankers, intermediaries, service providers and general hangers-on. Gareth wants the principals, the hedge fund managers: the *allocators.*

Gareth reads the crowd.

A man and two women have closed down a tall, serious-looking man wearing a gilet and frameless glasses. A few steps from them are two younger men who are listening in on the group without being part of it.

A little further away a number of groups are trying to move in on two older men who are engrossed in conversation. The men seem familiar in a *Bloomberg News* kind of way. Gareth moves onto the wing of one of the circling groups, and when he hears the men's voices, their names click. The taller one with the beard is Howard Simon, the mathematician-turned-founder of Prometheus Tech, one of the earliest quant funds. He's talking to Justin Roberts, founder of Saxon Capital. Roberts closed his own fund twenty years ago to focus on seeding new firms. Both are personally worth double-digit billions.

Gareth instinctively goes to straighten his tie, even though he isn't wearing one, and touches his jacket pocket to check his business cards are there. But as he makes a move towards the pair, the ballerina brushes past him.

'Oh, hi...' starts Gareth. The girl turns and looks at Gareth with indifference before continuing on her way.

Gareth follows her to the door and watches her make her way up the grand staircase. As she reaches the first landing, she looks up and stops to talk to someone who is on their way down. Gareth watches another ballerina, in a white leotard, follow the curve of the stairs down, and a few steps behind her is Aurelius Blois in a blue linen suit. After pausing briefly, the ballerina in gold disappears up the stairs, while the ballerina in white turns and gives

Aurelius a kiss before carrying on down the staircase. Aurelius's eyes follow her down into the atrium before catching sight of Gareth.

'My dear Gareth!' Aurelius's voice booms across the open space of the atrium.

'Mr Blois,' says Gareth, half walking, half jogging to the foot of the stairs and nodding politely to the ballerina as she passes him.

'Please, my name is Aurelius.'

Gareth extends his hand, and Aurelius instinctively extends his, before retracting it.

'I'm sorry, Gareth. I don't want to be rude, but I have a little semen on my hands. It would be amusing, but also disrespectful, for me to shake your hand.'

Gareth opens his mouth to reply but all that comes out is an exhale of breath.

'Come, we must talk; let's go somewhere quiet.'

As they walk across the atrium in the direction of the entrance hall, an unlikely pair emerge from one of the reception rooms. Chris Tan is athletic, baby-faced and ethnically ambiguous. He's wearing suede loafers and what could be a tracksuit. Melwyn Snoxall is a short, red-faced WASP. His concession to the weekend has been to remove the jacket and tie, while keeping the white shirt and red braces.

'Melwyn, Chris, look at you two, thick as thieves.'

Aurelius shakes Chris's hand, then turns and puts one hand on the back of Melwyn's neck while he slaps him on the arm with the other, turning his head momentarily to wink at Gareth.

'This is my good friend Gareth Eary. This is Chris Tan, Global Head of IB at Merrills, and Melwyn Snoxall, Head of Goldman's Delta One desk.'

Gareth smiles and nods. He knows a few people on Melwyn's team. They have the best clients and the fattest commission.

Chris starts talking, but Aurelius cuts him off. 'Gentlemen, don't let me divert you, but you *must* go and watch the prima ballerina in the ballroom. She's from the St Petersburg Imperial. She is *fantastic*.'

Gareth nods politely at Chris and Melwyn, then follows at a march behind Aurelius, who is already making his way towards the entrance hall. Two footmen pull the doors open as Aurelius approaches.

Minty is flirting with a security guard, who snaps to attention when Aurelius appears.

'Can I help with anything, Mr Blois?' asks Minty.

'Just keep up the good work.'

Aurelius opens another door and Gareth steps through after him, only to find that he is standing next to Aurelius in the toilet.

'Oh, sorry.'

'No, no, just pull the door,' says Aurelius as he starts to piss into the toilet bowl.

Gareth pulls the door to and coughs awkwardly as he stands facing the wall, with his back to Aurelius.

'Have you never seen a man piss before?'

Aurelius pumps a fistful of liquid soap into his palm and carefully lathers up his hands and wrists. Slowly, he rinses and dries his hands, before cupping them to his face and taking a deep breath.

'Ahhh, that's better. Now, where were we? Ah yes, the library, follow me.'

Aurelius ushers Gareth out of the toilet. Back in the entrance hall, Gareth catches Minty's eye and shrugs awkwardly.

Next to the toilet door is another door with a gilded sign that reads *North Library*. Gareth pulls the door open and follows Aurelius in.

The North Library is noticeably colder than the rest of the building, and most of the curtains are drawn. The room smells musty. As his eyes become accustomed to the gloom, Gareth sees that, unlike the other reception rooms which have been cleared for the party, this room is full of ornaments, photographs and floor-to-ceiling shelves of leather-bound volumes.

Aurelius points Gareth to a chair in front of the fireplace.

'Today is not for talking business, but please just a quick update on where we are at.'

'Touch wood,' replies Gareth, tapping the arm of the chair, 'it's all going like clockwork. We've split the position across the Limited Partnerships to keep each one below the three per cent disclosure threshold, and we're rolling and rebooking the positions periodically so that we can stretch out the effective settlement period… indefinitely.'

'Indefinitely?' asks Aurelius.

'Indefinitely.'

'I'm impressed. Well done,' says Aurelius, pulling open a section of curtain.

The English summer afternoon reflects off the giant gilded mirror hanging above the fireplace to bring light into the room. Gareth sees that the rain has stopped.

Aurelius continues, 'And tell me, what's the chatter on ALB? Give me some colour.'

'Volumes really dropped off at the start of last week, then Thursday, Friday, things started picking up again, but mostly it's been the smaller quant and momentum-type funds reducing their positions.'

'Quant funds are selling?' asks Aurelius.

'Looks like it.'

'And the buyers?' asks Aurelius.

'Retail money.'

'Retail investors are buying.'

'Exactly.'

'What the wise man does in the beginning, the fool does in the end,' says Aurelius.

'Sorry?'

'Sell the position.'

'How much?'

'Everything. Minimise the price impact, but do it quickly.'

'Everything?'

'Sell everything,' repeats Aurelius.

CHAPTER TWENTY-ONE

Friday the 4th of May, 2012

Jamie Dimon, JP Morgan CEO, has called the statements he made last month 'unfortunate', following the bank's announcement that it has lost $3.2bn in six weeks as a result of London Whale trading losses. In April Dimon had called speculation about losses incurred by trader Bruno Iksil 'a tempest in a teapot'. Iksil and his boss, JP Morgan CIO Ina Drew, have left the business.

9.21pm – Dan Trench, The Troxy, Limehouse

The wall of noise beyond the darkness is deafening. It throbs and pulses through Dan's body. Suddenly the noise cuts out. Silence brings stillness. It reminds Dan of being underwater. There's no pain, only a sharp backward motion and a sense of powerlessness, as the fist flies through the space where his guard should be to land cleanly on his chin. Beyond the darkness, eight hundred pairs of eyes see that Dan is dead on his feet. One clean shot will lay him flat on the canvas.

But the knockout doesn't come. After a furious opening volley, the fierce young man in the navy *Essex*

Boys vest has punched himself out. He takes a step back and stands with his bottom jaw wide open, chest heaving, sucking air into his lungs.

A heartbeat is all it takes for the survival instinct to kick in. Urgency is Dan's only strategy. Working his double jab, Dan forces his exhausted opponent back across the ring. Now his senses are returning, he can hear the riot of voices again. From Dan's corner, Marc is shouting something about keeping his guard up.

The bell goes. Dan's clothes are heavy with sweat and he's gasping for breath, but there's too much adrenaline in his blood for him to notice. He sits on the stool and Marc squirts some water into his mouth.

'Spit,' he orders, holding out the bucket.

Dan gulps it down.

'No! I said spit!'

Marc squirts the bottle into Dan's mouth again and this time Dan spits.

'Work the jab. Double it up. Jab, jab; jab, jab. And keep your guard up!'

Dan nods and Marc squirts some water on his head and then ducks out of the ring, pulling the stool back through the ropes as Dan stands up for the bell.

The bell goes, and Dan steps forwards into the ring, holding out his left fist to tap gloves with his opponent. The young man in the *Essex Boys* vest leans forwards as if to tap his glove, then snaps a quick jab into Dan's nose. It smarts and Dan grimaces. There's a murmur from the crowd; someone boos, but the referee says nothing, and Dan is quickly back on his toes, peering out from behind his guard with watery eyes.

Marc is shouting 'double jab' from the edge of the ring, and Dan finds himself instinctively lunging forwards: jab to the head, duck down, jab to the body and finish with a right to the head. The three punches flow in a sweet rhythm, with the second jab setting his body exactly true, like the cocked hammer of a pistol, so that he can throw all of his power into the right, which lands squarely in his opponent's face.

The other boxer takes a step back and then slips on the canvas, falling onto all fours as he fails to keep his balance. Now the referee jumps in to pause the fight and points Dan towards his corner. As he turns, he feels a sharp shove from behind. He tumbles forwards and his right shoulder bounces off the canvas before he jumps quickly back to his feet. The referee is pushing his opponent back into the corner and is shouting in his face. The man in the navy *Essex Boys* vest is unhappy with this and spits out his gum guard so that he can articulate more clearly.

'*Fuck off!*' snarls the boxer, before lunging at Dan. 'You want a fucking fight? Come on then!'

The referee jumps between them and waves his arms to end the fight. Dan's opponent plays up to the 'boos' from the crowd, waving his right arm in the air and shouting defiantly. The MC steps into the ring with the microphone.

'Now we'll have none of that. Not tonight. This is a good clean white-collar night. There'll be no misbehavin' and no fuckin' swearing… except from me.'

Dan leans on the ropes while Marc pulls off his head guard and unties his gloves.

'What just happened?'

Marc shakes his head. 'Anthony. He's got some kind of mental problem.'

'You know him?'

'I know all of 'em.'

Marc has pulled off the left glove and is untying the right one when he looks up and nods. 'Oh right, here we go.'

Anthony is walking towards Dan's corner, his gloved hands raised apologetically.

'No hard feelings, mate!' shouts Anthony as he approaches.

'Watch out,' warns Marc.

Out of impulse Dan springs forward, leading with his right hand, which he brings cleanly into Anthony's cheekbone. Without gloves, Dan feels the full sensation of his knuckle impacting on bone, followed by a sharp pain in his hand. The pain feels good, as does the slick, sweaty touch of Anthony's skin. It's a sensual feeling.

Anthony is caught off balance, which allows Dan to come in with a left hook that catches him on the nose. Dan feels the crunch of cartilage.

Suddenly Dan is on the ground and Marc, who has him in a kind of bear hug, is shouting in his ear. The referee is holding Anthony against the ropes. There is blood streaming down Anthony's chin and the front of his vest. Dan can smell it. For a second the two fighters look at each other, and Anthony offers a bloody grin. The audience, who were booing noisily a moment ago, have gone quiet.

The atmosphere in the hall is subdued as the pair are led out of the ring, a safe distance apart. Members of the audience avoid eye contact. Gareth, who is sat with Dan's colleagues on the City Financial Training table, shifts uncomfortably in his seat when Dan gives him the thumbs up.

'Psycho!' shouts an anonymous voice from the gallery.

Dan isn't sure if this is directed at Anthony or himself, but Anthony assumes the role of spokesman.

'*You fucking want some?*' he screams up at the gallery.

The corner man who is guiding Anthony towards the fighter's entrance walks more quickly.

When they reach the corridor, Marc passes Dan his kit bag.

'Showers are at the end on the left,' says Marc.

The pair stand in silence for a moment.

'I don't know what to say,' says Marc.

Dan says nothing. Marc turns and walks back out into the main hall, leaving Dan alone in the corridor.

Dan stands in the shower thinking about the young man in the navy *Essex Boys* vest, and then about Marc. He tries to keep Marianne out of his head for as long as he can, but eventually she comes flooding back in and Dan feels helpless and alone. The only thing that makes sense are the few minutes that he spent in the ring, lost in the moment, consumed by the violence. He wants to be back there.

Dan is anonymous when he returns to the hall. All he has to show is the beginning of a bruise around his left eye. In the ring, two short, stocky figures are slogging it out. At the City Financial Training table, Gareth sits alone in a sea of half-empty glasses.

'The champ's back!' exclaims Gareth, standing up and pulling his jacket off the back of his chair.

'Where is everyone?' asks Dan.

'Jackie walked out as soon as it was over. She was horrified. Monday morning's going to be interesting.'

'Yeah.'

'That Colin guy is a hoot. He was going wild for it. I think he would have climbed in the ring too, if they'd let him.'

'Yeah, that's Colin.'

'Now get me out of this shithole.'

Gareth puts his hand on Dan's shoulder and steers him towards the back of the hall.

Dan runs his fingers gently around his swollen eye socket.

'Well, I must say, it has been interesting to see life on the other side of the tracks,' Gareth chuckles, 'but I can't say I'll be coming back in a hurry…'

Dan watches a beer bottle making a lazy arc through the air. It stops abruptly in the back of a lady's head. She falls to the ground. There are flecks of her blood on the white T-shirt of her stout, middle-aged companion. He throws his thick tattooed arms in the air liked a crazed baboon and launches himself at a man standing a few feet away. Suddenly the bar is a sea of fists, bottles and chairs. Two bouncers edge slowly away.

Dan is transfixed by the scene unfolding a few yards from him. His adrenaline is rising. Then Gareth grabs his arm and pulls him towards the exit. Suddenly a man in an *Essex Boys* hoody steps in front of them. The man puts his hand on Gareth's shoulder and leans in to talk to him. Gareth shakes his head and turns to Dan. The man motions for Gareth to follow him, but Gareth turns away. The man leans in to talk to him again, but Gareth is already off. There's something desperate about the way Gareth pushes his way through the crowd, like a man struggling to keep his head above water.

Dan follows Gareth out of the main entrance and then has to run to catch up with him.

'Wait up! You OK?' asks Dan. 'What did that guy say?'

'Dunno.' Gareth shrugs, still walking quickly. 'Now let's get the fuck out of here.'

CHAPTER TWENTY-TWO

Monday the 7th of May, 2012

Fitch has revised the outlook on the UK's AAA credit rating from 'stable' to 'negative', warning that the government has 'very limited fiscal space to absorb further adverse economic shocks'. The news will put further pressure on George Osborne, the chancellor, as he grapples with a national debt burden which continues to grow despite his unpopular policy of fiscal austerity.

7.07am – John Gruff, Cheapside, City

Gruff looks out of the window while the chauffeur navigates the early morning traffic along Cheapside. Next to him in the back of the S-Class, Hugh Holmes slurps on a coffee. Gruff looks at his watch and then back out of the window. He pulls his Blackberry out of his jacket pocket, then puts it back and looks out of the window again.

'You OK, John?' asks Hugh.

'Fine. You?' snaps Gruff.

Hugh starts to shuffle through his case. 'Actually, I've just finished reading this book you might find interesting.

It's about sleep. You know, how important it is to sleep well to be the best version of yourself.'

'No.'

'No?'

'Look around you. People spend their whole lives asleep. Even when they're awake they're asleep.'

Hugh slowly puts the book back into his case. Gruff senses that there's something else he wants to say.

'Spit it out,' says Gruff.

'Well… I had that meeting with Paul Todd… about the earnings guidance.'

Now Hugh has his full attention. 'Yes? And?'

'I don't know how comfortable I am with some of his ideas.'

Hugh looks apologetic.

'Everything Paul mentioned complies with accounting standards. It's within the letter of the law, right?' replies Gruff.

'Look, these are areas where there is a lot of subjectivity.'

'Whatever is going on between you and your conscience is your problem. Don't try to make it mine.'

'Look, I want to make the numbers just as much as you do, but if we take shortcuts then next year we're going to have to pull another rabbit out of the hat. I mean… Enron, Worldcom, Parlamat… it starts off as a little aggressive accounting and then one day you realise that the gap between the story and the reality is just too big.'

Gruff is silent for what feels like a long time. When he talks again his voice is detached. 'I'm just disappointed. When I hired you, I thought I'd hired someone who understood the game. I guess I was wrong.'

'You didn't hire me, John. The *Board* hired me.'

The car is stopped in traffic at the junction of Cheapside and Threadneedle Street. Gruff looks through the back window to check for cyclists before opening the door.

'I'll see you at Green Knight at nine.'

Hugh nods.

Gruff pushes the door shut behind him and steps up onto the pavement.

A few moments later the black S-Class pulls past him and Gruff glances through the window at Hugh, who has a folder of management accounts resting on his knee. Hugh happens to look up at the same time and for a moment the two men stare at each other before the car accelerates away down Threadneedle Street.

It's a couple of minutes to The Mercer, and as he walks, John scrolls through his emails, firing off single-word replies. He stops just inside the front door to read the sales report from his head of international.

'Good morning, sir, do you have a reservation?' asks the maître d'.

'I'm meeting someone,' replies Gruff, without looking up from his Blackberry.

He spots Aurelius Blois across the room at a table tucked beside a pillar. As Gruff walks across the restaurant, Aurelius stands up. He's taller than Gruff expected, with three buttons of his crisp white shirt undone and a voluminous wave of hair across his head.

'John.' Aurelius stands and extends his hand.

'You must be Aurelius.'

Aurelius grips Gruff's hand and looks at him intently. Something about the way the hedge fund manager is looking at him makes Gruff feel uncomfortable.

'It's great to finally meet you, John,' says Aurelius,

walking round and pulling out Gruff's chair, 'although I've read so much about you that I feel I know you already.'

'And what do you think?' asks Gruff.

'I think… that this is a man who likes to win.'

Gruff shrugs. 'True, if not particularly insightful.'

Aurelius throws his hands in the air. 'My observation is banal! We all like to win, but the *interesting* thing is what compromises we will make to get there.'

The waiter arrives with a cafetière of coffee, a large bottle of still water and a tumbler of cubed ice. The waiter puts the tumbler of ice down in front of Gruff, who raises an eyebrow at Aurelius.

The smile on the Frenchman's lips is at odds with the focus in his eyes.

'Gentlemen, may I take your order?' asks the waiter.

'John, I'm sorry, you haven't even had a chance to look at the menu,' says Aurelius.

'I don't need to look at the menu,' replies Gruff.

Aurelius turns to the waiter. 'I will have the usual, please.'

'Of course, sir. And for you?' The maître d' turns to Gruff.

'Sure, the same.'

Gruff pops an ice cube in his mouth and crunches it between his teeth.

'Now what was I saying?' asks Aurelius when the waiter has gone.

'Winning.'

'Winning, yes. And you are a man for whom victory must come, no matter the consequence. Does that describe you, John? The will to win above all else?'

'Yes.'

'Why?'

Gruff sits back in his chair and laughs out loud. 'Why?'

Gruff waits for Aurelius to reply, but instead the hedge fund manager sits quite still and watches. For a moment Gruff holds Aurelius's stare before looking away and shaking his head.

'You believe in right and wrong?'

'I have values which guide me,' replies Aurelius.

'That's where we differ.'

'Coffee?' asks Aurelius, pushing the plunger of the cafetière.

'Black.'

While Aurelius pours the coffee, Gruff looks out between the marble columns at the cavernous space of the old banking hall.

'So, all of this… the money and the status, the Mayfair pied-à-terre, cars, women, whatever… whatever your thing is. You really believe it's pointless. You think you'd be just as happy without any of it. Honestly. I don't believe that for a moment,' says Gruff.

Aurelius shrugs. 'Actually, I don't own a car; I have no property. For me, property is… it's very bourgeois.'

Gruff starts to laugh and has to cover his mouth to stop shards of ice from spraying across the table.

'Sorry, did you just say *bourgeois*? A socialist hedge fund manager?'

'No, I am not naïve enough to be socialist. I am just anti-bourgeois.'

Gruff's brow draws into a deep furrow as he tries to understand what Aurelius has just said.

'So you're a hedge fund manager who doesn't care for… material things?'

'Everything beautiful is ephemeral. Permanence is an illusion that enslaves.'

Gruff shakes his head. 'You're fucking crazy.'

Aurelius leans back in his chair and starts to laugh. His voice booms around the restaurant. Gruff feels he is somehow being goaded.

'Last week I spent a night sleeping rough on the street,' replies Aurelius.

It takes a moment for Gruff to understand what Aurelius has just said.

'But… but… why would you do that?'

'It was for a homeless charity.'

Gruff shakes his head. 'Good for you. But why bother?'

'To understand how other people think. To see the world from a different angle.'

'I have no time for people who see the world differently. Those people are wrong.'

'What's your favourite fairy tale?' asks Aurelius.

'My favourite *fairy tale*?' repeats Gruff.

'You have a favourite?'

Gruff feels his temper rising. 'Are you taking the piss?'

Aurelius continues, 'Mine is *The Emperor's New Clothes.* I always enjoyed truth-to-power narratives the most, not least because the boy grows up to become the emperor one day.'

Gruff smiles and shakes his head. 'Then you are naïve. The boy doesn't grow up to become anything; he gets executed in the street. And the weavers become the emperor's spin doctors. That's how the real world works.'

Aurelius looks at Gruff silently across the table. Something tells Gruff that the hedge fund manager has found what he was looking for, even though Gruff doesn't know what.

'I'm glad we've had this chance to understand what makes the other tick,' says Aurelius. He seems to grow as he relaxes back into his chair.

‘Are you holders?’ asks Gruff. ‘We couldn’t find you on the register.’

‘I’m afraid I can’t answer that,’ replies Aurelius. His expression gives nothing away.

Gruff’s eyes narrow. ‘Short seller?’

Aurelius gives Gruff a blank expression and says nothing.

Gruff’s eyes narrow. ‘There’s nothing I hate more than a short seller.’

Aurelius smiles. ‘And if we were short your stock, what would you say?’

Gruff tips another ice cube into his mouth and stares at Aurelius while he crunches it. ‘OK, we’re done here,’ says Gruff.

Gruff pushes out his chair and stands up. Aurelius picks the starched white napkin off his lap and lays it across his side plate, then stands up too.

‘Thanks for your time, John.’

Gruff shakes his head and walks off. As he approaches the entrance, the maître d’ leaps across his path to pull the door open for him.

After he has left, Aurelius walks round to the other side of the table and sits in Gruff’s seat. He picks up the glass still half full of ice and turns it slowly in his hand. Looking back in the direction in which Gruff has just left, Aurelius pulls out his phone.

The first ring is not quite finished when a voice answers.

‘Aurelius.’

‘Melwyn.’

‘What can I do for you?’

‘Short ALB.’

‘Short Albourne, how many?’

‘Three hundred million shares.’

‘Three hundred million shares…’ there’s a pause, ‘… that’s twelve per cent of the free float.’

‘Can you do it?’ asks Aurelius.

‘How quickly?’

‘End of the week.’

‘OK, leave it with me. For the main fund?’

‘Yes, the main fund.’

‘I’ll keep you updated.’

Aurelius drops the phone back in his jacket pocket.

The waiter appears holding two plates.

‘Will the gentleman be returning?’

‘He will not. But his loss is my gain. You can just pile them both together for me.’

‘Pile them both together?’

‘Yes. Not too fussy. Here, let me do it.’

Aurelius uses Gruff’s knife to slide one steak tartare on top of the other, then takes the plate from the waiter.

‘Bon appetite.’

‘Merci.’

Aurelius slides his fork through the egg yolk and into the steak tartare. He studies the texture of the raw beef patty and grunts appreciatively before forking it into his mouth.

9.07am – John Gruff, Green Knight Asset Management, Knightsbridge

Gruff picks up two cubes of white sugar and drops them into his third coffee of the morning. He looks down at the two business cards and then back up at the two men sitting across the table. *Anthony Dye, Head of Research* and *Andrew Waite, Fund Manager*.

Tony Dye is trying to make small talk, something about cycling, something about having teenage children and living in Sevenoaks, dribbling words into the vacuum formed by the absence of the Gessner Bank broker-cum-chaperone.

Hugh comes off the phone. 'She's stuck in traffic.'

Andrew Waite glances at Hugh, then returns to shuffling through the pages of handwritten notes that sit on the table in front of him. Gruff has always found fund managers to be insufferably dull. Lacking either the testosterone of the investment banker, or the charm of the broker – lacking in fact any spark of personality at all – the fund manager is much like the accountant but with misplaced self-importance.

'Andrew Waite,' says Gruff out loud, looking at the business card.

Andrew appears alarmed at the sound of his name.

'Andrew *Waite*,' says Gruff again, now looking at Andrew. 'It says here, *Fund Manager*. Surely not.'

Andrew looks at Gruff and then at Tony and then back to Gruff. His face has turned a shade pink.

'Yes, that's right… I took over from Peter Mancroft last month.'

'Hmmm,' says Gruff, unconvinced. 'So will Francis be joining us?'

Tony raises an eyebrow. 'Francis… Portnoy?'

'Francis Portnoy,' repeats Gruff.

'I would say… unlikely. He's more on the business development side these days.'

'Do we wait for her?' asks Hugh.

'Wait for who?' replies Gruff.

'The broker. She's stuck in traffic.'

'No, we do not wait for the bloody broker.'

'Fine,' says Hugh, pulling a pair of investor presentations out of his case and sliding them across the table. 'We can run through the acquisition deck or take questions, whatever suits you best.'

Tony runs his hand over the cover of the presentation then flicks through it, eyes half closed, with a scowl of intense concentration. It appears that Tony is not actually reading the words or the numbers but rather divining their meaning.

Gruff looks at his watch. 'We have a meeting on Davies Street in sixty-two minutes. How do you want to do this?'

'Yes, right,' says Tony, flipping the presentation shut with sudden decisiveness. 'Andrew has prepared some questions, so we'll just jump straight into those, if that's OK?'

'Fire away,' says Hugh.

Andrew's paper shuffling increases in velocity and Gruff wonders if he will lose a sheet. But before he does, he comes to a stop.

'I'd like to focus on acquisitions, revenue recognition policies and intangible assets,' says Andrew, ticking off each bullet point as he speaks.

'Accountant, are you?' asks Gruff.

'No.'

'Well, you sound like one. And that's not a compliment.'

'Acquisitions—' says Andrew.

'You want to know about our acquisition track record?' interrupts Gruff. 'Let me tell you what you need to know. In twelve years, I have built this business into the UK's largest food producer. We supply every major food retailer in the UK, and our international business is growing at over thirty per cent. I think you'll find the numbers speak for themselves.'

'But you've paid for those acquisitions by taking on a lot of debt and by issuing new shares, and looking at the returns you're generating from the acquired companies it appears that you overpaid for these new businesses and failed to realise the promised synergies, which is to say there's been a great deal of… value destruction.'

Andrew rushes the words out, without taking a breath, looking down at his papers while he speaks.

While Andrew is talking Gruff feels strangely calm, even as he feels the anger rising inside him. Tony Dye is rubbing his hands on the cover of the presentation again and staring at Gruff and grinning.

Hugh is shifting in his seat.

'Thank you for that, Andrew,' says Gruff, calmly. 'I can only assume you've been looking at the wrong set of accounts, because the business *I* run generates fantastic returns, is operating well within its banking covenants and has an excellent record of shrewd acquisitions.'

Hugh shifts in his seat again. 'If I may add—'

'We're done on that question,' interrupts Gruff.

Andrew is shuffling his papers again.

'Are all of your questions ill-informed?' asks Gruff. 'Because we have a busy schedule and plenty of shareholders to meet who've actually done their homework.'

'Cash flow,' says Andrew.

'I'm probably the best person to take that one,' says Hugh, trying to strike a conciliatory tone.

'The business enjoyed significant growth in adjusted profits last year,' continues Andrew, 'but there were some chunky inventory write-downs and a big jump in accounts receivables and a large accrued income figure, which all add up to a significant cash outflow. The business has been steadily burning cash for a number of years. It seems to me that you're going to have to tap the market for fresh equity within the next year to eighteen months.'

'The adjusted free cash flow—' begins Hugh.

Tony, who has been grinning and rubbing the cover of the presentation throughout the exchange, suddenly becomes animated. 'Please! *Adjusted.* Adjusted free cash flow…' Tony is shaking his head. 'Cash is cash is cash!'

'Perhaps you can start by giving some colour on the accrued income,' asks Andrew.

'*Cash is cash!*' Tony shouts the mantra across the table.

Hugh stares at Tony before turning his attention back to Andrew.

'The accrued income relates to supply contracts in our international business, and the revenue recognition in that part of the business is something I'm looking at as part of stepping into this role. I would expect there to be a closer correlation between cash and profit going forward.'

Gruff turns and stares at Hugh. As the finance director's mouth opens and closes, Gruff feels hot blood rushing behind his eyes.

Andrew is nodding and scrawling in his Moleskine notebook while the other three men in the room watch him in silence. When Andrew becomes aware that they're waiting for him to ask the next question, he puts down his pen and starts to shuffle through the papers again.

'So, ummm… the next question is… to do with… intangible assets. I'd like to understand more about your policy on… capitalising expenses, in that there seems to be a surprising amount of it going on for what is a low-margin manufacturing business.'

Gruff feels something snap.

'We're done here,' he says, standing up. 'I've known Francis Portnoy for a very long time, and this is *bullshit*.'

Gruff is staring at Andrew, who is avoiding eye contact and instead seems to be focusing on Gruff's tie. Tony, still grinning, sits back with his arms crossed.

'Call yourself *Head of Research*,' says Gruff to Tony, 'it's a disgrace.'

Tony doesn't flinch but continues to grin at Gruff.

Hugh sheepishly packs his papers back into his case and stands up.

'Thank you so much for your time,' says Tony. 'Very informative… let me show you out.'

'We can show ourselves out,' says Gruff, pulling so hard on the meeting room door that it almost hits him as it bounces back off the doorstop.

Hugh bows apologetically before hurrying after him.

Andrew watches the door close behind them, then lets out a long sigh.

'Sorry. That was a disaster.'

'Oh no,' says Tony, 'not at all. I thought that was very good. Jolly clever all that accounting stuff. You really put the shits up them. They couldn't get out of that door fast enough.'

'But they barely answered the questions.'

'That's not the point,' says Tony, clapping Andrew on the back. 'It's precisely what they didn't say that was important.'

'What do you mean?'

'Dodgier than a double-glazing salesman, that John Gruff. Never liked the fellow. I think you might have saved us a lot of money. Well done.'

9.39am – John Gruff, Mayfair

'I understand you're upset, and we probably need to be more joined up going into these meetings, but this is my area, and the bottom line is: I'm not answerable to you; I'm answerable to the Board.'

Hugh is talking, quickly and earnestly, but all Gruff can hear is a persistent and irritating noise as he turns the morning over in his mind.

Breakfast with Aurelius Blois; a meeting with Andrew Waite. Two unconnected events but from the outset they were only ever going to go one way; no matter what Gruff might have said or done, the tide is already turning. Suddenly Gruff realises that, instead of being a disaster, the morning has been a gift. The edifice was always going to collapse; his final coup will be knowing when and how to jump.

Hugh is still talking. 'If you're not happy with my judgement then this is probably a discussion that we need to get the Board involved in,' says Hugh.

Gruff turns to the driver. 'Stop the car.'

'Sorry, sir?'

'Wait,' interrupts Hugh, 'this isn't Davies Street.'

'Cancel the meeting,' replies Gruff, 'and *stop the car*.'

Gruff opens the door while the car is still moving, and the driver breaks suddenly.

'*Wait!*' calls Hugh as Gruff steps out of the car.

'You're the finance director – you do what you need to do,' replies Gruff, closing the door behind him.

As soon as he is out of the car Gruff feels calm. For the first time this morning he is in control of the situation. In the inside left breast of his jacket is a button-down pocket, and in that pocket is a small mobile phone.

Gruff sends an SMS: *GREEN PARK 20 MINS.*

A few moments later the phone vibrates with a message: *OK. RITZ CORNER.*

Walking south through Mayfair, Gruff hardly notices the drizzle. His coat is still on the back seat of the Addison Lee. In his mind he's turning over his next few moves, looking for anything that might upset the plan. He pulls out his Blackberry and checks the live price for ALB. The shares are down a few basis points today but still within a whisper of their all-time high. A smile stretches across Gruff's face, and then he begins to laugh.

Gruff emerges from Bolton Street onto Piccadilly, then turns left towards the tube station where there is an entrance into Green Park. He crosses over the road in front of an empty open-top sightseeing bus. In front of him, the Ritz Hotel overlooks the corner of Green Park. Just inside the park entrance is a statue of the goddess Diana. A tourist is filling a water bottle from one of the trickles of water dribbling from the fountain. Gruff stands under the awning of a refreshment booth and types a message on his burner phone.

AT FOUNTAIN

John Gruff is lost in thought when Paul Todd arrives.

Paul looks worried. He pulls the collar of his overcoat tight around his neck. 'Everything OK, John? I just got an email from the IR team saying all your meetings are cancelled. And where's your coat?'

Gruff looks at Paul and smiles.

Paul looks more worried. 'John, talk to me.'

'Everything's going to be OK, but we've got work to do. This is our exit,' says Gruff.

'Exit? Is Hugh getting wise?' asks Paul.

'He is, but this isn't about Hugh. Livermore Capital are building a short position and Green Knight is going to exit. The market is getting wise.'

'Oh shit. When those break, it's going to be pandemonium. The narrative is going to switch like that.' Paul snaps his fingers. 'We're not going to be able to fight it, John.'

'I know.'

'You're relaxed.'

Gruff nods. 'I am. How much of the numbers is Hugh seeing?'

'Just enough to keep him in the dark, but our person in Accounts says he's asking a lot of questions. He's asking the right questions. He's going to work it out for himself soon enough, unless we do something.'

Gruff nods. 'Good.'

Paul is confused. 'Good?'

'Let him get the numbers, everything, the whole kitchen sink.'

'Are you sure about this, John? Hugh is straight down the line. The moment he sees what's going on he's going to inform the Board; the banks are going to come calling. It's going to be a big rights issue. You'll be out. The game will be up.'

Gruff stares at Paul for a moment, running the plan through his mind one more time before answering. 'I know. Let's do it. We need to kick the dominos before someone else does.'

Paul has gone pale; he puts his hands to his mouth. 'I'm two steps behind you, John. Help me out here.'

'We always knew this was going to happen eventually, but if we're smart, we get to choose when and how.'

'You want to crash the stock? I don't understand. This is your life's work.'

'If we do this right, it will be our biggest bet, but only if we do this right.'

Gruff waits for this to sink in. Slowly, the frown drops from Paul's face, and he begins to laugh.

'You're a genius, John. You're a fucking genius,' says Paul, shaking his head. 'You're calling our friend in Malta?'

Gruff nods. 'Wait for the stock to start sliding, then get our person in Accounts to help Hugh work things out. I don't think he's going to need much help.'

Paul is smiling and nodding. 'I'm going to enjoy this,

John. I'm going to enjoy this a lot... but I guess it means our adventure is almost at an end.'

'It's not over yet. Don't fuck it up,' says Gruff.

Both men stand in silence for a moment looking at the fountain.

'How long have we got?' asks Paul.

'Ten days, tops. Maybe a week.'

'A week? OK, then I better get to it,' says Paul. He shakes Gruff's hand before striding out from under the awning of the refreshment booth and back into the drizzle. The investment banker holds the collar of his overcoat up under his chin as he walks down the ramp into Green Park tube station.

Gruff watches him go, then pulls out the burner phone again.

He keys in a number and waits for the phone to ring. After a single ring someone picks up.

'Hello.'

'Hello,' says Gruff. 'The account is "Premier", that's "Papa, Romeo, Echo, Mike, India, Echo, Romeo".'

'Thank you, sir. Password please.'

'Amaretto.'

'Thank you, sir. May I have your instructions please?'

'I want to open a short position in Albourne, that's ALB.'

'ALB dot L, sir, that's Albourne PLC, LSE listed, currently trading at... ninety-three spot forty-two.'

'Correct.'

'May I have the size and type of order?'

'Short forty million shares at market, close it at... twenty-five.'

'Stop loss, sir?'

'No need.'

'Short forty million at market, close at twenty-five spot zero, no stop loss.'

'Correct.'

'One minute please.'

The line goes silent and Gruff waits. He feels his heart beating in his chest. This trade will make him over £25 million.

'It's a large order, sir. The dealer advises that it may take a few days to execute.'

'Fine, just get it done.'

Gruff hangs up and looks down at the burner phone in his hand. He turns it over and pops open the back. Under the battery is the sim card slot. Gruff carefully slides out the sim card with the tip of his index finger and turns the small piece of metal and plastic over between his fingers before snapping it in half.

On his way out of the park Gruff drops the handful of metal and plastic into a bin.

CHAPTER TWENTY-THREE

Wednesday the 9th of May, 2012

Thomas Cook is close to securing a £1.2 billion lifeline from its banking consortium that investors hope will secure the future of the debt-laden package-holiday operator. The deal will hand 5% of the company to banks in exchange for extending its loan maturities. Shares in the company have fallen 90% over the last year as a series of profit warnings led to the departure of CEO Manny Fontenla-Nova.

7.16am – Gareth Eary, Cannon Street, City

The Italian cafe on Cannon Street is rather out of the way and the coffee is functional at best, but Gareth likes to take the diversion when he has time because the three baristas are all cute Sicilian girls. He leaves with a tray of coffees in one hand and a bag containing three bacon sandwiches, an almond croissant and a can of diet coke in the other. A short distance down the street Gareth stops beside a bin and chucks the coffees. With a free hand he can now check his emails.

In the time it takes to cover the length of Gresham Street, Gareth skims the 7am corporate news announcements. He's just stepped into the ground-floor lobby and winked at the receptionist when his phone starts to ring.

'Good morning, Prek. Are you at the flat today?'

'I call to say I have to go home, sar. My uncle pass away last night.'

Gareth's first thought is that the bathroom won't be finished for the weekend.

'Oh… I'm sorry to hear that, Prek.'

Gareth is watching the numbers on the lift as it moves down towards 'G'.

'So you're going back to Poland?'

The lift doors open and people start to file in. Prek is silent for a moment on the other end of the line.

'…I from Albania, sar.'

'Sure.'

The last person steps into the lift and the doors are about to close.

'Don't worry, sar, in Albania we bury the person within one day. Funeral tomorrow morning, I back to finish your bathroom on Monday. You not worry, sar, I make everything good.'

Gareth skips into the lift. 'Good stuff, got to go.'

The doors close and Gareth's phone cuts out.

Jessica, Jabba and Martin are already at their desks when Gareth walks in.

'A bacon sandwich and a can of diet coke for Jabba, a bacon sandwich for you, Martin, one for me,' he passes the bag to Jessica, 'and an almond croissant for you, Jessica.'

'Much obliged,' says Jabba.

Gareth, Martin and Jessica all stop what they're doing and turn to Jabba.

'Much obliged,' says Jabba. 'Now fuck off.'

'Phew, that's the Jabba we know and love,' says Jessica.

Jessica takes the almond croissant out of the bag, then pulls out a piece of paper. 'Wouldn't want you to misplace this,' she says, handing it to Gareth. On the back of the receipt is a phone number followed by *Giovanna XXX*. 'If you're trying to make me jealous it's not going to work,' says Jessica.

Gareth laughs.

'Actually,' continues Jessica, 'one thing I am rather envious of is your comm numbers this month. You are smashing it. But there are a couple of clients I don't recognise.'

Gareth knew this conversation was coming, but it still catches him off guard. He feels someone staring at him and turns his head to see Jabba, his thin lips curled into a smile.

Gareth turns back to Jessica. Martin is looking up from his desk too.

'Those are Livermore Capital LPs,' explains Gareth.

'Ah, I see…' Jessica is nodding, 'and you've got them all signed off with compliance… the money laundering all checks out?'

'Yeah, yeah.'

'Hmmm,' replies Jessica, studying the list with a frown. 'So why isn't Livermore named as the client?'

'Oh, aren't they?' Gareth tries to sound casual.

'All we have are nominee accounts at Bank of Cayman.'

'Sure, but Livermore is the *underlying* client.'

'And all the paperwork checks out?'

'Of course.'

'And you have the order records?' asks Jessica.

'Sure,' Gareth lies.

'Email?'

'Calls mostly.'

'On the recorded line?'

'Ummm… yeah.'

'Something's going on in ALB,' says Jabba. He taps a few keys on the terminal. 'Looks like… Numis. Messy job. They're killing the price. What are they doing?'

Gareth and Jessica drop what they're doing and fall in behind Jabba.

'What's going on, Jabba?' asks Gareth.

'Who's the client?' asks Jessica.

Jabba flicks to a screen that shows the order book and shakes his head. 'I mean, look at this.'

Gareth knows he needs to call Aurelius Blois, but first he needs to know who's behind the selling and why they're getting out.

'Forty, sixty, seventy million on the screen, and you can bet there's more behind it,' says Jabba.

'Who's the client?' asks Gareth. 'What's going on?'

'Millennium?' suggests Jessica.

'No,' says Jabba, 'not through Numis.'

'Hawkbridge?'

'No,' says Gareth, 'spoke to them yesterday: they're happy holders.'

Jabba brings up the shareholder register and suddenly it jumps out.

'Of course,' says Gareth.

Jabba sees the same thing. 'Yeah, must be.'

'What's going on?' asks Martin.

'It's Green Knight,' says Gareth. 'They're dumping Albourne like there's no tomorrow.'

Jessica shakes her head. 'No way, that's not how they work, and they've held Albourne like, forever.'

'It's Andrew Waite,' says Gareth, 'he's running Mancroft's book now.'

'But the Mid-Cap Fund can't have more than twenty million,' says Jessica. 'You gonna call them?'

Gareth is already at the phone.

'Rest is in the Columbus Fund,' says Jabba.

'Hello?'

'Andrew,' Gareth tries to sound relaxed.

'Gareth.'

'So, umm, seeing much action today?'

'Why do you ask?'

'Well, a little birdy tells me that you might have lost your sweet tooth.'

Andrew laughs.

'Look, obviously I've got a vested interest in this one, because we do a lot of business in ALB. But as a friend I'm going to be totally honest with you. I know you guys get a great service from Numis, but when it comes to execution, with a job of this size, they're just not the best house. Truth is, Andrew, you're getting your face ripped off on this one.'

'*Did* a lot of business,' replies Andrew.

'Sorry?'

'You don't do a lot of business in ALB. You *did* a lot of business. Historically. Past tense,' explains Andrew.

'Right.' Gareth ignores the snub. 'Of course. But just one thing, for old times' sake… I can see seventy million on the order book, there's twenty million in the Mid-Cap Fund and…' there's a pause while Gareth taps at his Bloomberg terminal, '…it looks like five hundred and twenty million across all funds… are you shifting the lot?'

'You know that's price sensitive, Gareth.'

'I know, I'm sorry, look, I wouldn't ask, but for old times' sake.'

'Are you OK, Gareth? You sound kind of desperate.'

'Please.'

'We're getting out and, if I'm right, pretty soon everyone else will be too.'

Andrew hangs up.

Gareth looks up at Jessica who is back at her desk. 'They know something. They're dumping the lot.'

Gareth punches the speed dial for Aurelius's direct line. It rings once, then the line goes dead. Before he can punch the speed dial again his phone buzzes with a message from an unknown number.

ARE WE OUT?

Gareth holds up the message to Jabba. Jabba reads the message, then gives Gareth a wink.

CONFIRMED IN FULL, replies Gareth.

CHAPTER TWENTY-FOUR

Thursday the 10th of May, 2012

The Greek parliamentary elections delivered a fragmented result that highlighted public opposition to austerity and the challenges faced by political leaders trying to keep the country in the euro. Strategists at Citi see a rising risk of a Greek exit ('Grexit') from the euro within the next eighteen months, increasing their probability of this occurring from 50% to 65%. The odds available from Paddy Power yesterday suggested a 40% probability of a Eurozone break-up by the end of the year.

10.28am – Andrew Waite, Green Knight Asset Management, Knightsbridge

Mancroft once told Andrew the story of Portnoy's first job, as an analyst at Mercury Asset Management, where he worked for Richard Newbury. Later, it was Newbury who encouraged Portnoy to set up on his own, seeding the first Green Knight fund. Andrew reckons the pair must have known each other for forty years, and Newbury will have been managing money for over fifty, which, from where Andrew is sitting, is two entire lifetimes.

While Andrew is reflecting on this thought, the smell of ancient decay alerts Andrew to the fact that the manager of the UK Large Cap Fund is nearby. That Richard Newbury still manages Green Knight's largest fund is a testament to Portnoy's loyalty. At any other house he would have been shown the door years ago and replaced by someone younger and more marketable. Mancroft once wistfully explained to Andrew that there comes a point in one's career when age and experience stop being an asset and instead become a liability. Then Andrew made a joke about operating leases and Mancroft had called him an idiot, which Andrew later realised was just Mancroft feeling defensive about not understanding lease accounting.

'Hello, Richard,' says Andrew, without looking up from his screen.

Newbury shuffles closer.

'Oh, hello, Andrew.'

'Is it that time of day already, Richard?'

'Indeed! Important to keep fit, you know, especially at my age,' says Newbury, leaning heavily on Andrew's desk.

'Say, Richard, I've been meaning to ask about your tie.'

'Regimental.'

'You were in the Army.'

Newbury draws up to what's left of his full height, clicks his heels together and snaps his right arm into a smart salute.

'1951 to '57, 1st Battalion Sirmoor Rifles, Charlie Fire Support Company, Mortar Platoon Commander.'

'Who are the Sirmoor Rifles?'

'Gurkha Regiment. Doesn't exist anymore. All been amalgamated. Part of the British Indian Army until 1947.'

'What happened in 1947?' asks Andrew.

Newbury gives Andrew a withering look.

'Indian Independence,' interjects Jude, still typing at her keyboard.

'Very good,' replies Newbury. 'Smart girl. You should be doing *his* job.'

'I know,' says Jude, without looking up.

Out of the corner of his eye Andrew spots Lucia marching purposefully in his direction. Despite his recent change of fortune, the prospect of being called to see Portnoy still gives him a jolt of nerves. Newbury is still talking, but Andrew isn't listening.

Lucia is halfway down the floor when Tony Dye, the head of research, stops her. At the same time Andrew's phone starts to ring and he glances down to see that it's Gareth Eary.

He picks up the receiver, but as he starts to answer, the floor is cut with Lucia's scream.

'Jesus!' shouts Tony Dye.

'Oh God, is he dead?' says someone else.

Andrew and a dozen other people rush to the middle of the floor where Lucia is lying on her back, squealing, with Richard Newbury lying quite still on top of her.

'He just came out of nowhere,' says Tony. 'We were talking and then, smack! Stupid old bugger never saw her until he hit her.'

It would be funny except that Newbury appears to be dead.

'Get him off me!' screams Lucia. 'Get him off me! *Get him off me!*'

'Yes, yes, right-oh!' says Tony Dye, doing his best to take control of the situation.

'He's moving!' shouts someone.

'Hmmm, hmmm.'

'Are you OK, Richard?' asks Tony, kneeling down to speak to him.

'It's wet! Why is it wet?' shouts Lucia.

'Oh, hello, Lucia,' says Newbury, 'you smell nice.'

Lucia pulls a face.

'I seem to have found a nice spot here,' says Newbury, putting his face back down between Lucia's breasts.

'Are you OK, Richard?' says Tony again.

'Oh yes, quite well, thank you.' Newbury looks up at Lucia's grimace and then back at Tony. 'Marvellous. Closest thing I've had to sex in twenty years!'

'Oh God!' says Lucia. 'Just get him off me.'

'OK, Richard, Andrew and I are going to lift you up. Is that going to be OK?'

'Absolutely.'

'Lucia says something's wet – are you sure everything's OK?'

'Oh yes, don't worry about that, probably just my colostomy bag.'

'Oh God!' says Lucia again.

'Right-oh,' says Tony, motioning to Andrew to take Newbury's right arm.

After the excitement has subsided, and Newbury's assistant has taken him to Harley Street for a check-up, Andrew resumes his position behind the Bloomberg monitor. A few minutes later, Portnoy rolls out of his office. The CEO of Green Knight Asset Management is rarely seen on the main floor, preferring to direct his troops through Lucia and Tony. The room has become quite still. A wave of menace precedes his slow advance. He's looking for Lucia, who ran out of the building as soon as she was released from Newbury's soiled embrace. It seems that no one told Portnoy about the incident.

Portnoy frowns as Tony relays the story, and then when Tony has finished, Portnoy lets out a roar of laughter that fills the floor. Following Portnoy's lead, Tony starts to laugh too, shaking his head, while Portnoy claps him on the back. When the laughing has finished it takes Portnoy a moment to compose himself and to remember the errand that he'd sent Lucia on in the first place. From the corner of his eye, Andrew sees Portnoy pointing at him before walking slowly back to his office.

Tony catches Andrew's eye and waves him over.

Andrew slips the Prince-of-Wales-check jacket off the back of his chair and pulls it over his shoulders as he walks to Tony's desk.

'Nice tie,' says Tony. 'Hermes?'

'Thanks. You think Richard's OK?'

'Silly old bugger. I'm sure he's fine. It will take a while for Lucia to get over it though.'

They stand in silence while Andrew waits for Tony to tell him the news.

'Portnoy wants to see you.'

'Any idea what about?'

'Yes, but I'll let him tell you. Don't worry though: it's good news.'

Without Lucia there to wave him in, Andrew stands outside Portnoy's office, composing himself for a few moments before knocking.

'Come in,' shouts Portnoy through the door.

Andrew is part-way through the door when Augustus, the bull terrier, heaves himself onto Andrew's right leg.

'Come in and shut the door,' says Portnoy.

With the dog throwing him off balance, Andrew struggles to manoeuvre himself. Augustus is licking

Andrew's crotch, while vigorously rubbing his own crotch against Andrew's leg.

'Give him the bag!' shouts Portnoy.

'Sorry?'

'What are you waiting for? Give him the bag!'

'What?!'

'He's horny!' explains Portnoy. 'The dog's horny. Give him the bag!'

Portnoy waves at a filthy beige beanbag sitting on top of a cabinet.

Andrew reaches up and grabs the bag, which is crispy to the touch. He throws it into the middle of the room.

With a yelp of delight, Augustus releases Andrew's leg and waddles across to the bag, sniffing it vigorously before mounting it.

'Oh,' says Andrew, transfixed at the sight of Augustus shagging the beanbag.

'Sit down,' says Portnoy.

Andrew steps around Augustus. His crotch is damp with the dog's slobber.

'Congratulations,' says Portnoy.

'Thank you,' says Andrew.

'For what?' asks Portnoy.

'Sorry?'

'What am I congratulating you for?'

'Oh. I don't know. Sorry.'

'We won the mandate. The consultants have given the nod, and ADIA will be transferring one billion into a segregated mandate, mirroring our UK Mid-Cap strategy and managed by yourself. So, congratulations.'

'That's fantastic, thank you, Mr Portnoy.'

'Andrew Waite, you are now a big fucking deal. My advice is: don't let it get to your head, and don't ever, ever forget that it was me who made you a big fucking deal, because I can take it away just as quickly.'

Augustus, whose amorous moment seems to have passed, is now whimpering and gnawing tenderly on a threadbare corner of the bag.

'You know, you remind me of another promising young buck,' says Portnoy. 'Chap called Dan Trench. Please don't fuck this up like he did.'

CHAPTER TWENTY-FIVE

Friday the 11th of May, 2012

HSBC is facing allegations that its operations in Mexico deliberately failed to install the systems needed to identify money laundering and suspicious transactions. In one instance, the bank failed to raise any red flags when Drug Enforcement Administration agents posing as members of the Norte del Valle cartel deposited millions of dollars in a Mexican branch and then transferred the money to accounts in the US. Mexican traffickers are understood to use boxes specifically designed to the dimensions of the HSBC teller's window to deposit cash on a daily basis.

7.35pm – Dan Trench, Clapham Common, South London

Dan has been pacing around his kitchen island for almost an hour. In his hand is a faded scrap of paper with a phone number on it.

'Do it,' says Dan out loud. 'Just do it.'

Sarah is looking up at him from a photo frame on the worktop.

Dan lays the frame face down and slowly exhales. Then he punches the number into his phone and waits. It rings. It keeps ringing. Eventually, the number rings out.

Dan's disappointment is edged with a sense of relief. He presses redial. It rings once. Twice.

'Hello,' says a woman's voice.

'Hi, can I…' Dan hesitates, '…can I come tonight?'

'You've been before?'

'No.'

There's a long pause. It sounds like the woman is talking to someone.

'OK,' says the woman.

'Where is it?'

'Someone will meet you.'

The woman gives Dan a time and location.

'If you're late, he'll be gone,' says the woman, 'and come alone.'

'OK.'

At 9pm Dan meets a shirtless man at the number 41 bus stop near the entrance to Tottenham Hale station. The man's demeanour precludes small talk, so Dan walks alongside him in silence for ten minutes until they get to a corner shop. Then the man asks Dan for some money, buys a small can of Euroshopper energy drink and hands back the change. After walking in silence for another ten minutes they arrive at a derelict office block. The lower windows are boarded up. They walk around to the back of the building where the fire escape is open.

Following the man up the stairs, Dan studies the dark furrows that scar his bare torso.

'Why do you fight?' asks Dan.

The man turns and frowns. Bone and sinew ripple under his tight, pale skin. His tired, grey face has a patina of browns and blues.

'I fight because I lost everything and now all I have left is anger.'

The ketone funk of his breath rolls over Dan.

On the top floor, the man pushes through a set of double doors and turns right down the corridor.

Dan glances into empty rooms. In the murk of the emergency lighting he can make out chairs and filing cabinets, mounds of rubbish, paper, old PC monitors.

'I used to work in an office like this,' says the man.

At the end of the narrow corridor, double doors open into an empty space that might once have been a conference room. Two men in Lonsdale hoodies block the way. One of them nods at Dan's companion; the second man stands a few steps back with his arms folded across his chest.

'Hey, bruv, who's this?'

Dan's companion shrugs.

Tightening, straightening, silently posturing, the man looks at Dan. 'What d'you want?'

'I called up,' explains Dan.

'You called up?' asks the man.

'Yeah. I called up.'

The man talking to Dan turns to the other man in the Lonsdale hoody.

'Hey, Noah, he says he called up.'

'He called up?' replies Noah.

'Yeah.'

'I called up,' repeats Dan.

'I see,' says Noah. 'You called up?'

Making the assertion a fourth time seems unnecessary, so Dan just looks at the two men and crosses his arms.

'OK,' says Noah.

'OK,' says the other man.

A thick gold chain hangs from Noah's right wrist, and Dan can make out the dark markings of a tattoo showing above the neck of his hoody.

'We gotta be careful with new faces, you know.'

In the main room, cardboard has been taped over the windows, and all of the furniture and rubbish is pushed up against the walls. Dan's shoes stick to the filthy, threadbare carpet, which crunches with broken glass. In the middle of the room hangs what's left of a light fitting, wrapped in red tinsel. The ceiling is a patchwork of broken tiles, the kind that used to be made of asbestos, and fragments of powdered tile lie scattered across the floor.

In one corner a man is selling small bottles of alcohol from cardboard boxes stacked on top of a desk. At the far end of the room a single fluorescent tube illuminates a crowd of people. The damp air is heavy with adrenaline.

Dan stops for a moment to take it all in, then walks quickly to catch up with his companion.

'You're here to fight?' asks the man.

'Yeah,' says Dan, sounding more confident than he feels.

'You're gonna get fucked up real nice.'

The man throws his head back and laughs, showing gum where once were teeth.

'Do you get scared?' asks Dan.

'I get scared that I'll walk away from here without leaving enough of myself behind.'

'What about getting hurt?'

'This isn't a fucking cocktail party.' The man studies Dan. 'Are you scared?'

'Yeah.'

'Then you must have something to live for.'

Dan thinks about Marianne.

As they approach the crowd, people step aside for the man and Dan follows close behind. Someone thrusts a plastic bottle into the man's hand, and he takes a swig from it before passing it to Dan. Dan holds the bottle to his nose. It smells of rust. He passes the bottle back into the crowd.

Dan's companion pushes into a space at the edge of the ring, which is constructed from aluminium barriers. In the middle, two men, bare chested, bare fisted, are studying each other under the fluorescent glare. One of them, thin and very tall, all bone and sharp angles, takes a step back. He has the same sick, grey complexion as Dan's companion.

'Fucking get on with it,' shouts a voice from the crowd.

The other man – short, muscular, with neatly cropped hair – bounces on the balls of his feet, guard raised, elbows tucked tight into his abdomen. He wears red boxer's shorts with a thick white waistband and gold trim.

'Who's he?' asks Dan, nodding at the boxer.

The man shrugs.

'And the other guy?'

'Oh yeah, he's my boy.'

The thin man stands with his arms by his side, his feet quite still. The only movement is his chest rising and falling and a swinging motion across his bony chest and shoulders.

The boxer shuffles forwards on his toes, keeping just out of range. He feints a jab, ducks left, feints another jab, then shuffles right, dancing with sudden, awkward movements.

Suddenly the boxer flashes a double jab, smacking the thin man twice on the chin. The thin man reels backwards and coughs. A thick glob of blood lands a few feet away from Dan's foot. Dan looks at the floor. The carpet tiles are marbled with blood and shit and sweat. The boxer bounces back into range again and flashes another jab that grazes the thin man's cheek.

Dan can feel his chest tightening. His palms are damp. He imagines that it's him in the circle, bouncing and ducking, throwing the double jab.

'It'll be your turn soon enough,' says the man.

The boxer is getting into his rhythm. He feints a right hand, which causes the thin man to shift his weight straight onto the next punch, a left uppercut, which catches him sweetly on the chin. His head snaps back and his body follows, tipping his centre of gravity and throwing him off his feet. His head and shoulders hit the floor first and for a moment he lies perfectly still, eyes closed. The boxer skips a few steps back, staying on his toes, looking around for someone to step in to call an end to the fight.

'Are you going to finish the job or what?' shouts a voice from behind Dan.

'He's out!' shouts the boxer, looking in Dan's direction and, for a moment, looking straight at Dan.

There are a few more jeers, but mostly the crowd is silent.

On the floor, the tall man has opened his eyes and is starting to move.

'You'd better finish the fucking job,' shouts the voice again.

The thin man rolls onto his front, and the boxer takes a step back as his opponent slowly gets to his feet.

The boxer seems unsure what to do next. He extends his arm to tap fists. The thin man looks at the fist and then at the boxer. He curls his top lip into a sneer, snorts and then spits a mouthful of blood and phlegm, which lands across the boxer's shoulder and chest.

Looking disgusted and then furious, the boxer drops his guard and bounces back into range, taking a swing with his right arm. The tall man anticipates the punch and twists his shoulders, so that the fist flies past his face into empty air. As the boxer recovers his balance, the tall man extends his right arm, locking it around the boxer's neck, before bringing him down on his back in a chokehold.

And now the crowd begins to howl, like a pack of wild dogs. Dan looks at the faces on the other side of the ring, contorted in lust and rage. He looks at a screaming, red-faced, middle-aged man with thinning hair. His head is nestled in the fleece-lined hood of a green duffle coat, which is zipped up to his neck. The strip light picks out a purple vein running down his forehead. Dan imagines him at work on Monday morning, chatting about the match and the holiday his wife has just booked, and all the while thinking about his Saturday night, spent cheering while a person is beaten to a pulp. Dan wonders if the men leaning across these barriers have ever seen a person die here on this grey office floor.

'Good boy,' screams Dan's companion, 'you've got him now.'

The boxer is scrabbling to get out of the hold. He tries to peel back the arm that's locked around his neck, then swings his legs up to kick his opponent in the head. But the tall man's grip is tightening. Gasping for breath, the boxer is getting desperate. He reaches back and tears at the tall man's face, trying to gauge his eyes. His fingers pull at the tall man's cheeks and nose and mouth, and then he lets out a gasp and brings his hands to his chest. The tall man gives a final squeeze, then releases the boxer and slowly gets to his feet. There is blood running down the tall man's chin. The boxer is curled on the ground, with his left hand held tightly in his right. The tall man takes a few steps back and grins at the people gathered round, squeezing a fat stump, like a bloodied cigar butt, between his front teeth. With a shriek of delight from Dan's companion, the tall man pulls a piece of finger out of his mouth and throws it to the crowd.

There is a rising feeling in Dan's stomach. He wants to be sick.

The hall erupts like a prison riot. The middle-aged man in the green duffle coat snarls and clashes his teeth, lifting a piece of barrier a few inches off the floor and smashing it back down.

The boxer is back on his feet, his left hand curled into his chest. The white waist belt of his shorts is red with blood. Like a wounded animal he moves warily round the edge of the crowd, then finds a gap in the barrier and tries to push through.

'Let me out!'

Hands push him back into the ring. He slips then gets up and tries again, but the mob blocks his exit. The tall man watches silently, arms by his side, shoulders gently rocking.

The boxer stops trying to push his way out through the crowd and turns round to face his opponent. The crowd has become quiet.

'You're going to pay for this,' shouts the boxer, cradling his left hand. 'I swear you're going to pay for this.' But his voice has no conviction.

Dan looks at the faces in the crowd, out of their minds on cheap brandy and the sight of blood.

'When does it end?' asks Dan.

'It ends when it ends,' says the man, looking at the fighters, then turning to look at Dan.

‘What were you expecting?’ he says quietly.

The man is staring at Dan, waiting for a reply.

‘What were you expecting?’ he says a little louder. ‘It’s not a fucking cocktail party.’

‘I thought there would be rules,’ replies Dan.

‘Rules?’ The man shakes his head and frowns.

‘Rules keep strong men on their knees so that weak men can stand on their backs. Rules put a fist of notes in your pocket and left me with nothing. Rules go against nature. So you can fuck your fucking rules.’

With a shout, the boxer charges at the tall man, who jumps forwards, raises his right leg high into the air and strikes his heel into the boxer’s chest.

With a smack the boxer is back on the floor, winded from the kick. The tall man stands still, poised, insect-like. Then with a yell of excitement, he springs at the boxer, bringing his full weight through his knee into the man’s chest. Dan hears a sharp crack and a gush of air, like a tire deflating.

Now the tall man starts to pound the boxer’s face. Standing a few metres away, Dan can hear the snap and crunch. The boxer uses his forearms to block the blows and tries to wriggle out from under the tall man’s knees, but the tall man continues to pump his fists, like bloodied pistons, into the boxer’s face.

‘Having a change of heart?’ asks Dan’s companion.

Dan nods.

‘Shame.’

Dan turns and pushes his way through the crowd. Halfway to the door, he stops and looks back over the mass of heads. There’s still a gap near the front where he was stood a moment ago, and beyond that the tall, thin man continues pounding with his fists, and the boxer’s arms lie limp above his head.

CHAPTER TWENTY-SIX

Saturday the 12th of May, 2012

High hopes for the temporary power provider Aggreko sent it to the top of a re-energised FTSE 100 yesterday. The company, which will provide generators to the London Olympics, reported an increase in demand in the first quarter of 2012 and forecast-beating earnings for 2011. Aggreko's earnings last year were boosted by a contract to supply Tokyo Electric Power Company following the nuclear disaster in Fukushima, Japan.

7.14am – Marianne Bleekman, Broadway Market, Hackney

She spots him on Broadway Market, and she knows she has to give him a second chance.

The shuttered shopfronts shimmer gold in the low morning light. At the vegetable stall a man is unloading an old blue van. Dan is standing halfway down the road outside a cafe, eyes closed, face raised towards the rising sun, a haze of stubble across his jaw. He hears footsteps and turns to face her.

'Are you OK?' asks Marianne.

'It's amazing to see you. I didn't think you'd come.'

'I wasn't sure, but I'm glad I did. Have you slept?'

'Not a wink. I've been thinking everything through.'

Under his jacket Dan is wearing a tracksuit. A gym bag sits by his feet.

'Where have you been?'

'Tottenham.'

'Tottenham? What's in Tottenham?'

'I made a mistake, but it made me realise that you were right… about everything. I'm sorry about the other night. I'm sorry I walked out. There are things I want to change. I'm ready to change. I wasn't then but I am now. I want your help.'

'Good morning,' says the hipster, drawing up outside the cafe on his fixie. The chocolate colour of the small dog in the bike basket matches his beanie.

'You're a bit early,' he says, studying Dan. He turns to Marianne. 'Everything OK?'

Marianne gives him a reassuring smile.

He locks the bike and picks the small dog out of the basket, then turns to Dan. 'You look like you could do with a coffee. Or probably something stronger.'

'I could… murder a coffee,' says Dan.

'Ha, ha,' replies the hipster as he waits for the shop shutters to roll up. 'We don't open for half an hour, but I can do a takeaway.'

'Thanks,' replies Dan.

'What'll you have?'

'Flat white,' says Marianne. 'That's so kind.'

'Me too,' says Dan.

They watch the hipster through the glass frontage. There's so much to talk about, Marianne wonders where to start.

'What's in Tottenham?'

Dan rubs his hand along his jaw. 'It's a fight club.'

'What's a *fight club*?' asks Marianne.

'I want you to know everything, but I want to start at the beginning… and then you might see how I've got to here.'

'OK.'

Dan looks away and his eyes settle on the roofline of the buildings across the street. He suddenly looks tired. Marianne takes his hand.

'What's the beginning?'

'I want to tell you about Sarah.'

Marianne's optimism chills. She slips her hand from Dan's.

Marianne's tone is matter of fact. 'You told me you still love her. What's changed? Have you seen Sarah… have you spoken to her?' asks Marianne.

Dan shakes his head.

'Sarah used to make me laugh. All the time. She was graceful, and she was beautiful. I used to wake up beside her and think that it must be a dream. She was too perfect. What we had was too perfect.'

There are tears in Dan's eyes, but he is smiling.

'We met on a climbing holiday and things happened quickly. We moved in together, into a flat in North London. And then we went to Venice for a long weekend. It was April and I proposed in St Mark's Square. I thought I was being romantic. She thought it was hilarious. We'd only known each other for six months, but I knew it was right, and she said yes.'

Dan has been avoiding eye contact, but now he looks at Marianne.

'Sarah did a lot of climbing in North Wales. It was her passion; it was what she did. I started going with her. I was a beginner really. One weekend we were coming off a route. It was a tricky exit off the top. We were coming down, and…'

Dan's voice starts to crack. Marianne puts her hand on his back. Dan breathes out slowly.

'Sorry.'

He takes a few more deep breaths. 'We were coming down, and she slipped… and she fell… and she died.'

Marianne shudders. 'Oh God. I'm so sorry. I had no idea that she died. I thought…'

Dan's voice is trembling. 'And I… I… nothing's been the same since. I've just been drifting along, going through the motions… I've been depressed for a long time. The boxing, the fighting, the… violence has been the only thing that made sense… and then I met you.'

Dan turns and puts his arms round Marianne and squeezes her close. Marianne buries her head in his chest. She wishes that the world would stop, and they could stand like this forever.

A small dog starts to bark.

The hipster is holding a pair of paper coffee cups.

'Umm… two flat whites.'

Marianne takes the drinks, and Dan reaches into his jacket for his wallet.

The hipster waves his hands. 'On the house… I hope it works out!'

'So do we,' replies Marianne.

The hipster disappears back inside with the small dog at his heels.

'Thank you for telling me about Sarah.'

'I want you to know everything.'

'What do we do now?' asks Marianne.

'I really need a shower.'

'My place is five minutes away.'

'Look, I've got this crazy idea. Let's get out of London for the day. Let me go home, get changed, book a Zipcar. Will you come away with me? Come away for the day, just you and me. We'll talk about everything.'

Marianne looks at Dan and grips his hand tightly.

'I'll go anywhere, as long as it's with you.'

11.58am – Dan Trench, West Sussex

Dan feels the automatic switch down a gear as he breaks into the bend. Sand on the back seat and an ice-cream wrapper in the glovebox hint at yesterday's journey. Marianne is watching the countryside speed past the window. She looks across at him and smiles. A road sign comes into view.

'*East Grinstead*? It sounds…'

'…Dickensian,' Dan finishes her sentence.

'Yeah, Dickensian. What's in East Grinstead?'

'Just a place I know. I hope you like it.'

Flat whites on Broadway Market feel like a lifetime ago.

'Getting out of London, it feels like…'

'A fresh start?' says Dan.

'Exactly.'

He looks over at Marianne. 'You're so gorgeous. You're stunning.'

She smiles and blushes.

They pass a sign for Brighton.

'Are we going to the beach?'

'Do you want to go to the beach?'

'Sure.'

'We're not going to the beach,' replies Dan.

'I saw a sign for Gatwick Airport…'

'No!' Dan laughs, shaking his head. 'But we're almost there now. The food is great; the setting is great: you'll love it.'

The turning is just up ahead. Marianne sees the sign before he does.

'*Gravity Manor?*'

Dan laughs. 'I think it's pronounced *Grave-Tie*.'

'*Gravetye*, of course.'

They turn down a gravel drive. Marianne catches a glimpse of the old manor house through the trees and sighs. As they pull up outside, Dan wonders what it was like to live in a grand old house like this. Cold and dark, probably, back in 1598, with all of those small windows and the thick stone walls.

The restaurant is quiet. The waiter shows them to a table on the lawn.

'I love it,' says Marianne as the waiter pushes her chair in for her.

Dan sits down and runs his hand over the starched white tablecloth.

The waiter pours water from a bottle on the table. 'May I bring you some drinks?'

'Champagne!' says Marianne. 'Shall we?'

'Of course,' says Dan, 'and a double espresso.'

'Two glasses of champagne and a double espresso,' repeats the waiter.

The waiter leaves them, and Dan picks up the menu. 'I just realised I'm starving.'

'Me too.'

Over lunch Dan tells Marianne his whole story, right up until the moment they met.

'You're the only person I've ever told all this to. I've been in darkness. I've just tried to put it all out of my mind. To just take each day as it comes, and all the while falling further into this desperate place. And then last night someone said something that made me realise you have given me a reason for living again. You *are* my reason for living again.'

Marianne starts to cry.

'There is another me, a better me, in here.' Dan takes her hand and puts it on his chest. 'If you'll give me time – not much, just a little time – I can become that person again.'

'Yes.'

After lunch they hold hands and walk slowly round the gardens. As the afternoon draws on, Dan suggests they head back into town, but Marianne wants to stay a little longer, so they carry on walking through the nearby woods and then come back to the house for a late tea on the lawn.

Dan drains his coffee and slouches back in the wicker chair. A yawn escapes from his mouth. 'Sorry, I'm flagging.'

'Of course,' replies Marianne, standing up. 'Just give me two minutes.'

She runs her fingers through his hair as she walks past him towards the house.

An elderly couple sit at the next table. With the sun on his back and his eyes closed, Dan catches snippets of their conversation, about the garden and the seasons. The sun has dropped far enough that now, suddenly, it feels like evening. Just as Dan thinks to look for the waiter, he appears.

'I'll put this on the room, sir.'

'Oh, we're not staying.'

The waiter looks confused. 'It's Mr Trench.'

'Yes.'

'Robinson Suite.'

Dan laughs. 'No, no, I think there's been a mistake.'

The waiter looks up, and Dan feels Marianne's hand on his shoulder.

'I've… done something… naughty! I hope you don't mind,' says Marianne.

She turns to the waiter. 'Yes, put it on the room.'

'Well, that's woken me up!' says Dan, sitting up straight in his chair.

'You don't mind, do you?' asks Marianne.

'Bloody hell, it's an amazing idea.'

'Oh good. Give me ten minutes then come up.'

Marianne goes back inside and Dan stares at his watch for ten long minutes, then another five for decorum, before making his way into the house.

The oak-panelled lobby and the staircase smell of wax polish. He stops at the third-floor landing to look at an etching of a lady holding a parasol, with a Capability Brown landscape in the background. He takes a wrong turn and retraces his steps to find their room. He starts to turn the handle, then stops and knocks instead.

'Dan?' comes a muffled voice through the door.

He pushes the door open a crack. 'It's me.'

'Why are you knocking? Don't be silly!'

Dan walks in and closes the door behind him.

'I'll be two minutes,' says Marianne, through the bathroom door, which is ajar.

Dan looks out of the window, down onto the lawn below. The teapot still sits on their table. He sits in an armchair, then picks a leaflet off the table and tries to read it, but the sound of Marianne in the bath turns the text into squiggles.

He can hear her standing up and getting out of the bath and the gurgle of water in the plughole.

'I'm just going to dry my hair.'

For what seems like an age Dan sits in the armchair, looking down at the leaflet, listening to the sound of the hairdryer. His hands are cold, but his face feels hot and his heart is beating quickly.

The hairdryer stops and, with a waft of warm jasmine air, the bathroom door opens. Marianne stands in the doorway, wearing a white dressing gown. The collar is pulled up close around her neck.

'My pussy is really wet.'

Marianne walks over to the armchair and stands astride him, then pulls his hand into her dressing gown and slides it up her thigh. She guides his fingers towards her tender softness.

He pulls the dressing gown open.

'Just fuck me,' whispers Marianne.

CHAPTER TWENTY-SEVEN

Sunday the 13th of May, 2012

A decade after Renzo Piano's first sketches, external work on The Shard is at last complete. The final pieces of glazing and steel work were fitted last week by three workers known on site as Daz, G-man and Mr B. The final height of the building will be 310m, making it the tallest building in Europe.

8.33am – Gareth Eary, King's Road, Chelsea

Gareth scribbles the Tesco Direct order number down on the notepad below a list of train times, then closes the laptop. Sitting on the table next to him is a bottle of hair dye. He stands up and walks round to a drawer beneath the TV. Amongst the utility bills and takeaway menus is a stack of old photos bound with an elastic band. Gareth flicks through them until he finds one of himself. He grimaces. The haircut, that shy grin, the horrible, horrible tie. He holds the photo next to the bottle of 'dark chestnut' hair dye and studies the two hair colours closely.

Good enough.

In the bathroom he runs his hand through his carefully tinted 'dirty blond' hair. A shame, but it's got to be done. By this evening he'll have switched it back again. Gareth works confidently with the tint brush, and once he's finished he sets his Panerai Radiomir for twenty-five minutes.

Gareth drops onto the couch and idly picks the Farrow & Ball colour wheel off the coffee table. He does a mental tour of the flat, ticking off the colours. Master bedroom walls Mole's Breath, feature wall Rectory Red, picture rail Breakfast Room Green, architrave Pale Hound, ceiling Lime White. Prek has executed Gareth's vision masterfully in every room, but he really saved his finest work for the bathroom, where the silicone work round the shower tray left Gareth so moved that he left a gushing review on Trusted Tradesmen. Of course, he would have felt quite differently if he'd known the story behind the empty cans of Dulux the concierge had complained about finding in the basement.

The alarm on his watch tells Gareth that twenty-five minutes have passed. He washes and conditions his hair, then takes a deep breath and looks at the results. Not bad. He picks the photo off the bathroom shelf and studies it against his reflection in the mirror. Not bad at all.

At the bottom of his wardrobe is a bag of old clothes. Things that Gareth thought he might wear if he ever had to go paintballing or do DIY. Mercifully, he has done neither recently, but he finds a cotton sweater that should work with a pair of jeans and his gym shoes. And a black beanie which will help to avoid awkward questions if he bumps into any of his neighbours on the way out of the building.

Before he leaves the flat, Gareth stands by the full-length mirror in the hallway and checks himself over. The outfit is… ghastly, but just right. He pulls off the beanie and studies his hair. Not bad. There are two more things that Gareth needs to do before he can make his way across town to Liverpool Street station. Firstly, the Panerai. He pulls the watch off his wrist and drops it, with a satisfying thud, into the leather tray on the sideboard. Secondly, the pinky ring. Gareth twists it off his finger and places it on the tray next to his watch.

'Hi, Gareth,' he says to the mirror in a voice that will always be his.

9.14am – Marianne Bleekman, Gravetye Manor, West Sussex

Marianne wakes up smiling, wrapped in the snug embrace of coital satisfaction. Morning peeps through gaps in the curtains. It takes her a few moments to remember where she is and why. She looks across at Dan, who is lying on his back beside her, still fast asleep. She lies on her side for a moment, tracing his profile with her eye, watching his chest slowly rise and fall. She thinks about how they'll spend the day: maybe breakfast in bed, then a walk hand in hand through the woods, talking about what they've started and where it might go. She tries to push the thought of driving back into London out of her head. She wants to stay here forever, just the two of them, keeping the rest of the world at bay.

She slides off the bed and tiptoes to the bathroom, closing the door quietly behind her. She has a wee then glances at her Blackberry. Her plans for the day instantly evaporate. A bunch of emails, a couple of text messages and three missed calls from an unknown number. She doesn't even need to read them to know what it means. Of all the Sundays, why this one? She could cry.

She quickly scans the emails. Some of her team have been working over the weekend on a rights issue for one of their corporate clients, to be announced to the market tomorrow. Judging by the time of the missed calls on her phone, the Addison Lee cab has been waiting outside her flat in Hackney for twenty minutes.

She walks back into the bedroom. Dan is lying on his side.

'Everything OK?' he asks.

She lets out a sigh. 'Everything was *perfect* until a moment ago when I checked my emails. I know I shouldn't have.'

'You need to go to work.'

'I'm so sorry.'

'Don't be. I totally understand. I know what it's like in IB.'

'You don't mind?' asks Marianne.

'Of course not.'

'Well, that makes it a bit better, I guess… thanks for last night; it was *unbelievable*.'

Dan grins. 'Do you have to go now?'

'I have to make a call,' replies Marianne.

Dan rolls out of bed and opens the curtain. Light streams into the room. He looks at her standing naked by the bed, clutching her Blackberry.

'You're so fucking hot,' he says, then kisses her purposefully on the mouth. She feels her face go flush.

'I want to Dan… but I *have to* make a call.'

Dan goes to the bathroom and Marianne presses 'call back' and sits down on the edge of the armchair.

The phone rings once before Todd answers.

'Are you here?'

'I'm sorry, Paul, I just got the messages,' replies Marianne.

'Fine. The car's outside your flat. Just get here ASAP.' Paul is annoyed.

'I'm sorry, Paul, I'm not at my flat.'

The line is silent for a moment. 'OK,' says Paul slowly, 'then where the fuck are you?'

'I'm at… I'm in… Sussex.'

'Sussex?' repeats Todd.

'East Grinstead.'

'East Grinstead?' repeats Todd.

'With my… boyfriend.'

'OK,' says Paul, 'this is what you're going to do. You are going to call a taxi immediately, and you are going to come to the Club Quarters on Threadneedle Street. And in one hour from now you're going to be standing in front of me.'

'Yes, Paul.'

'Good,' says Todd, then hangs up.

'Everything OK?' asks Dan.

'It's shit,' says Marianne. 'I need to call a cab.'

'You gotta go now?'

'Yeah, right now. I'm so sorry.'

Dan shakes his head. 'Hey, don't worry, it's just one Sunday. There'll be plenty more, right?'

'Right.'

'And when I check out, I'll book the Robinson Suite again for next weekend, and we'll pick up again where we left off.'

'Oh yes please.'

'So, no worries.' Dan kisses her.

'You're right, no worries.'

Twenty minutes later Marianne is sat in a taxi, waving through the back window at Dan, who stands on the gravel outside the main entrance in a white hotel dressing gown and slippers. Dan puts his hands to his face to shout something that Marianne can't quite hear, then he puts his hands on his chest and then holds them up towards her with his fingers curled into the shape of a heart.

10.20am – Gareth Eary, Liverpool Street Station, City

Gareth is in a reflective mood as the train pulls out of Liverpool Street station. With the Essex–London sprawl rushing past the window, he has time to think about where his life is going, and the knotty situation with Jabba and Aurelius Blois starts to trouble him. For a moment Gareth wonders whether he really is as smart as he thinks he is, before quickly putting the moment of self-doubt down to skipping breakfast. But after the situation with the girls at Jabba's flat, nasty rumours have been going round, and although he despises Jabba so much that it gives him a headache to think about it, he has to admit that there is a terrible brilliance to Jabba's little scheme. He's been stitched up good and proper.

The line goes through Wivenhoe, Alresford, Great Bentley. The names are heavy with memories and guilt. Every time he comes back, things have fallen apart a little more.

Two elderly women sit down a few rows behind, and he catches snippets of their conversation. The familiar patois washes over him as he dozes off.

'I did the potatoes last night, so tonight'll be easy: I'll just give them to him with lots of salad cream…'

'Tonight, I'll watch *The Vet* and *Animal Hospital*, then I'll wash my hair and get things ready for tomorrow…'

'What's your husband?'

'Taurus…'

'…I don't blame him though, I'm sure we won't want to go to the old folks' home either.'

'That's because we're strong.'

'But in the end, we'll go.'

'In the end, yeah, we'll go.'

Gareth opens his eyes with a start and sees that the train has just pulled into his stop. He grabs his bag and hops onto the platform. The long way round from the station avoids the high street. The term 'high street' applies only for want of a better word. He used to enjoy coming back, mostly because it was a chance to show off. The place was less depressing then. He walks past a terrace of houses. A large cushion sits in a window. There's an embroidered picture of a cottage and underneath it says 'Home Sweet Home'. An unexpected wave of emotion catches Gareth, who stops in the street to stare at the cushion. An old man appears at the window holding a cat. Gareth quickly moves on and reprimands himself for confusing a sentimental moment with what was surely just an instinctive reaction to bad taste.

Gareth is keen to avoid seeing anyone who might still remember him, but as he turns a corner there's a familiar voice.

'Too good for me now?'

Standing in the doorway of a house is a man in a blue Champion sweatshirt. He's a little younger than Gareth but about the same height and build. It's the man who approached Gareth on fight night at the Troxy.

'I… I'm sorry. I wasn't expecting to see you there.'

'Why did you ignore my messages?' asks the man.

Gareth tries to think of a clever excuse, then decides against it. 'I'm sorry.'

'What you doing back here anyway?'

'You know,' replies Gareth.

The man nods.

'She doing OK?' asks Gareth.

'Same old.'

'Come with?' asks Gareth.

'Nah. Maybe I'll pop over later.' The man nods his head up the road. 'Go on.'

'Do you want to chat?' asks Gareth.

'Do you?' replies the man.

'There's stuff I need to say, but…'

The man shakes his head. 'There's nothing to say.'

Gareth feels a lump in his throat.

'Go on!' says the man again, this time with an edge in his voice.

Gareth carries on up the road and behind him he hears a door closing.

As the road leaves town, it peters out into a track; soon the buildings change to bungalows and then to temporary-looking structures. On an overgrown plot at the end of a cul-de-sac is the static caravan where Gareth spent the last few years of his adolescence after his father died and money became tight.

It's a clear day but inside feels damp.

The woman pulls Gareth in for a hug. Every time he sees her, she seems smaller.

'You smell nice, darling.'

'You been looking after yourself, Mum?' He pushes a strand of grey hair back from her face. 'You been looking after yourself?' he asks again.

'I get by. Can I get you a brew, darling?'

'Love one.'

The beige kitchenette looks bare. As his mum fills up the kettle, Gareth pulls two mugs out of the cupboard and puts them on the counter.

'There's nothing in these cupboards.'

'I'm fine, darling. I just buy what I need. I don't like to have too much food lying around; it just spoils, you see.'

'Does this work?' he asks, pointing at the Baby Belling single-ring electric hob and grill.

'I'm not sure.'

Gareth raises his eyebrows.

'Don't worry, darling, I'm just fine. Really.'

'Are you using the money I sent you?'

'Well, some of it. I don't know what to do with it, really. But I appreciate you helping out.'

'I wish you'd let me do more.'

She passes him a mug of tea, then pulls a large bag of white sugar from the cupboard. 'Sugar?'

'Not for me.'

He watches her adding sugar to her mug. Two, three, four teaspoons. He wants to say something but stops himself.

There's a rap at the door. 'Hello!' calls a voice.

Gareth opens the door. The delivery driver is wearing a blue fleece and on the track behind him is his van.

'Hi,' says Gareth.

'Tesco Direct,' the man says.

'Yeah,' replies Gareth.

'Name please.'

'Gareth Eary.'

The man checks his clipboard and nods.

Gareth turns to his mum. 'I just ordered you a few bits and bobs.'

'Had a bit of trouble finding this place,' says the driver over his shoulder as he walks back to the van.

He returns with a blue crate full of shopping bags. As Gareth transfers the bags onto the kitchen counter, the driver peers into the caravan.

'Do you… actually… live here?' he asks.

'God no!' says Gareth, letting out a laugh before checking himself. 'I mean…'

'I do,' says his mum.

Once the driver has gone, Gareth goes through the bags.

'OK, so there's a few bits of fresh veg here and some canned stuff. Baked beans, tuna, bean salad… here's some pasta and a few jars of sauce… tea bags of course, coffee, bread… there's some milk for the fridge…'

Once it's all stacked up in the cupboard, Gareth feels a little better.

Then he remembers the conversation he had with the assistant in Boots and starts to rummage through his bag.

'Oh, and I got you some vitamins,' he says, pulling a small box out of his bag. 'Vitabiotics, these are for… *older women.* Osteoporosis… menopause… you know, stuff like that…'

She turns the box over in her hand, looking at the front and the back before placing it on the counter next to Gareth's bag.

'That's a nice bag, dear.'

'Thanks, Mum. It's a travel bag from William & Son in burgundy leather. Why don't I get you one? A ladies' one. I'll have it monogrammed for you.'

'Oh, that's very kind, Gareth darling, but what would I do with a nice bag like that?'

The bag costs more than the caravan they are standing in. Gareth instinctively goes to twist his signet ring then remembers, with relief, that he left it in Chelsea along with the Panerai.

She takes his hand.

'It's so nice to see you, Gareth, and it's lovely, darling, such a treat to be looked after. And I'm pleased that you're making a success of your life and doing well in your work. Why don't we sit down for a bit and drink our tea, and you can tell me about your life… and when I can be expecting some grandchildren!'

Gareth puts his tea down on the counter, then takes the mug from her hand and puts it down beside his. He wraps his arms round her and hugs her close.

'Oh, Mum. I love you. But don't hold your breath for grandchildren. Seriously!'

They sit on two small benches, beneath the cloudy Perspex window, facing each other across the folding table. Gareth's shoulder rests against the wall, which is damp with condensation.

'Have you seen your brother?'

'I bumped into him.'

Her eyes light up. 'Oh, I'm happy to hear that. He… missed you, you know. For a long time, he really missed you.'

Gareth nods.

'He always looked up to you,' she continues, 'particularly after Dad died. And when you left, I think he just felt like everyone had… abandoned him.'

'You've always been here for him.'

'Yeah, but it's different at that age, when a boy is growing up. He needs a man around.'

They sit in silence.

'I'm proud of you. What you've achieved. The important work you do. It makes me proud to know I brought you up. That you were… one of us.'

'Were?'

'I mean, your life's moved on… I'm happy for you.'

They both look out of through the Perspex at the back of the shack on the next plot. When Gareth has finished his tea, he stands up and puts the mug on the counter.

'I meant what I said at Christmas, about getting you a proper place to live.'

'I know, darling. We can talk about it another time.'

3.23pm – John Gruff, Club Quarters, Threadneedle Street, City

Paul Todd is waiting in the lobby.

Gruff shakes Paul's hand and leans in to talk quietly in his ear. 'Well, this is sooner than I thought.'

'We left a few crumbs and Hugh found the path.'

'He knew what he was looking for.'

'And Malta is sorted?' asks Paul anxiously.

'We'll clear twenty-five bar at twenty-five.' Gruff smiles.

Paul looks relieved. 'Excellent. Then I'll leak it this evening, so the story is in the headlines before the announcement is out. That should get us halfway to twenty-five at open.'

'Good. And if we need another leg down, I can do that at the presentation.'

'Is there anything else we need to think about, John? Any holes in the plan?'

'I've been asking myself the same question,' replies Gruff. 'Hugh's got the bit between his teeth now and he won't stop until he's finished the job. We just have to make sure he doesn't realise we're delighted.'

'We seem to have hired the right finance director after all,' says Paul, as the lift door opens.

The pair step out of the lift and into a warren of meeting rooms.

They turn the corner and see Hugh in the corridor.

Hugh looks up from his Blackberry. 'John, I'm sorry we had to call you into town on a Sunday, but this is material. I've spoken to the banks, and we need to get the statement out first thing tomorrow.'

'What do I need to know?' asks Gruff.

Paul pulls open the door and Gruff follows Hugh into a large, windowless meeting room. Hugh's financial controller is slumped across two chairs in the corner of the room. Two associates from Gessner Bank, still wearing jackets and ties, stand up when Gruff enters the room and scurry round the table to introduce themselves. Gruff shakes his head and waves them back into their seats. Paul goes to close the door, but before he does, another member of the team appears in the doorway, holding a can of air freshener.

'Ah yes, this is Marianne. She's taking over from Calum and Casper.'

'Hello,' says Marianne, holding her hand out to Gruff.

Gruff takes her hand. 'Marianne. I don't think we've met.'

'I'm fairly new to Paul's team.'

Gruff wants to say more but Paul cuts in, 'Actually, this is probably a good time to hand over, Marianne, if you're happy you're up to speed.'

'Sure.'

'Calum, Casper, anything else we need to know before you go?'

'No, Marianne's fully up to speed on the model,' replies Casper, pulling on his jacket.

The junior bankers are out of the door at double-speed, as if they might be summoned for another thirty-hour shift at any moment.

Gruff falls into a chair next to Hugh.

'Lay it out for me.'

Hugh takes a deep breath. 'OK. So the debt on the Warburtons deal has various covenants, pretty standard stuff really, but the issue is that we never really had a chance of meeting them. The assumptions in the model that Gessner prepared,' he points at Marianne's laptop, 'are nonsense.'

'Let's… keep it professional,' says Paul.

'I mean… day one, shut down Albourne's flour mill, consolidate mill operations with Warburtons. Put through above-inflation price increases… when has any supplier ever got Tesco to accept above-inflation price increases? I mean, the supermarkets are in the middle of a fucking price war!'

Gruff starts to laugh. 'Hugh, I don't think I've ever heard you swear before. This is quite an episode.'

'Look, I haven't seen my family all weekend and I haven't had more than three hours' sleep. I'm done.'

'I get the picture. We overextended and we did a bad deal.' Gruff looks at Paul. 'We can play the blame game later. Right now, you guys just need to work out how much we need to raise, and I'll sell it to the market. I don't need to get involved in the numbers. You guys know what you're doing. What's the plan, Paul?'

Paul stares at his Longines for a long time.

'Paul?'

'Yes, sorry. Umm… Marianne is finalising the announcement to the market, pulling together the deck and liaising with the lawyers. Then we need to do a full review before we put out the statement at 7am.'

'Sounds easy.'

'Not much fun, but all very doable.'

'The numbers are done,' says Hugh.

Gruff looks at Paul, who nods.

'Marianne's going to pull it all together. John, you need to write a CEO statement, or I can do that if you prefer. Hugh's done his bit.'

'I'll do the statement,' says Gruff.

‘Then I’m going for a lie-down,’ says Paul.

‘Me too.’ Hugh sighs, then lifts himself from the chair and wakes up his financial controller. Together they walk slowly towards the door. ‘I’ll be happy when tomorrow’s over.’

Gruff watches the pair file out of the room, with Paul close behind.

Now Gruff and Marianne are alone.

Marianne looks up from her laptop.

‘OK, I’m going to go and write this statement,’ says Gruff. ‘Come up to my room in forty minutes and I’ll have a draft.’

Marianne looks at her watch. ‘Sure, I’ll be up.’

Gruff makes his way back to the lobby to collect his room keys, then up to his suite, which is much like all the other suites in the hotel. He wonders which young lawyer he might have fucked on this particular bed. In the shower, Gruff thinks about holding Marianne down and pushing himself inside her.

There’s a knock at the door and when Gruff opens it Marianne looks surprised to see him in his dressing gown, hair still wet from the shower.

‘Oh sorry, shall I come back?’

‘No, perfect timing.’ Gruff smiles. ‘Just go through to the lounge area; I’ll be with you in two minutes. Help yourself to the minibar. Mine’s an Amaretto with ice.’

Gruff’s eyes follow Marianne into the lounge.

‘Minibar’s under the TV.’

Marianne opens the cupboard, then crouches down to look inside.

‘They should have put a large bottle of Amaretto in there for me… and pour yourself something.’

Gruff turns back to the door and quietly clicks it shut.

CHAPTER TWENTY-EIGHT

Sunday the 30th of August, 2009

Dan Trench, Snowdonia, North Wales

Sarah and Dan are on the ledge at the base of the final pitch.

'You sure about this?' asks Sarah. 'We've got options.'

Dan takes the guidebook. 'No big deal. The crux is only a 5a.'

'You know that doesn't mean the same thing as it does at the climbing wall.'

Dan shrugs.

'OK,' says Sarah, 'focus on your gear placement. The traverse is about fifteen metres, then when you hit the crack, you're through the crux. From there it's straight up to the finish.'

'How about gear?' says Dan.

'Oh, you're interested in gear now?'

Dan smiles sheepishly. 'Maybe I'm coming round to your way of thinking.'

Sarah unclips three racks of nuts and picks out all the smallest ones.

'These are for the traverse. It'll help if you put a quickdraw on each of them now. It's quite crimpy and there's a bit of overhang so try to keep moving. Put plenty of gear in and you've got nothing to worry about.'

While Dan prepares his rack, Sarah sorts out the ropes to belay him up the final pitch. Dan studies the route. The traverse takes them off the slab and onto a vertical face. It's really exposed. *Difficult and committing* says the guidebook. He feels his stomach churning.

'Ready when you are,' says Sarah.

'Right. OK. Right,' says Dan, taking a deep breath.

'You OK?' asks Sarah.

Dan winks at her before making a start, moving his fingers along the flake and smearing his toes on tiny dimples in the rock.

'Gear,' says Sarah quietly.

Dan unclips a nut and slides it behind the flake. He puts a rope through the quickdraw, then tests the placement by pulling down on it until the gear is taking most of his weight.

'Feels good,' he says.

A little further along the traverse, Dan peers down at the drop below. His forearms immediately tense up, and he instinctively grips harder with his fingers. He feels his heart rate jump. Watching him closely, Sarah seems to know exactly when he needs to be told to trust his feet, while also describing from memory the rock features and the best spots to place bits of gear.

At the crux, Dan has to reach round a corner with his left hand for a hold that he can't see. Leaning out to the left, Dan feels his body tense up, and as he puts more weight through his left foot, his leg starts to shake.

'Shit,' says Dan quietly to himself, shifting his balance back to the right, his right hand gripping a little tighter.

Sarah's voice floats across to him.

'There's a great hold for your left hand at head height, just round the corner. Take a breath and reach for it. Trust me.'

Dan closes his eyes and takes a breath, then shifts his weight again and slowly reaches his left hand up and across, running his fingertips along the rock face. Soon all of his weight is over his left foot. Another inch and he'll be totally committed to the move.

He hears Sarah's voice in his head – *trust me* – and with that he reaches a little further and then his left hand curls over a large, satisfying flake.

Dan lets out a relieved 'whoop!'

'There you go,' says Sarah, 'you could hang off that all day! Just some easy moves now to finish.'

As Dan moves round the corner, Sarah disappears from view. His arms are burning with lactic, but the last few metres up the crack come easily. Dan heaves himself onto the ledge and kneels there for a moment, catching his breath, exhilarated and relieved. The view down to the lake is spectacular. A couple of metres back from the edge are two old steel rings that have been bolted into the rock. When Dan has finished setting up the anchor, he calls for Sarah to follow him up.

Sarah is hidden from view behind the corner of the traverse, but he feels her progress through the rope. Every now and then she stops, most likely to knock out a firmly wedged nut. Eventually he can see her at the bottom of the crack, and soon she is pulling herself up beside him on the ledge.

'Amazing traverse,' says Dan.

'You nailed it.'

'Only because of you. Thanks for getting me through the crux.'

'Back down for lunch?' asks Sarah.

'You read my mind.'

'It's a scramble across there,' Sarah points south, 'to the gully. The gully's pretty wet, so we'll abseil it.'

Dan coils the ropes while Sarah pulls a pair of approach shoes out of her rucksack. The deep-lugged Vibram soles are perfect for scrambling on loose or damp rock.

'You left your boots?' asks Sarah, looking at Dan's smooth-soled climbing shoes.

'I like to go light,' says Dan. 'I'll be fine.'

When Dan's finished coiling the rope, he ties it over his back, like a rucksack, and then follows Sarah on the scramble to the top of the descent gully.

As they approach the top of the gully the ground starts to slope down steeply.

'There's a dicey climb down before the last scramble to the bottom,' says Sarah. 'Probably worth roping up.'

Dan is still a few metres above Sarah when his shoes slip on a patch of wet grass. He lands hard on his side, grimacing as he cracks his hip on a sharp edge.

'You OK?' asks Sarah.

'Oh fine,' says Dan, bouncing back to his feet like a boxer trying to beat the count. But Dan doesn't quite regain his balance on the steep slope and stumbles forwards into Sarah.

He sees her in slow motion: looking straight at him, her back to the edge of the cliff. And then she's gone.

There's a scream which ends with a dull thud, like a feather pillow being hit against a wall. Dan freezes. His mind goes blank.

Then everything becomes quiet. Dan doesn't move. He can hear the blood pumping through his ears, he can see the hazy blue sky dabbed with puffy white clouds and, under his fingers, he can feel the hard, damp rock.

Then the silence is broken by the sound of Sarah screaming again. It's a step back in time, the echo from a few moments ago when Sarah was still alive, falling, screaming, watching the ground race towards her.

Dan is at the bottom of the gully. He can't remember how he got here. He saw Sarah's body from a distance, but now that he's here he is unable to look at her. Instead, he just kneels beside her, with the heel of her shoe in his hand. The numbness which had cloaked him is slipping away and now everything is becoming vividly, terribly real. He gasps a lungful of air and lets it out in a shrill wail. He crawls round to look at Sarah's face, which sits in a nest of hair and blood. Her mouth is open, her jaw pointing out at an unnatural angle from her head.

Now Sarah's voice is in Dan's head.

'You did this.'

CHAPTER TWENTY-NINE

Monday the 14th of May, 2012

City scribblers have been playing the guessing game over the weekend with rumours that a major UK company will announce a rescue rights issue this morning. Some sources believe it could be a financial stock, with parts of the sector still looking fragile. However, given the intense focus on financials in recent years, we believe that the equity raise is likely to come from elsewhere. Answers on a postcard...

8.47am – Dan Trench, London Wall, City

From across the road, Dan can see people gathered in the main atrium. As he walks into the building, Colin's voice rises over the growing crowd. Dan moves to the front to find his colleague pushing the decomposed remains of the office photocopier across the marble floor. Colin's leather-soled shoes slip on the polished surface as he shunts the sorry mangle of metal and plastic across the atrium.

'Fucking cunt. Bullshit. *Fuuuck!*'

'Everything OK, Colin?' asks Dan.

'If I'm going down, I'm taking this motherfucker with me.'

A security guard stands back, unsure. Dan catches his eye.

'He's insane,' explains Dan.

The security guard nods.

With a howl and a run-up, Colin crashes the photocopier into the revolving door, landing on top of it. The obstruction brings the door to a halt. The space is too tight for Colin to push the photocopier forwards, and the photocopier stops him from moving the door backwards. He beats his fists against the glass in frustration like a wild animal caught in a trap, then slouches, sobbing, over the mangled carcass of the machine.

The crowd begins to lose interest and people start to head for the lifts. Dan knocks on the glass.

'You OK, buddy? Can I do anything?'

Colin shakes his head. He looks exhausted.

Dan calls over to the security guard, 'Can we get him out of here please?'

The security guard shakes his head. 'Not until the police get here.'

'Police?'

'He's a danger to himself and others. I can't let him out until the police get here. Right now, I think that's the safest place for him.'

The security guard is probably right.

'Sorry, Colin, you're stuck for now, but we'll get you out soon. Do you want me to call anyone?' asks Dan.

Colin shakes his head and lets out a long sigh, then looks up at Dan, past Dan, to something behind him.

'So, what the fuck?' says Jackie, walking across the atrium towards them.

Colin becomes agitated again and lets out a long scream, like a war cry.

'Maybe you should go back upstairs,' says Dan to Jackie. 'I don't think you're helping.'

Colin is beating the photocopier with the leather heel of his shoe. Fragments of plastic bounce round the glass cage.

'I'm done,' says Jackie, 'this is absolutely the last time I do a people business. You guys are all fucked. There's something wrong with you.' She's talking to Dan, then walks up to the glass. 'There's something wrong with all of you; you're all fucking crazy. I've never met such a bunch of neurotic dickheads in all my life.'

Colin has dropped the shoe and now his face is pressed up against the glass.

'Yes, Jackie, yes! Let it out, let it all out, it feels good, doesn't it?' His face has left a greasy smear. Dan starts to snigger. He tries to stop himself but then it comes out, uncontrollably. He's laughing so hard that his abs hurt. He's laughing so hard that he has to gasp for breath. Colin starts laughing too. Beating the glass with his fist and laughing.

'Is everything OK, ma'am?' asks the security guard.

'No, everything is *not* OK. I'm done.'

Jackie throws her pass at the guard and walks out through the second door and into the street.

'I don't suppose we'll see her again,' says Colin, who has become calm suddenly.

'It wasn't her fault, you know that,' says Dan.

'I know.'

A van pulls up in the street outside and three policemen in riot gear jump out. The security guard walks out to meet them.

'I guess a man stuck in a revolving door makes a nice change from beating Occupy protesters.' Colin sighs.

Dan's phone starts to ring. It's Marianne.

Dan turns to Colin. 'I've got a call – are you going to be OK?'

'I'll be fine.'

Dan looks at the policemen, then turns back to Colin. 'Don't do anything stupid.'

'I'll be fine. Go.' Colin is slouched in the small space next to the machine.

Dan picks up the phone. 'I'm already looking forward to next weekend! How did you get on?'

'Hi.'

As soon as he hears Marianne's voice, he knows that something is wrong.

'Are you OK?'

'Dan.'

'What's wrong? Where are you?'

'I'm just going into a presentation.'

'What is it, Marianne?'

'I did an all-nighter.'

'Albourne, yeah I saw. Did it go OK?'

'And I was working with…'

Dan feels his body go cold. 'Gruff. You were working with John Gruff… are you OK?'

'He asked me to come to his hotel room and…'

'He what?' His voice has become loud. 'What!' Dan says again, but he already knows what.

'I didn't want to. I said no. But he did it anyway.'

'Gruff… he…' Dan can't bring himself to say the words.

'I'm so sorry, Dan. I wanted to stop him. I tried to stop him, but he wouldn't stop.'

'Are you safe? Where are you?'

'I'm so sorry, Dan.' Marianne hangs up.

And now Dan breaks into a sweat. His body is trembling. He throws his phone across the street. It hits the curb and shatters.

8.56am – Gareth Eary, Gresham Street Capital, City

Gareth usually avoids breakfast meetings on a Monday: a breakfast meeting means that by the time he gets to his desk he's starting the week on the back foot. But this was an intro to a new hedge fund, and he's always found that investing at the beginning of a relationship pays dividends later. He read the Albourne profit warning on the walk back from the tube station and made a mental note to send something to congratulate Aurelius on the well-timed exit. The stock opened this morning at thirty-five, down almost 60%.

Gareth walks onto the floor with his chin raised to the maximum angle. It's almost 9am and the morning meeting has come and gone. The desk is empty, apart from Martin.

'Jessica left you in charge?'

Martin looks up. 'I guess so.' He looks tired.

'What you up to?'

'Got my FSA exams next week.'

'Then we can set you loose on clients.'

'Yeah.'

'Just keep your hands off mine!'

Martin laughs half-heartedly.

'You OK, Martin?'

'Yeah, I'm OK.'

'Look, just remember Rule 101 and you'll be fine!'

Martin smiles. 'I think I'll have more success following that one than you have!'

Jabba eases back into his seat. 'Sharing a final joke with the condemned?'

'Oh, I don't know. I don't remember those FSA exams being quite that bad,' says Gareth.

Now Jabba starts to laugh. Martin looks uneasy again.

'You're in a good mood, Jabba.'

'You saw Albourne?'

'Oh yeah. Timing on that one, eh!'

Jabba laughs again. 'You could say that.'

'A few per cent off the all-time high and just before a massive profit warning. You can't time it better than that!'

Jabba is staring at his screen and says nothing.

'I don't remember seeing the confirms, Jabba. What did we get out at in the end?'

Jabba is still staring at his screen. He says nothing, but Gareth can see that he's smirking.

Suddenly Gareth has a bolt of panic.

'Wait, wait, wait. Jabba. We're out of ALB… right, Jabba?'

But before Jabba can answer, Jessica appears at Gareth's desk. She is biting her lip. She leans in close and talks quietly, 'Would you come with me please, Gareth?'

Gareth turns to look at Martin, whose eyes are heavy with tears.

'I'm sorry,' says Martin.

'Oh my, my, my. My dear Gareth,' says Jabba.

Gareth looks at Jessica, then at Martin, and finally at Jabba. The game is up.

'You're in as deep as I am, Jabba.'

'We'll see about that.'

Gareth stands up and Jabba starts to slow clap. A few people look up from their desks.

Jessica walks down to the boardroom at the end of the corridor. Gareth follows her. The head of compliance and legal counsel are sat on the other side of the table.

'Would you like to explain what's going on?' says the head of compliance.

'Are you asking about our business with Livermore Capital?'

The head of compliance consults a pile of contract notes in front of her.

'OK, so we have a contract note here for Livermore Capital on the 19th of March, purchase of twenty million shares. The account opening papers were received on the same day, but the money laundering and KYC checks were only completed on the 22nd of March. Is that right, Gareth?'

'I don't remember the exact dates. I'm sure you're right, but look, everyone in this room knows Livermore Capital.'

'It was a bad call, Gareth, in breach of company policy and not to mention illegal. You could be disciplined by the FSA for that. That breach alone could cost you your Approved Person status.'

'Come on, guys, let's keep things in perspective here.'

'People have been fired for less,' says Jessica.

The legal counsel is scribbling copious notes on a pad of yellow paper. The head of compliance continues leafing through the documents. Gareth looks at Jessica, who is sat at the head of the table. She holds his gaze for a moment, then looks away.

'So, let's move on to... a series of trades in Albourne PLC between the 20th of March and the 7th of May executed for a number of accounts registered in Switzerland. Here we have email orders from a law firm... Rex-Ferris LLP on behalf of an unknown client. There is no record of the underlying client and no KYC or money laundering checks have been carried out; incomplete account opening papers have been filed and the Swiss accounts are registered at Banque Esprit Cantonal, who are on our blacklist.'

The legal counsel looks up from his notepad. 'The blacklist exists for a reason. I would say that these trades carry a very high money-laundering risk.'

'These trades are also for Livermore. It's the same client, but they're dealing through segregated accounts.'

'Where is the evidence, Gareth, that these trades were for Livermore, that Livermore is the client? We can't find any call records or emails to that effect. Help us.'

'There are no records. I had dinner with Aurelius Blois, and he left me the order.'

The legal counsel frowns. 'Wait. Stop, stop. I don't get it. Jessica, help me out here, were you aware of this?'

Jessica shakes her head. 'I don't know anything about this. What the hell were you thinking, Gareth?'

'I'm sorry. It was Aurelius Blois. I had to go the extra mile to get the business. You know what these hedge fund types are like sometimes.'

Jessica shakes her head.

'Anyway,' the head of compliance continues, 'this is all just footnotes really.'

'Footnotes?' repeats Jessica. 'Oh, Gareth, what have you done?'

'Jabba's as deep into this as I am. It's his trading book.'

'Yes, he said you might say that,' says the legal council. 'Sorry to ask, Jessica, but would you mind asking Jab… Nigel if he would join us? And Martin too?'

Jessica spins out of her chair, and Gareth listens to the clip of her heels down the corridor as the boardroom door slowly closes behind her. The room falls silent. The head of compliance is still flicking through the call and email records and contract notes piled up in front of her.

'You know, Gareth, when we're finished we're going to know everything. Every piece of dirty laundry, every little thing you thought you'd swept under the carpet. It's all going to come out in the end.'

The three of them sit in silence until the door opens and Jessica leads in Jabba, with Martin following a few steps behind.

'He's got nothing to do with any of this,' says Gareth, gesturing at Martin.

'Oh, but I think you'll find he does,' says Jabba.

'Sorry, Gareth,' says Martin.

'Stop apologising,' says Gareth.

'Nigel… is there anything you'd like to say?' asks the head of compliance.

'I think this gives a pretty clear picture,' says Jabba, taking his phone out of his pocket. He taps the screen a few times and places the phone on the table. Gareth recognises his own voice.

Look, Blois is going to make a huge difference to your bonus and mine. So, I think we're going to be on the same page with this… Blois needs to stretch out the settlement period on his trades, so rather than T+3, he can settle in, say, ten days… Look, this is zero risk. In exchange for extending a few days, we're going to get so much *business. It's just a* no-brainer.

So, you need me to warehouse the stock without compliance catching on.

Yeah. I need you to park it in your trading book.

Park it in my trading book? It's a fucking stupid idea. You know I can't do that.

Look, we both know that management don't give a shit as long as you're making money.

Jabba picks up his phone and stops the replay.

'And what happened after that, Nigel?' asks the legal counsel.

'After that I told him to fuck off.'

'But you ended up going along with the plan anyway?'

'He blackmailed me.'

'That's bullshit and you know it,' snaps Gareth.

'He blackmailed me,' repeats Jabba.

'Sorry, Nigel, how *exactly* did Gareth blackmail you?'

'He turned up at my house one night with drugs and prostitutes and said that the police would find drugs in my house unless I did what he said.'

'Oh my God!' exclaims Jessica.

'That's bullshit, Jabba, and you know it!' shouts Gareth.

Jabba shakes his head and turns to Martin. 'Martin saw everything.'

'Is it true?' ask Jessica. 'Is Jabba telling the truth?'

Martin hesitates.

'Did you see Gareth bring drugs and prostitutes to my house?' asks Jabba.

'Yes,' says Martin. 'Sorry, Gareth.'

'I think this is out of our hands now,' says the legal counsel, abruptly standing up and leaving the room. The head of compliance follows a few steps behind.

'It wasn't like that! This is bullshit.'

'Gareth, after all these years I thought I knew you,' says Jessica.

'There, there,' says Jabba, 'don't blame yourself. I don't think even Gareth Eary knows who Gareth Eary is.'

'I need some air,' says Jessica, leaving the room.

Gareth and Jabba face each other across the boardroom table. Martin sits nervously between them.

'You planned this from the beginning, didn't you, Jabba, from our first conversation in the pub, you planned to set me up all along.'

'You set yourself up, Gareth. You were so obsessed

with becoming someone else, you were always going to tie yourself up in your own bad decisions.'

The legal counsel returns with two security guards.

'Gareth, please come with us.'

Gareth is taken down through the fire escape to the loading bay, and soon a police car pulls up outside. As he steps into the back of the car, an ambulance races past, heading towards St Paul's.

9am – John Gruff, The Lincoln Centre, Holborn

Gruff looks down from the stage at neat rows of analysts, fund managers and investment bankers: pale, bespectacled men, clicking purposefully on Blackberrys. In the front row is Paul Todd, and next to him sits Marianne, who avoids Gruff's gaze.

Marianne and Gruff have a secret. Only they know that a buttoned-up shirt collar, some carefully applied make-up and a misplaced sense of shame conceal the rape that took place in room 704 of the Club Quarters last night.

Gruff glances at his phone. The shares are steady at 36.2. They need to come off another third to close out his shorts. Paul catches his eye and winks.

The Chairman stands up, which means that it is exactly 9am.

'Thank you all for coming… at such short notice… and on a Monday morning too. It's *unusual*, clearly, to call an analyst presentation in conjunction with a trading statement, but… on this occasion… given the nature of the update and the… implications, the Board was… of the view… that this would be the most appropriate format…'

The Chairman is nervous.

Hugh called him late yesterday afternoon to tell him

of the update, and his flight from Edinburgh only landed ninety minutes ago.

'So… thank you for coming… and I will now hand over to John Gruff, CEO, for a summary before we, ummm, I think…' the Chairman glances across at Hugh, who nods, '…yes, before we open up to questions. Yes. Thank you… ummm… John…'

The Chairman waves towards Gruff before sitting down.

Fifty expectant faces watch Gruff stand up and he feels overcome with self-satisfaction. The words that come out of his mouth over the next few minutes will destroy hundreds of millions of pounds of shareholder value and make him rich. This is power.

'The shares are down sixty per cent this morning, and you are expecting us to tell you that this is an overreaction… but we're not going to give you that comfort… we can't give you that comfort. Things have come to light over the last few days. New information has come to light. And what it boils down to is that the position of the Warburtons business, at the time we acquired it… the state of that business was misrepresented to us.'

Hugh taps Gruff's elbow. He pulls it away.

'The position of the Warburtons business was misrepresented to us, the due diligence carried out by our advisors was sub-standard, and the synergies that we expected… it's become clear that before we can talk about synergies, we need to understand what must be done to stabilise the Warburtons business.'

Around the hall, men with thinning hair and expensive ties tap frantically on their Blackberrys. Someone shuffles apologetically along their row to the aisle where they half walk, half jog to the exit at the back of the room. But as the man approaches the double doors, he pauses for a moment, then takes a step back. There's shouting coming from the other side and the sound of a struggle.

People at the back of the hall have started to turn round. A few are out of their seats, and as Gruff looks up, the rest of the audience follows his stare in the direction of the commotion.

With a bang, two men come flying through the double doors. One of the men, a security guard, hits the ground. The other man pauses to look round the room and draws up to his full height. Gruff recognises him without remembering why.

'Is that Dan Trench?' asks the Chairman to no one in particular.

'Dan!' screams Marianne from the front row.

Now Gruff knows why Dan Trench is charging towards him. Gruff stands up and grabs a tumbler from the table. He launches the glass at Dan, who is halfway to the stage. But the throw is off, and it strikes the Credit Suisse consumer goods analyst just above his left eye. The analyst reels back in his chair, emitting a sharp squeal.

'His research was never that bad,' shouts a voice in the audience.

Gruff spots the fire exit to the side of the stage and decides to make a run for it, but as he turns, Hugh pushes his chair out to stand up, and Gruff trips on the leg.

'Get out of my way, you fucking retard!' shouts Gruff, pulling himself off the floor.

'What's going on?' asks Hugh.

Gruff is back on his feet, but by now Dan is on the stage, and all that stands between him and Gruff is the table.

'Security!' shouts Gruff.

'Dan Trench?' asks the Chairman.

Dan picks up the table and throws it over his shoulder onto the floor below the stage.

'Look here,' shouts Hugh. 'I don't know who you are or what you're trying to achieve, but this isn't going to get you anywhere. The police are on their way, so the best thing you can do right now is stop, take a deep breath…'

But Hugh doesn't finish the sentence, because with a shove of Dan's left hand, he is lying winded on the floor.

Dan hasn't laid a finger on Gruff but already the CEO feels defeat. Like the soldier who emerges with their arms in the air before a shot has been fired. Dan looks at Gruff and comes to a halt, as if he needs an action to trigger reaction: a spark for his own consuming anger.

Then Gruff starts to laugh.

'I can't even begin to understand a man like you.' Gruff is shaking his head. 'This is about the girl, isn't it… a *whimsy* like that…' Gruff shrugs, spitting his words with relish, knowing that Dan will show no mercy either way. 'Just a tasty snack to me. A cheap and tasty snack.'

Time slows down. Gruff watches Dan compress his frame, bringing his left foot forwards and swinging his right shoulder down towards the floor, with his chin tucked down into his chest, like a spring coiling up. Then at his point of maximum compression, Dan springs forwards, his right shoulder swings back and his left arm shoots up, like a steel bolt, into Gruff's chin.

Gruff feels the teeth at the front of his mouth explode, and a sharp snap as the back of his head whips back against his spine. And then John Gruff feels nothing.

9.04 – Dan Trench, The Lincoln Centre, Holborn

As he connects with Gruff's chin, Dan remembers the boxer with his arms lying limp above his head. For a moment Dan is stood in that ring, under the glare of the fluorescent tube, while the crash of a metal riot barrier echoes around him. And while his arms set to work pulverising the meat, cartilage and bone that form Gruff's face, the fury and desperation in his heart starts to lift.

He remembers lying on the grass next to Sarah, his fingers entwined with hers under the gentle, mottled shade of the high cirrus.

He remembers the feeling of sand between his toes and the Indian Ocean lapping his ankles as a tropical storm builds on the horizon.

He remembers the sound of thunder echoing through heavy rain.

And he feels peace.

The Credit Suisse consumer goods analyst, clutching a bloodied napkin over his left eye, interjects that Dan might at least leave Gruff alive because he would like to sue the CEO of Albourne for assaulting him with a tumbler. And Hugh tries again to reason with Dan. But eventually there are no dissenting voices.

The police arrive to find people standing around eating miniature French pastries. It takes them a few moments to ascertain that an assault is still underway at the far end of the hall.

In the end it took half a can of mace to slow Dan down and fifty thousand volts from a taser to stop him.

CHAPTER THIRTY

Tuesday the 15th of May, 2012

An armed response unit from the Metropolitan Police was called to an incident at the Lincoln Centre in Holborn yesterday morning. Eyewitnesses report that the incident took place during a presentation by John Gruff, CEO of Albourne PLC, a food manufacturing business, and that a man was tasered by police at the scene. The Metropolitan Police have confirmed that Mr Gruff, fifty-seven, was the victim of an assault, and that Dan Trench, thirty-five, is currently in police custody. Mr Trench is widely recognised for having been the face of a high-profile advertising campaign as the manager of the Columbus Fund, which was at one time the UK's largest retail investment fund. Mr Trench is understood to have left the investment industry in 2009 following the death of his girlfriend in a climbing accident. Earlier in the morning Albourne PLC had issued a profit warning and indicated that a rights issue would be required to plug a gap in its balance sheet. Mr Gruff had pursued a debt-funded M&A strategy which saw the business promoted to the FTSE 100. Mr Gruff is currently a patient at Guys & St Thomas hospital, where his condition has been described as critical. Shares in Albourne PLC closed down 64% at 35p yesterday, having traded as low as 26p during the day.

The City of London Police have praised the actions of whistle-blower Nigel Oakheart in providing evidence that led to the arrest of Gareth Eary, a banker at Gresham Street Capital, on charges of fraud and money laundering. It is alleged that Mr Eary used drugs, prostitutes and blackmail to launder money through financial counterparties on the Cayman Islands, while also trading illegally on Gresham Street Capital's account. Separately, the FSA is investigating the solvency of the bank, following allegations that Mr Eary's actions may have impaired Gresham Street's regulatory capital.

6.38am – Aurelius Blois, Gulfstream G650ER, unknown location

Aurelius doesn't feel himself this morning.

Maybe it was the message from his security consultant to let him know that he was subject to an Interpol *Red Notice*. Maybe it was the 2am race to Biggin Hill. Or maybe it was just that in all the commotion he had skipped his usual Côte de boeuf. Whatever it was, it was serious, because when Ursula had emerged from the master suite at the back of the plane, knelt between his legs and grappled with his cock through his white linen travel chinos, Aurelius had not felt like fucking. Not one bit.

Ursula is flicking through a magazine and Aurelius is watching her.

‘You and me, Ursula.’

‘Hmmm?’

‘You and me. We will rebuild Livermore Capital.’

Ursula looks up. ‘First you need to disappear for some time, while things blow over.’

He tries to show his usual insouciance with a shrug. ‘I pay for the best lawyers.’

‘Of course, but in the meantime, we need to consider your extradition status and which countries are going to work best… as a French citizen.’

It is only 7am, but already this is the worst day that Aurelius can remember in a very long time. And it has just got worse.

‘I have a confession to make, Ursula.’ Aurelius can feel a lump rising in his throat.

‘As we are on this adventure together now, you deserve to know.’

Ursula leans forwards and takes Aurelius’s hand. ‘Baby, you can tell me anything.’

Aurelius takes a deep breath. ‘I am from Görlitz.’

‘Görlitz?’

‘Görlitz. Saxony.’

Ursula frowns.

Aurelius shakes his head. ‘I know. I have lived with this deceit for many years. Can you find it in your heart to forgive me?’

Ursula says nothing.

Aurelius puts his face in his hands. ‘It was Jacques Chirac. As a young man, I saw his suave gangsterism, and I knew this was the man I must emulate. I took that Gallic charm and I made it my own. If people knew that I am actually German-Polish, I would be ruined.’

Ursula starts to laugh, then puts her hand over her mouth.

Aurelius is desolate. 'I know. This changes everything. Can you ever forgive me?' asks Aurelius.

Ursula takes Aurelius's hand. 'I forgive you.'

'Oh, Ursula, you have a pure heart.' Aurelius kisses her hand, then he becomes serious. 'But you must tell *no one*.'

Ursula nods. 'Of course. No one.'

'*No one*,' repeats Aurelius.

Behind Ursula, the cockpit door opens.

'Good morning,' says the pilot.

'*Bonjour*,' replies Aurelius.

'Just to let you know that we have left European airspace.'

'Very good. *Dankeschön*.' Aurelius winks at Ursula.

The pilot nods and steps back into the cockpit, pulling the door closed behind her.

Suddenly Aurelius feels a lot better. In fact, he is starting to feel a lot like Aurelius again. He flexes his pecs and flashes the shining arc of his hyperdontia at Ursula.

'This day is looking up. Let's fuck.'

CHAPTER THIRTY-ONE

Friday the 9th of November, 2012

Aurelius Blois, the financier wanted for questioning by the City of London Police, is believed to be in Thailand after a man fitting his description, accompanied by an unknown female companion, was identified in footage from Chang Mai International Airport. He is believed to be travelling under an assumed identity.

A jury at the Old Bailey today found the former fund manager Daniel Trench guilty of manslaughter. Company Executive John Gruff died at St Thomas' Hospital in May from injuries sustained when he was attacked by Trench at an investor presentation in the City. Trench has been remanded in police custody while he awaits sentencing.

4.40pm – Jude Delaney-Hall, Daunt Books, Marylebone High Street

'No one would believe it really happened,' says Marianne.

Jude raises an eyebrow. 'It didn't… remember!'

Marianne looks thoughtful. '*I* can hardly believe it happened.'

'I wanted to say, again, thank you. For letting me write your story, too.'

Marianne nods, and the pair stand in silence for a moment.

'I wasn't sure how it would feel,' says Marianne, 'but I think it feels… cathartic.'

There's a commotion by the front door.

'*Darling!*' shouts Patrick.

Behind him is an assistant from the publisher laden with banners, and another carrying a case of books.

Patrick marches across the bookshop, grabs Jude by the shoulders, air-kisses her vigorously, then takes Marianne's hand.

'My darlings, how are you both? What a wonderful day. A momentous day. The Great City Novel has arrived. I stopped by *Liberty* to pick up a new cravat *specially* for this evening. What time do we start?'

'People should be here from five.'

'Oh goody. I do love, love, *love* a book launch! Can I get my Extinction Rebellion banner out? Burn the Bankers! Burn the Wankers! And all that.'

'Patrick, *be-have*,' replies Jude. 'You know perfectly well that Marianne is an investment banker… and as you also know, having, presumably, actually *read the manuscript*, that *that* is *not* what this book is about. And most of the guests this evening work in the City. So you are going to be on *best behaviour*.'

Patrick tugs an imaginary forelock and bows his head. 'Yes, m'lady.'

'That's better.'

Patrick winks at Marianne.

One of the publishing assistants thrusts a book into Patrick's hand.

Patrick smiles and passes the book to Jude. 'Jude Delaney-Hall. A published author. This is officially my proudest moment. I feel as if I sired you from my own loins.'

Jude ignores him and puts her arm round Marianne, who runs a finger down the dust jacket.

'It's perfect.'

'Any similarities with real people and events are coincidental,' reads Jude aloud.

Marianne and Patrick both laugh.

'And I love the title,' says Patrick. 'I guess I really must get round to reading it.'

White Collar.

When I was seven, my parents gave me a Royal 203 typewriter. I remember feeling so inspired by the promise of words and the possibility of the blank page. I've tried my hand at different things. I've been a fund manager in the City, a business school lecturer, a white-collar boxer and an Army officer. But I always come back to that typewriter and those feelings of promise and possibility. I wrote the first draft of my novel, *White Collar*, on that Royal 203. I spent the early part of my career in Dundee, London and Mumbai, and now I live with my family in North Wales. My first book, *Salt, Sweat, Tears*, was shortlisted for best new writer at the Cross British Sports Book Awards, 2015.

Adam Rackley, 2026.